2017
To Brother Odo
with all my love
& thanks for your [...]
Barbara [signature]
AP[...]

I See Things

BOOKS BY A. R. ALAN

The House of Cupcakes
The CB (Chocolate Brown) Social Club
Manhattan Madness
The Mad House on Sutton Place
The Flight of Snookems
Kisses to Die For
Fireflies
Fireflies Two—Vat 9
Do I Flaunt My Fat, or Jump Off a Bridge?
If You Really Loved Me, You'd Take Out The Garbage
Love is for the Birds
Confessions Of A Slut

The Delaney and O'Dell thriller series:
The Index Killer
The Past Rushes Forward
I See Things

A.R. Alan's books can be purchased at Amazon.com,
BarnesandNoble.com, booklocker.com, bbcarter2@aol.com, or
aralanbooks.com

I See Things

by A.R. Alan

© 2017

This is a work of fiction. All the characters and events portrayed in this book are either fictitious or are used fictitiously.

Gray Rabbit Publications
1380 East 17 Street, Suite 2233
Brooklyn, New York 11230
www.FantasticBooks.biz

ISBN 10: 1-5154-1018-8
ISBN 13: 978-1-5154-1018-8

First Edition

ACKNOWLEDGEMENTS

The author wishes to acknowledge the invaluable assistance of the following people who have helped her research the facts for this novel, and if she's gotten anything wrong, she says it's entirely her fault.

Dr. Reinhard Motte—Palm Beach County Medical Examiner, Dr. J.H. Byrd—Forensic Entomologist, Officer Herbert Kota—Ballistic Expert, Officer Richard Carnaggio, and Dave Murdoch at Florida Helicopters.

She would also like to thank the following people at the West Palm Sheriff's Office for their time and assistance: Marylou Doss and Marilyn Stokes—Evidence Analysists, Rafael Duran—Deputy Sheriff, Laurie Menard—Forensic Expert, Elizabeth Lancaster—Crime Scene Investigator, Doctor Cecelia Crouse—Doctor at the Crime Lab., Christine Rangel—Evidence Processing Technician, and Lieutenant James Putnik.

Last and equally important for the success of this book, she would like to thank her many friends who read and critiqued this book over and over again and supported her during her ups and downs and struggles with writer's block: Liz King, Michelle Putnik, Rosemary Hillary, Barbara Kreiger, Audrey Levine, Audrey Leader, Ina Kota.

Last, but the most important thank you and love goes Allan Carter—the author's best friend and brother who is always there for her.

CHAPTER ONE

"Catherine, some woman called you four times since 4:00 A.M. and she sounded frantic. I had those messages put on your desk," the admitting officer said when she dashed into the police station.

Homicide Detective Catherine Delaney nodded, then quickly headed into the inner offices. She was soaked to the skin from the driving rain, and exhausted from working through the night. Ernesto, a category-five hurricane still had 48 hours before it was supposed to slam into Florida with its full force, but the wind and drenching rain was already tearing palms off the trees, and people were going crazy.

"There's a call on the line for you," Detective Betancourt said as she neared his desk. He held the phone out to her, but covered the mouthpiece so the caller wouldn't hear him. "The woman sounds like a real nut job. She just keeps rambling on about it coming true and she told you so."

Catherine grabbed the receiver. "Detective Delaney, can I help you?"

"Did you see the papers this morning? I told you I saw it happen, and I told you it would come true. It always does, but no one listens to me. You all think I'm crazy."

"Who is this?"

"Amanda… Amanda Plummer. I spoke with you two nights ago. I told you it would happen, didn't I?"

Catherine swiped the dripping water away from her eyes. "I'm sorry, Amanda. Tell me again what you said."

"I told you I see things happen in the middle of the day and at night, and they always come true. I told you," she continued, sounding out of breath. "That I saw a young woman being abducted outside the Target on Hagen Ranch Road, and she was being held in a dark place that had lots of snakes crawling around."

The hairs on Catherine's arms rose. "Hold on a minute, Amanda." She pressed the phone against her chest. "Dexter, did you see today's newspaper?" she whispered.

He nodded. "Yes. The front page of the *Sun Sentinel* is asking for anyone who may have seen eighteen-year-old Hillary Blackstone in the Boynton Beach Target parking lot. The parents say she didn't return home after she went shopping two nights ago. I think Cody's checking out the missing person's report."

"Shit!" she brought the phone back up to her ear. "Amanda, can you come into the station? I'd like to talk to you about this."

"No. I don't want to ask anyone to drive me in this miserable weather. There are palms and things all over the road in front of my home. Can you come here?"

"Sure. What's your address? I'll be there as soon as I can."

After jotting down the woman's Delray Beach address and clicking off, Catherine headed to her partner's office. Cody was just getting up from behind his desk when she entered the small, cluttered room. "Cody, do you remember the phone call I got the other night from a woman who said she saw someone being abducted outside a Target store?"

"Yeah. I know," he said, tugging his fingers through his dark hair. "It looks like it really happened. I just got off the phone with the kid's parents. I told them we'd be right over."

"We need to see this Amanda woman," Catherine said. "She won't come here, so I got her address."

"First we have to talk to the Blackstones. The Chief told me to get a current picture of their daughter. He's arranged a press conference at the station at noon, and he needs that picture and whatever other information we can get him."

"Do you believe in psychics?" she asked Cody when they were seated in their unmarked car with their seatbelts buckled.

He shrugged, started the motor, then backed the car out of the parking lot and into the littered street. "Are you cold, Delaney? Do want me to adjust the air-conditioning?"

"No. I'm fine. Cody, what if this woman really does see things?"

"I heard some cops actually work with psychics, but I've never dealt with one," he said, swerving the car away from a large palm frond that was lying across the road. "Goddamn it. It's coming down so hard, I can hardly see through this windshield."

"Be careful. Slow down."

Cody pulled the car to the curb, got out, and then dragged the heavy palm onto someone's lawn.

"You didn't answer me," she said when he was back in the car. "What do you think?"

"Maybe she is what she says she is. I don't know. I've never been into that science fiction or ESP stuff."

Catherine bit on her bottom lip for a couple of seconds. "Cody, what if this woman's not a psychic? What if she actually helped someone abduct this teenager, and she's just another crazy son-of-a-bitch who wants media attention?"

"I don't know what to believe, but I'm willing to listen to anyone who can help us find this kid. And hopefully find her alive," he added, unaware that at that very same moment, a long, multi-colored snake was winding itself around Hillary Blackstone's neck.

CHAPTER TWO

The ride to the Blackstone residence in the Costa del Sol community on 19th Street was a long and arduous one. Some of the traffic lights weren't working due to downed power lines. Massive six-lane intersections were clogged with cars and trucks, because some drivers didn't know how to deal with the problem. The situation was becoming so dangerous, that Cody pulled the car over three times to direct traffic until another officer arrived to relieve him. Catherine was behind the wheel the last time he got into the car. For once the big man didn't flex his muscle and insist that he drive. He just sat in his soaked clothes, and bitched about the weather and lunatics who abducted defenseless young women.

"Cody, why don't you wait in the car?" Catherine said after parking in front of the sprawling Spanish-style house. "There's no need for both of us to question them."

Instead of answering, he unbuckled his seatbelt, opened the door, and quickly got out of the car.

Catherine practically ran to keep up with Cody's quick stride up the winding brick path. The front door was opened quickly.

"Mr. Blackstone? I'm Detective O'Dell and this is—"

"Come in. Come in, please," the man said, opening the door wide.

An attractive, dark-haired, middle-aged woman rushed down the hall in a flowing, red caftan. "I'm so thankful that you came after we spoke. I wasn't sure if the police were still searching for our daughter in this miserable weather."

"We are looking for her, and that's why we're here. We need your help."

"Thank you so much. Come inside, please."

Catherine was about to take off her wet, soggy black shoes, but was told not to bother. She and Cody followed Mrs. Blackstone into a large kitchen/family room, and sat at a round, glass-topped table. Mr. Blackstone left them, and his wife walked into the kitchen area.

"Would you care for some coffee, or a glass of water?" she asked.

"We're fine," Catherine answered for herself and Cody. She watched the woman's hands tremble as she poured water from a plastic bottle into an amber-colored glass.

"On the phone, you said you'd like to have a couple of recent photographs of Hillary," Harvey Blackstone said, when he walked into the room. He handed one of the gold-framed pictures to Catherine, and the second one to Cody. "Those were taken about a month ago, at her girlfriend's graduation pool party."

Mrs. Blackstone quickly put the glass down on the counter with a clunk.

"She's beautiful," Catherine said, looking at the missing young woman's long, dark hair and shapely figure as she posed in a skimpy bikini that barely covered her large breasts. She exchanged photographs with Cody, as Mr. Blackstone stood behind her. The second photograph was obviously taken that same day, because Hillary was wearing the same bathing suit, and standing to the right of her was the same young girl. "Mr. Blackstone, we need to ask you and your wife some important questions. The police chief and the mayor have scheduled a press conference at noon. We hope whatever you tell us might help us find your daughter."

Mrs. Blackstone joined them at the table without the glass of water. Her husband sat to her left.

"My daughter is beautiful," Mrs. Blackstone said. Her eyes teared up, then spilled over and down her cheeks. She pulled a napkin out of a napkin holder, and dabbed it against her pale face. "She was just accepted to compete in the Miss Florida Pageant."

Catherine gave Cody a quick glance.

He nodded for her to continue the questioning.

"Mrs. Blackstone—"

"Please, call me Claire, and my husband is Harvey."

"Tell us about the night your daughter went missing."

"I can't believe this is happening. This is a nightmare. A horror. No mother should ever have to go through this."

"Claire, why did your daughter go to Target? It was terrible outside. According to the missing person's report that you and your husband filled out it was late."

She covered her face and started to sob.

"She went out to buy some moisturizing cream," Harvey Blackstone said, casting an angry glance at his wife.

"Excuse me." Catherine blinked. "Did you say she went out in that weather for moisturizer?"

"My wife told Hillary that her skin looked dry," he said bitterly. "That's all it took."

Mrs. Blackstone grabbed some more napkins, and sobbed louder.

"Harvey," Catherine said after shaking her head. "Do you know if your daughter picked up a friend to go with her?"

"I doubt that, but I can't be sure. Hillary said she'd be right back, so I don't think she would have wasted time to pick someone up in that downpour."

"Does Hillary have a boyfriend?"

"No," he answered a little too harshly. "She was too busy competing in beauty contests, so she could qualify for the Miss Florida one. She was also getting her college stuff ready, because she's starting her freshman year in Florida Atlantic University in a few weeks."

"Did she have any enemies, or have a fight with someone recently?"

"Everyone loves my daughter," Claire said, sniffing and wadding the wet napkins into a ball. "Her girlfriends are always here after school and weekends, chatting about clothes, make up, and boys."

"The latest topic was breast implants," Harvey added.

"Harvey!"

"It's true, Claire," he burst out. "In the last six-months, Hillary and four of her friends had that procedure, and you did nothing to talk those girls out of getting it done."

Catherine glanced at Cody again. "Are you saying Hillary recently had breast implant surgery?"

"She didn't really need to have that done," Mrs. Blackstone argued, "but Hillary said all of the other girls who were competing for Miss Florida had large breasts or other cosmetic surgery, so I let her have it done."

"She didn't need to be in any of those beauty contests. It's because of those damn contests that she didn't apply to any of the out-of-state colleges."

"Harvey, Hillary loved being in those contests. She wanted to stay in Florida."

"Hillary had no choice. You started her off, before she could even crawl," he said bitterly. "And you kept signing her up for them. She went to that store because of you, Claire. If something happens to her…"

Mrs. Blackstone clutched the blouse over her heart. "You can't be blaming me for what's happened. I won't let you. I love my daughter. Hillary told us this competition was important. That if she didn't win Miss Florida, she wouldn't qualify for Miss America, and then possibly Miss World. It was Hillary's decision, not mine. She said those titles might get her a job as a newscaster. You know that," she said, as a fresh batch of tears streamed down her pale face. "I don't want you blaming me. Do you hear me, Harvey? I won't have it."

There were a few moments of tense silence, before Catherine proceeded. "Harvey, when did you first discover Hillary was missing?"

He gulped. His face was ash gray; his chest rose and fell rapidly, like he couldn't breathe.

"Are you all right," she asked, placing her hand on his arm. Catherine's heart ached for this man. He was the opposite of her father, who had been cold and distant after she'd been raped by a man who had climbed through her bedroom window when she was twelve. "Mr. Blackstone, do you need medical assistance? Shall I call for help?"

"No, I'll be fine," he said, pulling away from Catherine's hand. "I knew something was wrong when my daughter hadn't come home by 1:00 A.M., so I drove over to the Target store. Hillary's car was the only one left in the parking lot, and she wasn't in it. I walked to the store. All of the doors around the entire building were locked. I banged on the back door, hoping a security guard would hear me and open up. No one did. I didn't know what to do at that point. I had called Hillary's cell phone at least a dozen times before and after I went to the store. She never answered, so I left messages to call me back immediately," he said, wringing his hands together on top of the table. "I left her car in the lot, thinking she might have met a friend in the store, gone off for a while, and then would return to her car and drive home. Then I thought she might have stayed over at her friend's house."

Catherine watched his eyes fill with tears. He made no move to brush them away when they fell.

"My wife and I drove over to the Target the following morning, after waiting up all night," he went on. "When we saw Hillary's car was still parked in the lot, we went into the store and spoke to the manager. He wasn't able to help us. Immediately after looking inside Hillary's car, I called the police. I..." He stopped. His hands were now clenched so tight, his knuckles were white.

"Go on. What were you going to say?" Catherine prodded.

He stared down at his hands. "I should have looked inside Hillary's car when I first saw it sitting there, but I didn't. If I had, I would have called the police right away, and you might have found her close by. Hillary's pocketbook was on the floor in the front, along with the gold locket necklace we'd given her for her birthday. And the chain... the chain was broken like it had been ripped off. I... I..." He turned back to Catherine. "I knew then that something terrible must have happened to her."

"Mr. Blackstone, did you take Hillary's phone out of the car?"

He shook his head. "No. We were told not to open the car door, or touch anything inside. We waited for the police to arrive, but I looked through the windows. I didn't see the phone. She... she may have it, or it could still be in the car."

As a jagged streak of lightning flashed through the darkened sky and thunder boomed above the Blackstones' home, Harvey Blackstone sobbed into his hands, and his daughter, Hillary, slipped into a black void.

CHAPTER THREE

A beam from his flashlight lit the way, as he slowly climbed up the splintered steps to the second floor landing. He smiled, almost laughed out loud as he stood outside the locked bedroom door, because he heard them slithering around on the wooden floor.

As he drew closer to the door, the hissing beyond it grew louder. "You know I've brought you food, don't you?" he said in drawn-out, whispered words that blended in with the dozens of soft hisses.

He set the large metal pail down on the floor, then checked the bands around his trousers to make sure they were secured around the tops of his high rubber boots. After that, he inspected the thick, padded gloves to make sure they completely covered his hands and went over his long-sleeved leather shirt that had been custom-made to fit tight.

The padlock on the door was new and easy to open. He pocketed the key after opening it, then shut off the flashlight, picked up the pail, and slowly inched open the door so he wouldn't injure any of his precious snakes.

"Move away," he said, gently toeing a black eastern indigo snake away from the door before it could wriggle out of the room. He tossed the contents of the pail across the room, and suddenly a frenzy of black, brown, and striped snakes quickly slithered toward the beetles, lizards, and cut up rodents that were waiting for them.

He shut the door again, then stood there and listened in the darkness. The rain hammered against the metal-barred window and the wind howled outside, but he didn't hear a sound coming from the girl. He waited a few moments more, then flipped on the light switch.

Her nude body was curled on top of the pile of cartons where he knew he'd find her. He'd deliberately set up the boxes that way so she'd climb up onto them to get away from the snakes—snakes she didn't know were harmless. He almost wished he were an artist as he looked at her. If he were, he would have taken the time to paint the lovely sight. A common garter snake with a pattern of yellow stripes on its green background had wound itself around the girl's neck, and a long olive-colored ring-necked snake was slowly winding its way up her long leg. He studied her shapely body and her firm, rounded breasts a little longer. The snakes hissed around his booted feet. Her body had changed from its lush, pink color when he was plunging his erection inside her untouched womanhood, into a faded-pink with splotches of purple under her buttocks and feet, where her blood had settled after she expired.

He slowly removed the snakes from her body, and then gently placed them on the floor next to some of the scattered food he'd provided. More snakes wriggled into the room from the doggie door he'd constructed between this room and the adjoining bedroom. It was in that larger bedroom that he bred—and experimented on—his non-poisonous snakes. The poisonous ones were kept in the master bedroom, the room that faced the fallow sugarcane fields.

"And now to you," he said, looking her over again. "It's too bad the venom I injected into you worked so quickly. I wanted to suck on those ripe breasts a while longer, and then have you a couple more times. What a shame Grandpa. I'll just have to do better the next time."

He picked up Hillary's limp body, folded her over his shoulder, then left the room and locked the door behind him.

CHAPTER FOUR

By noon, the conference room in the police station was packed with news reporters and police officers who were waiting to hear the latest details on the Target abduction. Police Chief Stephen Delaney, Mayor Eugene Clarkston, and Sargent Mark Goldfarb were standing in front of the room where two microphones had been set up. Mr. and Mrs. Blackstone, Catherine, and Cody were standing behind them.

"Mayor Clarkston, what can you tell us about Hillary Blackstone," asked a very tall reporter from station WXEL.

The short, plump mayor who was dressed in an expensive designer suit and tie, stepped in front of a microphone and cleared his throat a couple of times before answering. "Ladies and gentlemen, Hillary Blackstone was abducted two nights ago in front of the Target store on Hagen Ranch Road, in Boynton Beach. The—"

"Did you get Target's security tape that filmed the parking lot?" a young, bearded reporter called out.

"As I was about to say, we did get a tape."

"What was on it?" the same reporter called out again.

"Unfortunately," the mayor said gruffly, glaring at the reporter who had the audacity to interrupt him. "It was raining very hard, so the camera got nothing but a gray sheet of rain. Therefore, we are unable to ascertain what actually happened to Miss Blackstone."

Murmurs filtered throughout the room, and feet shuffled. Sergeant Goldfarb sneezed three times into a crumpled handkerchief, and the mayor took three steps to the left, which made Chief Delaney also move to the left.

"I hear Miss Blackstone qualified for the Miss Florida Pageant. Do you think that had anything to do with her abduction?" a female reporter called out from the right side of the room. She didn't wait for a reply, and fired off another question. "Could a competitor be responsible for her being missing, like the attack on that Olympic ice-skater?"

The mayor turned right, so the sergeant could take that question, but Goldfarb couldn't, he was sneezing again. Chief Delaney stepped forward.

"We have no idea who abducted Hillary or why, or if she actually was abducted. It is possible that she went off with a friend, however her parents believe otherwise, and that's why we're asking for your help. If anyone saw Hillary in Target, or the parking lot, or any other place that evening, or if you've seen her within the last two days, please call our hot line immediately."

"With the hurricane about to hit us, will that hamper your search, Chief Delaney?" asked Samuel Ward, a reporter the chief knew well.

"It certainly will, Sam."

Catherine loved how her uncle was respected by the press, and how he called them by their names.

"With the hurricane only hours away from us," he went on, "it's urgent that we find this young lady as soon as we can. That's why we're asking the public to provide any information they may have as quickly as possible."

Mr. Blackstone walked up to the chief. "May I say something to them, please?"

"Yes. Of course," he answered, placing one of the microphones in front of him.

Harvey Blackstone looked out at the audience. "This is our daughter, Hillary," he said, holding up her graduation picture so it could be filmed and broadcasted. "My wife and I are frantic with worry for her safety. Hillary, sweetheart if you can hear me, please… please call home. We love you. And whoever you are, if you have taken our daughter, please call us. Don't hurt her. We'll give you money, anything to get our Hillary back unharmed. Please," he begged. Then he looked around, like he didn't know what he should do next.

Catherine assisted him back to his crying wife.

The mayor stepped forward, pulled a folded sheet of white paper out of his pocket, opened it, and then read: "I want to thank Chief Delaney and the fine men and women in his department." He didn't bother to look at any of them. "I'm sure they'll do everything humanly possible to find this teenager. And now on to hurricane Ernesto. Listen carefully. If anyone is planning to stay in one of our church or school shelters, you must bring your own food and water with you, as well as your children's necessities and your medications. During the worst of this hurricane, emergency services such as police and fire rescue will be on hold," he said, then turned and rushed out of the room, ignoring the many questions that were still shouted out.

The chief, Catherine, and Cody followed the mayor to the front door, where three female assistants were waiting for him.

"Thank you, Mayor Clarkston. I appreciate your finding time in your busy schedule to come to this conference," the chief said, extending his hand.

"Glad I could help. Must run," the mayor said, ignoring the hand and condescendingly patting the chief's shoulder. "If I don't show up at Annabelle's charity luncheon, I'll never hear the end of it."

One of the mayor's assistants opened the door for him. Another held a wide umbrella over his bald head, and then led him to the waiting black limousine.

"Pompous asshole," the chief mumbled as the limo drove away, and reporters and cameramen rushed past them. "Come into my office you two. There's something I need to tell you." He turned and then walked down the hall, grumbling about the mayor and the impending election. Catherine and Cody looked at each other, smiled, and followed behind him.

"You're still smoking," Catherine said when she entered her uncle's office. "I can still smell the smoke. Didn't you hear the doctor warning you to stop? For God's sake! You had a stent inserted in your artery. Doesn't that tell you something?"

In answer, the chief picked one of the cigar stubs out of the filled ashtray on top of his desk, and stuffed it between his lips.

"What did you want to tell us?" Cody quickly asked, derailing the old argument.

The chewed-up stub was taken out of the chief's mouth. "We got a wrinkle in this abduction case."

"What kind of wrinkle?" Catherine asked.

"Cathy, Chris went to the Target lot to tow Hillary's Nissan—"

"Chris?"

"You know, from our garage. He went to tow in Hillary's car for a forensic overhaul, and found it had a flat tire."

"A flat tire," Cody said. "How come Mr. Blackstone didn't mention the car had a flat?"

"The man was upset. Maybe he didn't see it? Whatever, it's the front tire on the driver's side that's flat."

"That kid drove over there in that pouring rain and suddenly her tire went flat? No way," Catherine said, her hands balling into fists at her sides. "Maybe someone deliberately flattened that tire, so he could offer her a lift home,"

"Why would she go off with a stranger, instead of phoning her parents?" Cody asked.

"She didn't call them, because that son-of-a-bitch wasn't a stranger. He was someone Hillary knew and trusted."

"But she must have struggled with him. Her necklace was broken, and her handbag was still in the car," Cody reminded her.

"I think you're right about there being a struggle," she said, walking across the room and then turning back to them. "She must have known him, but then he had to have said or done something that scared her enough to try and fight him off."

"You got it. Knew you would. That's exactly what I thought had happened," the chief said. "Marty is going through the in-store tapes now to see if Hillary spoke to anyone. We'll know later today when I get his report."

"Uncle Steve, Hillary's father said he didn't see her cell phone in the car. She may still have it with her and try to call 911, if she gets a chance."

The chief sighed, then turned to Cody. "Cody, Sergeant Goldfarb's sick and going home, I'm making you the lead on this case."

Cody nodded.

"Have someone check the phone company to see if their cell towers can trace her phone's signal."

"I already have Rinaldi on that," Cody responded.

"Well, then that's a start. Any questions, you two?"

"No," they both answered.

"Good. Then get out of here."

"I'm going to send Betancourt and Alvarez over to the girl's high school to get a list of Hillary's friends and teachers, so they can add them to the few names we got from the Blackstones. The sooner they're all questioned, the quicker we might get a lead," Cody said, as they walked out of the chief's office. "I'll only be a few minutes. Then you and I will be going back to the Blackstones'. I have a feeling there are still things that we haven't been told."

"Fine. I'll be in Whitehall and Wilkin's office when you're ready to leave."

He grabbed her arm to keep her from walking away. "What are you up to, Babe?"

"I'm going to ask them to search for pet shops that carry snakes. Then to check out the owners to see if any of them have a criminal record."

Cody stared down at her. "You believe that woman and her snake story?"

Catherine shrugged. "It can't hurt to check it out. Who knows? She may really see things. And don't forget, I promised to go and see her."

As Catherine and Cody were assigning jobs to the four detectives, Hillary Blackstone's body was being dumped into the cold water of a debris-littered canal that was rushing through a fallow sugarcane field.

CHAPTER FIVE

Mr. Blackstone's mouth dropped open when he opened the front door and saw the two detectives back on his doorstep. "Did you find her?" he asked.

"No. I'm sorry. Not yet," Cody answered. "May we come inside?"

"Yes… yes, of course." He stepped to the side and opened the door wide for them to enter the foyer.

Cody and Catherine unzipped their black rain-slickers. "Where do you want us to put these," Catherine asked, looking at the man's almost white face. "Mr. Blackstone, we don't have bad news. We just have to ask you some more questions."

"Harvey, who are you talking to?" his wife called out.

"The detectives," he called back, not moving, and not taking their dripping-wet slickers.

Mrs. Blackstone rushed to them, looking as pale as her husband. "Have you found Hillary? Where is she? Is she all right?"

"Mrs. Blackstone, we haven't found Hillary, but our men are out searching for her," Catherine said.

"Oh. I see. Harvey take their things. We'll go inside."

"Mrs. Blackstone… Claire, would it be all right if we looked in Hillary's room?"

She nodded, and after their jackets had been put away, she turned and led them down a long hall that was lined on both sides with family pictures. Catherine glanced at some of the photographs as she followed her. Most of the pictures were of Hillary at different stages of her life. Her baby and toddler pictures were adorable. In her cheerleading and pageant pictures—where she wore glittering, tight-fitting gowns and skimpy bikinis—she looked stunning. Catherine stopped in front of one of the bikini pictures for a moment, noting how much smaller Hillary's breasts were before her implants.

"Catherine," Cody called out from the end of the hall.

Catherine hurried to him.

"This is my daughter's room," Mrs. Blackstone said, pointing into a bedroom. "You're welcome to look around. My husband and I will wait for you in the family room."

After the couple left them, Catherine and Cody entered the room. "Wow," Catherine said, peering around the all-pink room. Floor-to-ceiling shelves on two walls were filled with glittering crowns and trophies. Colorful winning contest ribbons were tacked onto another wall, and the pink lace-covered bed was filled with stuffed animals and well-dressed dolls that looked very expensive.

"Come and look at this," Cody said from inside a walk-in closet.

Catherine joined him in the massive closet. "Wow again. This looks like the Blackstones cut through another bedroom to make this huge closet."

"You're probably right. I've never seen so many gowns. They could open a store with all of this stuff."

"Cody, this stuff must have cost them a fortune. You can't buy gowns like this off the rack. They have to be custom-made," she said, fingering a silver-sequined strapless gown. Catherine walked to the far side of the closet and rifled through some everyday blouses, slacks, and skirts that could have been purchased at a T.J Maxx, or a teen store like Forever 21. She removed a printed blouse from one of the hangers.

"What are you doing with that?" Cody asked.

"I'm taking it to Amanda. I want her to see and touch something Hillary wore."

"You're joking, right? She's probably a nut case."

Catherine folded the silky blouse and tucked it into her pants pocket, then looked up at Cody. "You may be right, but what if she is a psychic? I want to see what happens when she touches it."

"Are you going to tell the Blackstones that you're taking that blouse?"

"No, and I'm not going to tell them about Miss Plummer or her snake story. Those two are worried sick as it is. I don't want to make it worse for them. Let's get out of here."

"What about questioning the Blackstones?"

"The snake lady is waiting for us. We'll come back after we talk to her."

CHAPTER SIX

Crime Scene Detectives Dexter Betancourt and his partner Ricardo Alvarez not only looked different, but their demeanors were complete opposites. Dexter was a tall, muscular black man with long, thick dreadlocks that he'd flip over his shoulders when he got pissed-off. He was silent and serious, the one who'd shoot first and ask questions later, whereas his partner, Ricardo Alvarez, the Latin womanizer with the shiny, bald dome and small goatee, was quick to spout raunchy jokes to anyone who'd listen.

"Hey, Dex, you shoulda seen the redhead I scored with last night."

"Yeah, yeah, I heard it before," Dexter said, staring through the rain-drenched window that the wipers could barely keep up with.

Ricardo smiled. "Man, this one was special."

"They're all special to you. So what else is new?"

"Nah, this one really was special, I tell you. This broad was a natural redhead. Her collar and cuffs matched. I had to take time to pluck the red hairs out of my goatee this morning. That's why I was late," he said, fingering his well-groomed goatee and smiling.

"Yeah, well, you should have taken a shower while you were at it, because you smell ripe, buddy."

Ricardo's smile widened. "Boy, do I wish I could bottle that smell. I'd make a friggin' fortune."

"Crap!" Dexter yelped, when their car hydroplaned across the road. When he got it under control again, he let out a deep sigh and slowed down. "I wish it hadn't taken us so damn long to get Spencer's address. I wanted to be home already, and not driving around on these goddamned flooded roads. Look around. Lyme Road should be coming up on the right. I don't want to miss it."

"When do you think they're going to start developing this area west of Route 441?"

Dexter didn't answer; he was concentrating on the flooded road ahead.

"Slow down. There's a mailbox comin' up on the right. That may be it. Yeah, yeah, that's it," Ricardo said, leaner closer to the window so he could see the numbers 13307 painted on it. "Turn right. This is it."

When Dexter turned right, they found themselves driving down a narrow, winding dirt road that sucked at their tires, and nearly sent their black-and-white sliding into the trees and bushes that bordered it. The all-stone, two-story house was almost hidden by a thicket of tall pines, its windows were shuttered, and broken tree limbs lay on top of the dark, slate roof. Off to the right was an old, sun-bleached wooden barn. The door was padlocked shut, the roof looked repaired, and a mud-splattered Ford pickup truck was parked in front of it.

"This place is creepy," Dexter mumbled, unfastening his seatbelt after he shut off the engine.

"The principal's probably creepy, too," Ricardo said, unbuckling his. "Probably an old fart like the one I had in high school. I wonder what this one's wife looks like."

"Let's go, Casanova. Let me do the talking. I want to get out of here fast, before that muck on the road turns to quicksand and we're stuck out here for days."

Since the wind was too strong to open umbrellas and neither had raincoats, the detectives were soaked down to their skin when they reached Daniel Spencer's front door.

"He'd better be home," Dexter said, pounding on the wooden door. He did it four more times, before two locks were turned, and the door was opened a few inches.

"What is it?" the man said curtly, peeking through the space. Then he noticed the parked patrol car. "You're police?"

"Are you David Spencer, the principal at the Boca Raton High school?" Dexter asked as the wind-driven rain slashed against him.

The principal nodded.

"Can we come in? We'd like to ask you some questions about Hillary Blackstone."

"Yes, I'm sorry. Please do come in," he said, opening the door wider. "It was very rude of me to keep you outside, but I rarely get visitors." He let them enter, but didn't invite them past the small foyer.

"Now, what is it you wanted to ask me?" he said, pushing a lock of dripping wet hair away from his forehead.

Dexter matched the man's six-foot-three height, so he looked straight into his light-blue eyes. "Do you have any idea where Hillary Blackstone might be?"

The man didn't flinch. "She's probably run off with someone, I'd guess."

"Why would you guess that?" Ricardo asked, giving him a once over.

Spencer flexed his well-toned biceps before answering. "I thought she had a thing going with another student, because I caught them kissing in the girl's locker room.

Ricardo blinked. "First of all, what were you doing in the girl's locker room? And second, who did you see her kissing?"

"I went in there because the custodian had set some rodent traps, and later that day a student said she saw something caught in one of them," he replied, clearly annoyed. "He was gone, it was after school hours, and no one was supposed to be in there."

"But Hillary was," Ricardo went on, looking at the pecs that bulged beneath the man's black T-shirt—pecs that meant he could easily lift and carry off a young teen like Hillary Blackstone.

"Are these questions necessary? I was very busy when you interrupted me."

Dexter flipped some dreadlocks off his shoulder, and his lips tightened. "Mr. Spencer, if you'd prefer answering our questions at headquarters, we'd be delighted to transport you over there."

"No. No." A crash sounded in another room. Spencer quickly looked back, then faced them again. "That won't be necessary."

"Sounds like something broke back there," Dexter said, trying to see past the principal.

"It's just my cat. She's always getting into something. Now, about Miss Blackstone. I hesitated to answer your question, because it might embarrass Hillary's family if my answer were made public. I found Hillary kissing Deborah Logan. She's the same age as the lovely Hillary, and the girls graduated together. I suggest you go and talk to her. Perhaps Hillary is with her."

"We'll go and talk to that girl smart ass, but we'll be back," Ricardo said, buckling his seatbelt. He turned to his partner. "Dex, what did you think about that guy calling Hillary lovely?"

Dexter turned the key in the ignition, but didn't shift into drive. "I picked up on that, too. Did you notice his hair was dripping wet, and his shoes had left footprints on the tile floor behind him when he let us inside?"

"Yup! Saw that. Why do you think he was out in this weather?"

Dexter switched on the windshield wipers. "Looks like we need to question Deborah Logan, and then some of the girls in that school about their very young and handsome principal."

CHAPTER SEVEN

If this Amanda Plummer ever acted in a movie, it would only have been in a horror film. Catherine had tried to hide her shocked reaction when she first saw the woman's puckered and scarred face, but she was sure Amanda had heard her soft gasp when she and Cody were let into her home.

"Hang your jackets on those hooks," Amanda said, pointing to the wall on their left.

"I'm sorry we're making such a mess on your floor," Catherine said, hanging up her dripping-wet slicker and then hanging Cody's.

"Don't worry about the floor. The tiles will dry. Why don't you come into the kitchen? I was just about to have some coffee. You can join me."

Catherine and Cody followed Amanda's wheelchair into a brightly lit kitchen that was papered in flowery wallpaper. Large and small ceramic pots filled with an array of flowering plants lined the window sill and most of the granite counter tops.

"Mmm," Catherine said. "That coffee smells wonderful. Can I do the serving?"

When Amanda smiled, the left side of her mouth pulled down like she had had a stroke. "Sure," she said, "It'll be nice having someone serve me for a change, since I don't get out to restaurants these days." She wheeled herself over to the table, and then adjusted the small blanket that covered her legs. "Take the cups and plates from the top tier in the dishwasher. Don't take any of the bottom ones, they're dirty. The flatware's in the drawer, and the milk and sugar is in the fridge. Oh! And there's some leftover apple pie in there. Take it out. There should be enough in the tin for the three of us."

Cody sat across from her at the table. "Are you sure about that, Miss Plummer," he said with a wide smile. "Apple pie's my favorite."

Amanda gave him a crooked smile back. "Miss Delaney, cut the pie slices at the counter before you bring the plates over, or we might not get our fair share."

Cody chuckled and rested back against his chair. "Please call us Catherine and Cody, and if you don't mind, we'll call you Amanda."

"That sounds good to me," she said, blushing and turning toward Catherine.

"That dishwasher system you've set up for yourself is brilliant," Catherine said, depositing three mugs of coffee on the round table. She walked back to the counter for the plates of pie.

"I can't reach any of the overhead cabinets, so that works for me."

Catherine placed the rest of the things down on the table, and then sat with them. "Amanda what do you do with the dirty dishes while there's still clean dishes on the top shelf?"

"I pile them in the sink until I've used all of the clean ones, then I put the dirty ones back in the dishwasher and wash them for the next round."

"Cody, that's a fabulous idea. I think I'll try it. It's a perfect system, and fast."

Cody swallowed his mouthful of pie. "Really, Delaney? You don't cook, so you have no dirty dishes."

"I make coffee in the morning," she said, about to stab her fork into her pie.

"You'd need a hundred cups before you'd fill your dishwasher. By the way, when's the last time you used that thing? It probably doesn't even work by now."

Amanda's head turned from side to side as she watched their teasing banter. "Are you two a couple?"

Cody said yes, Catherine said no. Both glared at each other.

Amanda set her mug down on the table, then pushed it and her pie plate toward the center. "Do you want me to tell you what I see for the two of you?"

Catherine's fork hand froze halfway to the dish in front of her.

Cody just stared at the woman with his mouth agape.

Amanda closed her eyes, and placed her palms on top of the table. Cody and Catherine waited. "Catherine, I see you in a lovely white-lace wedding dress."

Now Catherine's mouth dropped open.

"Cody, I see a long line of police officers, and you waiting at an outdoor altar."

Cody smiled and glanced at Catherine.

"I see a man… he has a crooked nose. Tears are wetting his face."

The hairs on Catherine's arms rose, and her pulse quickened. "That's my uncle Steve."

"I see… I see…"

Cody and Catherine watched as Amanda started to rock forward and back in her wheelchair. Seconds later, her fingers twisted and untwisted together on top of the table.

"Catherine… you brought me something," she said, her breathing labored, her body rocking faster.

Catherine reached down to touch her pants pocket where she'd put Hillary's folded blouse.

"It's too late! I can't help her," Amanda suddenly cried out. Her arm swung to the side and swiped her cup and plate off the table. It crashed down onto the floor with a loud bang. Her eyes flew open. She stared straight ahead. "She's dead. The girl," she said in a strangled voice. "The one I saw with the snakes is dead."

Catherine's hand grabbed one of Amanda's. "Amanda, who killed her? What does he look like?"

"He's just a shadow," Amanda answered, staring ahead as if in a daze. "A dark shadow surrounded by an evil, shimmering, blue aura."

Catherine squeezed her cold hand. "Amanda, please look harder. You have to tell me what he looks like. Give me a name. Give me something. Anything so I can find him."

"He's making plans," she mumbled with her fingers splayed on top of the table, her eyes staring straight ahead. Amanda suddenly gasped, and clutched her throat.

"Amanda! Amanda," Catherine shouted, as the woman's eyes rolled upward until only the whites showed. "Amanda, what do you see? Tell us. Please."

"He's planning to do it again. I can feel it. The snakes are waiting in that dark place."

CHAPTER EIGHT

Although frigid air was pouring out of the car's air-conditioning vents, Catherine and Cody were sweating as their unmarked vehicle drove away from Amanda Plummer's small, one-story home. The wind had picked up again, and the few remaining palms that were still left on the trees looked like they'd soon join the others that were lying across the roads and on top of puddled lawns.

"Do you believe what she said about him making plans to do it again?" Cody asked.

Catherine watched the waves of water rise up on both sides of the car as it drove through the heavily flooded street, and how the traffic light swayed back and forth as they passed under it. "Yes, I believe her. Did you see her eyes? Did you see how they rolled up until only the whites showed?"

"Yeah," he said, making a slow right turn. "It freaked me out."

"Cody, she described Uncle Steve's broken nose, and she's never seen him."

Cody smiled, and cast a quick glance to her.

"What's so funny?"

"You forgot to mention the part about her seeing us getting married."

Catherine slid down in her seat and said nothing for the rest of the trip to the station. Cody drove on with a wide grin on his face.

"I thought you two would be home," the chief said, when they walked into his office.

Catherine plunked herself down on the corner of his desk. "We just came back to drive you home, Uncle Steve."

"Thanks, but I'm not going home." He walked behind his desk and sat down. "I'm staying in the station with a couple of our boys."

Catherine got up and turned to him. "You just had a stent put into one of your arteries. You're not even supposed to be here," she said, watching him pull a cigar stub out of the filled ashtray and then stick it into his mouth. "You're going home, and that's that."

Her uncle looked over at Cody. "When did she get so bossy?"

"Cathy's right this time. You're going home to wait out the storm, just like the rest of us."

"But—" His phone rang, and he picked it up. "Chief Delaney... Yeah... Yeah... You don't say. That's good news. Call me back on my cell phone if you find something else," he said, glancing at his niece. "Looks like I'm being taken home."

He hung up.

"Want to share the good news?" Catherine said.

Her uncle dropped the cigar stub back in the ashtray. "They found the broken tip of a knife lodged in the Blackstone girl's tire. It's a definite slash job."

"What about the in-store surveillance videos?" Cody asked, as the chief rose.

"Our lab has them. On one of the videos, they saw Hillary talking to a young man who looked to be around her age. They said he had his arm around her waist and was smiling at her."

Catherine's eyes widened. "Does he work in the store? If not, why was he out in that weather, and so late?"

"Cathy, hold on. That's all we know for now. Our lab guys are looking through some of the other tapes to see if the boy walked her out of the store."

"Mmm," she mumbled, chewing on her bottom lip.

"What are you thinking, Delaney," Cody said, poking her arm.

She turned to him. "We need our guys to see who not only walked out of the store, but who walked in, and what time they did that. Maybe our tire-slasher followed Hillary into the store a few minutes later. Maybe he and the boy were in it together. Cody, we have to get a photo of that boy over to the Target manager and employees. Maybe someone can ID him."

"I'll be back in a minute," he said, heading to the door.

"Where are you going?" Catherine called after him.

"To push the guys in our lab."

CHAPTER NINE

The full force of the hurricane hit around midnight. Winds over a hundred and twenty miles an hour tore roofs off homes and businesses, smashed unprotected windows, and swept debris and metal signs against anything that stood in its way. The last of the palms were ripped off trees, and downed power lines left a large swath of the eastern coast of Florida in total darkness. The deluge of rain flooded the streets. Canals and lakes overflowed their banks and seeped into homes. Mobile homes lifted off their cinder block foundations and smashed into one another. Cars and trucks floated down the streets, and the ocean's fury deposited large and small boats up on the beaches. Sirens blared, but their sounds were muffled by the howling wind.

Catherine stood by the bedroom window, her eyes closed, her hand splayed on the vibrating glass. She didn't turn to Cody. She knew he was awake and watching her. "Do you think Hillary's still alive?"

"Come back to bed," he said softly, patting the warm space she had just vacated.

Catherine turned around. She could barely see his outline in the bed, but she could smell his muskiness. "If she's alive, she must be terrified."

He said nothing.

Something hit the roof with a bang. Catherine gasped and ducked. "What was that?"

"Probably a palm frond. Come back to bed, Babe," he said, lifting the top sheet in invitation.

She walked over and climbed in beside him. His body was warm and wet with perspiration, a combination of their love-making and no air-conditioning. She ran her fingers through the dark, curly hairs on his chest, something that had taken her almost twenty years to do to any man after she'd been raped.

Cody pulled her close and kissed her forehead. "If the girl is still alive, he's probably making sure she doesn't get hurt," he said, pressing her head down on his chest. "And if he's doing that, we'll find her after the storm lets up."

"How can you say that?"

"I'm hoping, Catherine," he answered with a deep sigh. "That's all we can do now: hope that she's still alive and that we can get him before he hurts or kills her. Now relax. We need to get some sleep. Tomorrow is going to be a very long day."

Catherine wrapped her arm around his waist, closed her eyes, and listened to the steady thumping of his heart. Should she move in with him? Was she ready for that? Moving in with Cody would be a commitment—a promise of a tomorrow together. She knew she loved him, but she was just coming to terms with knowing that the man who raped her when she was twelve was dead and no longer a threat. But would he ever be out of her mind, and would the endless nightmares stop? She bit her bottom lip, and drew in a deep breath. Maybe she needed more time to recover, she thought, placing a kiss on Cody's chest.

That was all Cody needed. A moment later he was kissing Catherine passionately, and all thoughts of sleep were replaced by a burning hunger and need. As Catherine and Cody's slick, over-heated bodies thrust against each other's in the rumpled bed, Hillary Blackstone's body that had been dumped in a raging canal snagged onto the limb of a fallen log.

CHAPTER TEN

Getting to the police station was a monumental task for Catherine, Cody, and the chief the following morning. The roads were still flooded and littered with everything from fallen trees to whole sides of buildings. Many residents and business owners stood out in the streets, assessing the damage to their property. Emergency Florida Power and Light trucks were already working on the fallen power lines, and to make things even more chaotic, ambulances flashed their lights and blared their sirens so they could rush down those same roads to the over-stressed local hospitals.

"Uncle Steve, I'll catch up with you in a few minutes, after I check to see if I have any messages."

"Thanks for picking me up."

"Chief, there's a call for you," the officer at the front desk said, holding the phone out toward him. "It's the mayor, and he says it's urgent."

Catherine and Cody waited by his side.

The chief made a face, and took the phone. "Yes, sir, what can I do for you? Uh huh… Uh huh… That's terrible… Uh huh… I'll have someone look into that immediately.… Yes.… Yes.… I'll give it my personal attention.… Bye." With a heavy sigh, the chief handed the phone back to the officer.

"So?" Catherine said, shifting her weight from one foot to the other. "What does he have you giving your personal attention to?"

The chief sighed again, and shook his head. "His son's pharmacy was broken into."

"Really?" Cody said. "It was broken into during a category-five hurricane?"

"Probably had its roof torn off, like half of the buildings in this area," Catherine said, disgusted.

"No," the chief said. "This storm didn't steal three-hundred bottles of Xanax, Percocet, and Oxy-something-or-other."

"Just drugs," Cody asked.

"Would you believe the bastards actually chiseled the large safe that held those drugs out of the concrete floor? And all of that happened while the storm was going on. And since the surveillance camera was out of commission, there's no chance of us getting a look at who did it. Sonny," the chief said, turning to the admitting officer. "See who's patrolling that area, and have the dispatcher signal them to check it out and then get back to me."

"Will do, sir."

As Catherine, Cody, and the chief made their way toward the interior door, Sonny called out again. "Chief, hold up!"

They all halted and turned back.

"Don't tell me he's called back again."

"No, chief, it's not the mayor. Dispatch says a body was just found in a canal."

CHAPTER ELEVEN

The unmistakable stench of decomposing flesh grew stronger as Catherine and Cody neared the bank of the swollen canal just off Route 441.

A team of three men from the West Palm Beach Marine Unit were already on the scene. One of them was putting on a wetsuit; the other two were uncoiling ropes that would be used to retrieve the body that was still snagged on a tree trunk.

"Gentlemen," Cody said when he reached them. "Can someone tell me who called this in?"

"Hi, Cody," the taller of the three said after turning around. "I got word on my way over here that you're the lead on this case."

"Yeah, lucky me," Cody said, smirking and pulling a small pad and pen out of his shirt pocket. "So, Joe, do you know who called 911?"

"I'm not sure, but I think it was a couple of teenage boys. Dispatch said some kids are being hauled over to your station for questioning."

Cody jotted Joe's name down on the pad for the official record, and added his two teammates.

"Cody, the CSIs are here," Catherine said, watching Ricardo Alvarez and Dexter Betancourt emerge from a white crime scene van. "The medical examiner just pulled in behind them."

Cody turned around, and they waited and watched the CSIs and the ME and his assistant put on protective white Kevlar suits, booties, and rubber gloves. Two more patrol cars pulled up and parked. Four officers from their homicide division got out of them. Cody added all of their names to the growing list.

Burt, the medical examiner, was the first to reach the group. Silently, he peered out at the nude corpse. Because the body was bloated by a buildup of gasses due to putrefaction, it bobbed in the quickly flowing water like an ocean buoy.

"That palm tree got partially pushed up on the bank," Joe said, "That's why the body didn't float farther downstream."

"Retrieve the body first," Burt directed, "Then have that tree transported to your facility for testing. There might be something important embedded in the bark."

"Hold on, everyone," Dexter called out as he drew nearer. "I need to photograph the perimeter and body before anything is touched or moved."

After photographs were taken of the corpse and the surrounding area on both sides of the canal, the scuba-clad officer waded into the water. To keep him from being pulled downstream by the force of the water, the ends of two ropes had been attached to his waist. They were being held by officers on both sides of the canal. Everyone watched him lift up and unhook the body from the tree, then push it toward the bank where they waited.

Burt and his assistant, Paul, pulled the body onto the sandy embankment. Shiny, metallic green blowflies swarmed above the ragged gashes on the back of the corpse's head, legs, and torso. Samples of the blowflies and the eggs that were hatching in the wounds were collected and sealed in plastic evidence containers.

Catherine and another detective standing to the right of her visibly gagged when the ME rolled the body over. The corpse was not only missing its face, but two large, jagged flaps of flesh from the chest to the pubic area lay open, exposing part of the intestine and most of the pelvic bone.

"Doc, could this be a female?" Cody asked. "There's still some long, dark hair on its head."

Burt rotated the almost-bald head from side to side, feeling the shape of the skull as he did so.

Catherine and two of the other detectives looked away when they saw the skin on the corpse's chest slip back and forth.

The ME looked up at his assistant, who had risen. "Paul, I'm ready. Let's get started. Make sure you get everything."

Everyone silently waited while Burt examined the corpse's pelvic area and then flexed the arms for rigor mortis. "This is a female. Her skull is rounded, and the posterior ramus...the jaw bone is straight. Also, her pelvis is wider than a male's and her sciatic notch is also wider. Yes, this is definitely a female. She's fairly young, and she's never had any children. However, I see some signs of vaginal tearing, so I suspect this young lady may have been raped."

"Burt, do you have any idea what the cause of death is, and when it may have occurred?" Catherine asked.

Burt rose. "Obviously this young woman didn't take her clothes off and jump into the canal for a swim in a hurricane. When I do the autopsy, I'll check to see if there's any water in her stomach or skull sinuses to be absolutely certain she was dead before entering the water."

"Anything else?" his assistant asked.

"Based on the rigor mortis and flexibility of her arms, I'd say she's been dead for more than eighteen hours. It's too soon for me to tell you how she died. However, I'm quite certain it didn't happen in this immediate vicinity."

"Why do you say that?" Catherine asked.

Burt knelt down again, and rolled the body over so her back was visible. "See the lividity on the bottom of her feet, right palm, and buttocks? Those mottled blue and purple splotches mean she was sitting with her knees pulled up when she died." He turned her over again. "Now look at the lighter blotches on her thighs. When she turned over in the water, the blood started to seep to the new area. She had to be sitting down when she died, and if her knees were pulled up as I suspect, it means she must have been leaning against something. Look around. There are only fields as far as we can see, which eliminates her leaning against any kind of tree, or structure in this area."

"Burt, is it possible that she died of natural causes, and someone panicked and got rid of her?" Cody asked.

"There's always that possibility. Like I said, I'll know more after I do the autopsy."

Before Burt could rise, Catherine asked if there were any tattoos, or other marks on her body that might help to identify her.

"Identification won't be easy on this one. Her fingertips are missing, so fingerprints are out. I'll scan her body and her teeth. Eventually, dental records might identify her as well as her bones and DNA. There is one other thing that might help…" He hesitated a moment, then pulled the two flaps of skin on her chest together. "See those two faint silvery lines? I'd say this young lady recently had implant surgery. The implants are gone, but those lines were made by a skilled surgeon."

Catherine gasped and grabbed onto Cody's arm. She didn't need any veri-fication of this corpse's identity. She was certain this was Hillary Blackstone.

CHAPTER TWELVE

"Cody, let's stop at that drugstore that was robbed. It's on our way to the station, and it won't take too long," Catherine said.

Cody kept driving. "How come? Our robbery unit is already looking into it."

"I know, but since we're passing the place, I'd like to look around."

"Delaney, what are you up to?"

"Listen here, Grumpy. I just want—"

"You just want what?"

"I want to meet the mayor's son. Doesn't it seem strange to you that someone broke into a boarded-up store and stole all of those whoopee drugs while a category-five hurricane was tearing through Florida?"

"Fine, but make it quick. We have a briefing in forty-five minutes, and I don't want to be late."

"Okay, now what's on your mind? Spill it, O'Dell. You're not usually this cranky when we leave a crime scene."

"Just thinking about the Blackstone kid, and how we're going to break the news to her parents when the ME confirms it's her."

"So you did connect the surgical lines to her. I thought you would."

"Shit, Delaney. I'm not only thinking about that kid. It's obviously too late for her. I'm remembering what your psychic friend said about the bastard planning another... Fuck! Another girl's murder."

"She didn't say it was going to be another girl."

Cody pulled the unmarked car into the strip mall's parking lot and parked in front of the Barnes and Noble Bookstore which was to the right of the pharmacy. He turned to her. "It will be another girl if this guy kills again. Those creeps don't pick someone who can fight back. They're cowards. They prey on the defenseless, like old people or young girls. And if he does kill again, then we might be looking for a serial killer. Defenseless people are their mojo, according to the FBI's profiles on serial killers."

"I know." She unbuckled her seatbelt, still looking at him. "Cody, maybe we got a lead on the boy who was with Hillary in the Target, and someone's questioning him as we sit here. Also, there's the couple of teenage boys who were brought to the station. Maybe they witnessed her being dumped, and can give us a description of who did it."

Cody gave her a wan smile. "And maybe your friend Amanda will call, and give us something to nab the bastard before he kills again. Come on, Babe. Have your quick look, and then let's get out of here." He opened the door and got out of the car.

Catherine followed him past two young men who were prying a sheet of plywood off the store's front window and into the CVS. The interior of the pharmacy was a dripping-wet mess, because part of its roof had been ripped off. There were puddles all over the tile floor, and soggy merchandise lying in them. Water still dripped off the stacked metal shelves, and employees were tossing everything that was covered in paper or cardboard into large, black trashcans.

The pharmacy area was also a wreck when they stepped into the enclosure. Not only had the roof been torn off in the entire area, but the ceiling had come down and knocked all of the metal shelves and what was on them onto the floor.

Catherine looked up at the clear blue sky, then coughed a couple of times to let the man who had his back to them know they were there.

The pharmacist—who was dressed in a white lab jacket and wrinkled, beige slacks—turned around from his blank computer screen. "You're not supposed to be in the pharmacy. You—" He didn't finish what he was about to say when he spotted Catherine holding up her badge.

"Are you Mr. Clarkston?" she asked, staring at the balding, stubble-faced man who stood around five-feet-ten.

"Sorry. I didn't realize you were officers," he said. "Yes, I'm Sheldon Clarkston. What can I do for you?"

"Tell me about the robbery," Catherine said.

"Your men just left here," he said, his shoulders drooping. "I told them everything I know."

Cody's back stiffened. "Good. Now you tell my partner what you told them."

"I wasn't here when it happened. I was at home with my family, making sure they were safe. When I got in around 6:00 this morning, I discovered the mess, and…" He pointed down at the heavily cracked concrete floor, and the wide, jagged hole that was partially filled with water and floating gray chips. "This hole is where the safe used to be. I always locked those drugs in the safe at closing time, so none of them would go missing."

"Mr. Clarkston, how often do you get opiates delivered?"

"Sometimes once a week. Sometimes not at all. It depends when our supply starts to run low."

"Who usually orders those drugs?"

"I'm the only one who places pharmaceutical orders. Yesterday, that delivery came in a few minutes after the store opened for business."

"Who else knew you were getting that delivery?"

Clarkston drew in a deep breath before answering. "Everyone who works in this department, but none of them... not a single one of my people would have done this. I'd vouch for each of them."

"Did you or any other employee notice someone hanging around this area that looked like they were shopping, but ultimately bought nothing?"

"You've got to be kidding. Yesterday was crazy back here. We had lines of customers waiting to pick up their drugs before the storm landed. My staff and I didn't have time to breathe, let alone look at people who may have been hanging around."

"Mr. Clarkston, what's the name of your store manager? I'd like to speak with him."

"The manager is Emily. Emily Patel. But I'm afraid she's not in today. Her daughter called a little while ago to say she'd been injured, and is getting her broken arm set in the Delray hospital."

Catherine pulled a card out of her pants pocket and handed it to him. "If you think of anything else, please call me. Also, please tell Ms. Patel to give me a ring as soon as she's able to."

He nodded. "Yes, of course. Is there anything else?"

"No," Catherine answered. "Good luck with cleaning up this mess. Come on, O'Dell. I want another look around, and then we'll get out of here."

Halfway down an aisle, Catherine stopped and looked from right to left, and then back at the pharmacy.

Cody silently waited by her side, and watched her looking from one place to another.

"Okay, I'm ready," she said, turning and heading toward the front door.

"What was that about?" he said, keeping up with her.

"I just wanted to see what Clarkston was going to do with my card."

"And?"

"He's just like his asshole father. He tossed it down on the wet floor."

CHAPTER THIRTEEN

Since the power was still off in the police station, the old, barely working generator was only turned on when the interior temperature reached 80 degrees. The large squad room where a dozen or more officers were gathered for their daily briefing was barely lit by the sun that streamed through two dirt-streaked front windows. The room was uncomfortably hot, smelled of sweat, and the sheen of moisture on the rows of metal folding chairs made them sticky to the touch.

The chief was standing in the front of the room when Catherine and Cody entered. He immediately turned to them, nodded, and then called out: "Everyone grab a seat and let's get started before we all melt."

Conversations ebbed to silence as everyone found a place to sit.

"As you can see, Hillary Blackstone, our missing young woman's picture is taped on the board behind me. We've just been told that a young woman's body has been pulled out of the canal…" He looked across at Cody who was sitting next to Catherine in the front row. "Cody O'Dell, who's leading this case, has informed me that the corpse may be Hillary Blackstone. However, I urge you not to make this information public, as the identity of the victim has not been confirmed. Cody, why don't you fill us in on what the ME told you."

Cody rose and faced the group. He swallowed first and then began. "The body was pulled out of a canal by our scuba team. The ME said the victim is definitely a young female, and based on her pelvic bone structure she hasn't had any children. He's uncertain how she died and will know more after he does the autopsy. Based on the victim's lividity and the blowflies…" He swallowed again. "Burt feels she must have been dead for more than eighteen hours. Delaney and I believe this victim may be Hillary Blackstone…"He cleared his throat. "We believe it may be Hillary, because her parents told us that she recently had breast implant surgery, and there were surgical scars on the female's chest." He nodded to the group, and then sat down.

"Dexter Betancourt," the chief called out. "Bring us up to date on what you and your partner found out?"

Dexter rose. "Ricardo and I went to see Daniel Spencer at his home. He's the principal at the Boca Raton High School where Hillary just graduated. The school was closed, and we wanted to find out if he remembered Hillary, and if he did, could he gives us some names of the school kids she hung around with. He certainly remembered her," he said with a smirk. "He called her 'lovely Hillary'."

Murmurs flitted around the room.

"Spencer said rodents had been seen in the girls' locker room, so the custodian had set some traps in there. After one of the students claimed she saw something caught in a trap, he went into the locker room after the school had closed for the day to check it out. Hillary was in there, and not alone. Seems she was kissing a girl, Deborah Logan, and she wasn't kissing her cheek, according to him."

"Anything else?" the chief asked, wiping his brow.

"Could be. The principal was tall, young, and physically fit. Strong enough, in my opinion, to easily lift someone Hillary's size. Also, it was pouring like crazy outside, but it looked like he had just returned to his home, because his hair was dripping wet and his shoes left puddles on the tile floor. Ricardo and I are going to interview Deborah Logan after we leave here. We'll get some information on Hillary's friends, and try to get the scoop on Daniel Spencer. That's it for now," he said, then sat down again.

The chief looked to his far right. "Joe, tell us about the knife."

A tall, slim, young man with his hair pulled back in a ponytail stood up. "Rick, Armando, and I examined the abandoned car after it was towed into our garage. A purse and gold locket were found on the front floor, and the driver's license we found in the wallet was Hillary Blackstone's. We took the fingerprints off the interior on the vehicle, and we're running them through our data base now to find some matches. No prints were found on the outside of the car, because they were washed away by the rain. The front driver-side tire had been slashed, and the tip of the knife was still embedded in the rubber. It's a common hunting knife, so that's a dead end, unless we can find the rest of the knife with some prints on it."

Whispered murmurs filtered around the room, and chairs creaked as officers and lab technicians tried to get comfortable on the hard seats.

"What about the video tapes?" the chief asked.

Joe turned to the back of the room. "Mary, that's your area. Take it." Joe sat down, and a tired-looking plain-clothed officer rose.

She cleared her throat, and looked down at the white sheet of paper she was holding. "We have a video showing the girl in question entering the store, and shortly afterward she was seen talking to a young man. I printed out his picture. Officer Dudley has just taken a copy of it to the Target to find out if anyone recognizes him. Another video shows that same girl taking a bottle of something off one of the shelves in the cosmetic area. The next image I have of her is when she's leaving the store."

Catherine turned around. "Was she alone when she left the store?"

"Yes," Mary answered. "The store was almost empty at that time of night, because of the storm, and because it was almost closing time. However, I did print pictures of those few who were in the store, as well as those who exited the store shortly before or after the girl was in there."

Catherine rose and faced the lab technician. "Mary, please look at those videos again. See if anyone looks strange… a guy just milling around… killing time… someone who looks like he's not there to shop."

"I plan to keep looking at them, Catherine. I'll let you know if I find anything else."

"Thank you."

They both sat down.

"Wait," Catherine said, rising again and looking around the room. "Where's Stan? I asked him to check on the pet stores that carried snakes."

"Snakes," someone called out. "Catherine, it's hot as hell in here. What the hell do snakes have to do with any of this?"

"Cathy, you might as well tell them," her uncle said.

She nodded and walked up to stand beside him. "We have a psychic working with us."

"You've gotta be shitting me," the same officer shouted. "Next we'll be messin' with witch doctors and voodoo shamans?"

Cody jumped up. "Clark, shut that trap of yours, before I shut it for you."

"Cody, calm down," Catherine said, grabbing his arm. "Listen, guys, I don't blame you for being skeptical, because I was when I got her phone call saying she envisioned a young woman being abducted outside a Target store."

The room quieted, and all eyes were directed at Catherine.

"She added that the young woman was being held prisoner in a dark room that was filled with snakes. I didn't believe a word she said, until we found out that Hillary Blackstone was missing after going to a Target store. I believe this woman has a gift, and now… now she says he's planning to kill again."

"So this guy likes snakes?" someone in the back of the room called out.

Catherine shrugged. "I don't know, but I think it's worth looking into."

"Did she say when this new abduction is supposed to happen?" Dexter asked.

"He's making plans as we speak," Catherine said. "Time is running out for another young girl, unless we can stop him."

CHAPTER FOURTEEN

Deborah Logan's house was directly across the cul-de-sac from the Blackstones' house. Like most of the homes in the area, the windows were still shuttered closed, and the lawn was littered with ripped-up shrubs and torn-off palm fronds.

Catherine knocked twice on the Logans' front door, while Cody waited beside her. An extremely thin, dark-haired woman who was wearing a skin-tight latex gym outfit opened the door.

"Mrs. Logan?"

"Yes."

"I'm Detective Delaney, and this is my partner, Detective O'Dell," Catherine said, holding up identification. "We'd like to ask you and your daughter some—"

"Yes… yes, of course. You're here about Hillary," she said, stepping to the side so they could enter. "Deborah! Deborah, come into the den. The police are here about your friend." She shut the door, then led them into a small room off to the right. "Have a seat. I'll just be a minute. My daughter probably has those ear things on again and didn't hear me call her."

When Mrs. Logan left the room, Catherine turned around to look at three large family photographs that were hanging on the wall. "Mmm. Seems like the Logans have two daughters."

Cody had just moved over to Catherine's side when Mrs. Logan returned. "This is my daughter, Deborah." They both turned around. The girl, who was dressed in jeans and a tight, multi-colored T-shirt stood a head taller than her mother, and probably weighed thirty or thirty-five pounds more than she did.

"Deborah, I'm Detective Delaney. I'd like to ask you some questions about Hillary."

Deborah nodded, then walked over to the sofa and sank down on the cushions. "Did you find her? Is she all right?" she asked, staring up at Catherine while wringing her hands together in her lap.

Catherine sat beside her, then took one of the girl's nail-bitten hands into her own. "Deborah, I know you were very close to Hillary," she said softly, watching the girl's eyes not only fill with tears, but also fill with fear. Fear that her secret of being gay might come out. "Deborah, did you talk to Hillary the day she disappeared?"

The tears slipped down Deborah's pale cheeks. "I speak to her every day. Sometimes three or four times a day. That is…" She hesitated to catch her breath. "We were very close friends."

Catherine squeezed the girl's trembling hand. "What did you talk about the day she went missing?"

Deborah looked across at her mother, who was leaning against the door frame, then pulled her hand free and stared down at the white tile floor. "We talked about my going on a diet, because my mother was on my case to lose some weight before I left for college. Then we talked about her mother, and some other things."

"Go on. Please."

Deborah turned to look at Catherine. "She wanted to go to Stamford with me," she said, her voice choked with emotion. "Hillary had the grades. They were fabulous, even better than mine. She got accepted to Stamford. She pleaded with her mother all the time, but her mother refused to let her go, because she wanted her in those damn pageants."

"Deborah, watch your mouth," Mrs. Logan called out.

Catherine took a folded sheet of paper out of her shirt pocket. After opening it wide, she showed the teenager the picture of the boy who'd been seen with Hillary in the Target. "Deborah, do you know who this boy is?"

She nodded. "That's Randy."

"Randy who?"

"Randy Dixon. He went to school with us."

"Were Hillary and Randy friends? Did they ever date?"

Deborah's back straightened. "No! They didn't date. Randy had a crush on her, but Hillary just laughed about it. She…" She shut up then, and picked at her thumb nail.

Catherine saw the turmoil and fear in her eyes. "Deborah, was Randy angry with her when she turned him down? Do you know if he ever followed Hillary, or if they ever had an argument?"

"I don't know if they had any arguments. Hillary told me that he asked her to go to the prom with him, but she told him that she didn't believe in proms, and went to the movies with me that night."

Catherine pressed on. "Think, Deborah. It's important. Did Hillary ever tell you that Randy was angry about being turned down for the prom? Did she ever say she was afraid of him?"

"I don't know," she stammered, twisting and untwisting her fingers together on her lap. "Hillary never mentioned him getting angry, or any of that. She only told me that he asked her out, and that she always told him no when he asked her. If he was angry, you'd have to ask Randy."

"What about Hillary's other friends? Did she mention having a fight with anyone? Did anyone bully her?"

Deborah's eyes widened. "I think once something may have happened, because Hillary told me one of the girls in her science class was giving her a hard time. I don't remember the girl's name, just that it had something to do with Randy breaking off with her."

"Are you saying the girl thought Hillary was the reason Randy stopped dating her?" Catherine probed.

"I don't know for sure. Whatever it was about, Hillary told me the principal took care of the problem, and the girl stopped bothering her after that."

Catherine cast a quick glance at Cody before resuming. "Deborah, do you know what the principal did to correct that problem?"

Deborah shook her head. "No. The principal's a neat guy. All the kids like him."

"One last question. Is there any chance that Hillary ran away?"

"No. I'm her friend," she said adamantly. "Her only friend. She would have told me if she was going to do that. You need to find her," she said, bursting into heart-wrenching sobs. "I know something's wrong. Please. Please, you've got to find her."

Cody's cell phone rang, and he stepped out of the room to take the call. Catherine couldn't hear what he was saying, but a few moments later he gave her a high-sign saying they had to leave.

CHAPTER FIFTEEN

"What's up?" Catherine asked when they were back in the car.

Cody started the engine, pressed down on the gas pedal, and drove away. "They picked up a migrant who's been making calls on Hillary's phone. He's at the station, waiting for us to question him."

"What do we know about him?"

"Not too much. Just that he's an illegal. They fingerprinted him, and found he has no criminal record."

"Where did they pick him up?"

"They traced the calls to a soup kitchen in Boynton Beach, and caught him with the phone in his hand."

A short, deeply tanned Hispanic man in soiled clothes was sitting behind a metal table in interrogation room three. He looked up when Cody and Catherine entered, then placed the half-filled plastic bottle of water that he had been drinking on top of the table.

Cody sat directly across from him. Catherine pulled her chair to the side of the table and sat down. "Julio, I'm Detective O'Dell, and this is Detective Delaney. Do you understand English, or do you need an interpreter?"

"I speak English," he answered with a thick Spanish accent.

"Good. Now let me tell you that this interview is being recorded. Do you understand what recorded means?"

He nodded.

"Julio, because this interview is being recorded, it means you have to answer the questions and not just nod your head. Understand?"

"Si."

"Good. I was told you have been read your rights. Do you understand that what you say in this room may be held against you, if you have committed a crime?"

"I understand," he said, nodding rapidly. "But I did nothing wrong."

"Good. A little while ago, two officers found you making a telephone call to Mexico on a cell phone."

"Si. I was making a call, but I found that phone. I did not steal it," he said, leaning forward so that his stomach pressed against the table.

"Where did you find it?"

One side of Julio's lower lip twitched as he glanced from one detective to the other.

"Julio, where did you find that phone?" Cody repeated.

The man's dark brown eyes widened, and his chest rose and fell repeatedly as he looked at Cody. "In the garbage. This morning. I didn't steal it. I swear. I was just going through one of those big metal garbage things looking for bottles or cans to sell, or food to eat if I found any. I'm sorry. I didn't mean to do something wrong. I just wanted to talk to my wife, my mother, and my two children for a few minutes. I don't have no money. It was important those calls. I didn't mean to do something wrong, I swear I found that phone. When I have money, I'll pay for those calls. I promise."

Cody motioned to Catherine.

"Julio, we need to know exactly where you found that phone," Catherine said, softly. "You see, a young girl is missing, and that's her phone."

Julio bolted up, knocking his chair over and onto the floor with a loud bang. "I found that phone," he shouted, waving his hands around. "I don't know nothin' about a girl. I found that phone. I swear it on my children's lives."

"I believe you." Catherine said, as Cody righted the fallen chair. "Please, sit down."

"Am I going to jail?" he asked, sitting again.

Catherine leaned forward and placed her palms on the table. "Julio, all we want is for you to help us. Understand?"

He was breathing hard now, and his legs were nervously jumping under the table. "Si."

"Where is that dumpster?"

"Behind a supermarket. I go there all the time, because they throw good food in there, and sometimes I don't make too much money to buy what to eat."

"Okay. Here's what we're going to do," Cody said, taking over. "We're going to have some officers drive you over to that dumpster where you say you found the phone."

"Am I arrested?"

"Julio, where did you get that black eye," Cody asked, looking directly at him and not answering his question.

"I got into a fight with a man."

"And that long scratch on your face, and the cuts on your knuckles?"

"We were fighting. He hit me, and I hit him back. Am I arrested?"

"After you show us where you found the phone, you'll be turned over to the U.S. Immigration and Customs Enforcement Department," Cody said, rising. "Officers will be in shortly to drive you to the supermarket. Thank you for your help."

When Cody and Catherine left the room, and the door was locked behind them, they headed down the hall to arrange Julio's ride.

"That's it? We're just going to let him go?" Catherine said, keeping pace with Cody.

Cody halted and turned to her. "Delaney, we'll grab that water bottle for his DNA, but we have nothing to hold him on."

"He's all bruised and cut up. He could be the one who snatched Hillary."

"Cathy, I don't like it either, but we have no choice. ICE can hold him for 45 days while they do a background check. If their records show he's been deported once before, they can prosecute and jail him for two years."

"Shit! That means we only have 45 days to nail him."

"That's if we can prove that he grabbed her. We still have the Dixon boy and the principal to check out. Let's see where that leads us."

"And it might not be any of them," she said, walking on. "Cody, I researched snakes on the internet. Did you know some of them eat rodents?"

They stopped at Cody's desk. "So? What are you getting at?"

"The principal told our guys that the custodian had set rodent traps, and that's why he went into the locker room. Could the custodian be a snake collector? What did he do with the ones he caught?"

Cody sighed. "Snakes eat rodents… hmm… okay. Find out who the custodian is and where we can find him. I need a few minutes to arrange Julio's ride to the dumpster, and get Betancourt to pick up the Dixon kid for questioning. After that, you and I will pay a visit to the rat catcher."

CHAPTER SIXTEEN

The custodian was found later that afternoon at the Boca Raton High School. Cody pounded on the green metal door for ten minutes, before a man who matched his height unlocked and pulled it open.

"Summer school is over. The school is closed," the man snapped, one hand gripping a mop stick, the other the door.

"Are you Anton Erickson?" Cody asked, as the custodian was shutting the door in his face.

Cody pressed his hand against the door to keep it open. "Yah. What do you want?"

Catherine held up her police shield. "We'd like to talk to you."

The frown lines on the man's caramel-colored forehead deepened. It was obvious that he wasn't happy, but he stepped aside to let them enter. "Is this about the girl?" he asked, letting the door close.

"What girl are you talking about?" Cody asked, standing an arm's length away from him.

"Look, I don't have time for games," the custodian said, his brown eyes staring directly into Cody's. "I have all of these floors to wash, and the chewing gum that's stuck on 'em is driving me nuts."

"What girl are you talking about?" Cody repeated in that same even tone, not budging an inch, and staring back at him.

Erickson lifted the sopping wet mop, and dropped it into a large pail that was filled with sudsy water. "That girl who is missing. That's who I'm talking about."

"Do you know her?" Catherine asked.

He shook his head. "No, I saw the mayor talking on TV, and saw her picture."

"Did you recognize her?" Catherine asked, taking over.

"Yes. She was one of the real pretty girls," he said, brushing away a curl of black hair that had fallen over his right eye. "You couldn't help but notice her."

Catherine noticed he wasn't wearing a wedding band. "Did you ever speak with her?"

"I saw her in the halls a few times when I had to come in early for some emergency cleanup, but I never talked to her."

"Anton, may I call you Anton?" Catherine said softly, hoping she'd get more out of him if she acted friendlier.

He nodded.

"Anton, the principal told us that you had set rodent traps in the girls', locker room. Is that right?"

"Yes. Mr. Spencer said a girl saw a rat or a mouse in there, so he called and told me to set a few traps to catch it. I set three of them before I went home that night."

"Did you catch anything?"

"Mr. Spencer said he emptied one of the traps before I got to work the next night, and I found another one after that. I set the traps again. They're still in there. Do you want to see where I put them?"

"No. That won't be necessary. Anton, were any girls in the locker room when you set those traps?"

"No, definitely not! No one was left in the school, and all of the doors were locked, just like you found them today."

"I see," Catherine said, noticing his muscular arms and how his chest bulged beneath the navy, short-sleeved shirt. "If you usually work later in the day, how come you're in here so early today?"

"Mr. Spencer called me," he said, sounding annoyed. "I was supposed to be off today, but he told me to check things out to make sure the school wasn't flooded from the storm. Since I had to come in, I decided to get these floors washed up today, instead of waiting to do it next week. This way I can take off a couple of extra days to visit some friends."

Catherine nodded. "Is there anything you can tell us about Hillary Blackstone? Something that might help us find her."

"Sorry. Wish I could tell you more, but I can't. It's too bad what happened to her."

"What do you mean, 'it's too bad what happened to her'?"

Anton's eyes blinked rapidly a few times, and his hands clenched and unclenched at his sides. "I mean the girl is missing, and something coulda' happened to her. That's what I mean."

Catherine nodded.

"I hope you find her," he added, raising one hand and wiping the sweat off his brow.

"This is my card," Cody said, slipping a card into the man's shirt pocket. "Give me a call if you think of something."

"I will... If I think of something."

Catherine turned back before leaving. "Anton, do you have a pet?"

"A pet? No. I don't have a pet."

"What about snakes? Do you like snakes?"

"Snakes?" He cringed. "I hate those ugly things."

Catherine, nodded, thanked him, and then walked out of the school.

Once they were back in the car, she swiveled on the seat to look at Cody. "Cody, did you pick up on him saying: 'the girl who *was* missing'?"

"Yup! Past tense. He also said she *was* one of the pretty ones. Past tense again."

"You think he had something to do with Hillary's disappearance?"

"He's big enough," Cody said, starting the engine. "Strong enough, and I definitely don't like him."

"So what are we going to do about him?"

"We're going to check out where he lives, Delaney."

"Sounds good to me, O'Dell. You be my lookout, and I'll peek in the windows."

Cody smiled. "I like that. You can peek in my windows anytime, Delaney. Just let me know when you're going to do it, so I can put on a good show for you."

CHAPTER SEVENTEEN

"Damn," Catherine muttered as they slowly cruised past the custodian's house. "Take another turn around the block. Maybe the neighbors will go back in their house, after they've finished stacking their wet stuff and trash cans on the curb."

"I think we need to forget that peek for now," Cody said, picking up speed.

"Cody, drive around the block again."

"Forget it. The gate on that chain link fence has a lock on it. You'd have to climb over it, and one of the neighbors would see you."

"So what? I'm a cop."

"So, you don't have a warrant. Let's forget it for now. We'll think of something later."

"Fine," she said, "But, humor me. Just one more drive by so I can take a good look at his house."

Cody drove around the block one more time, and stopped in front of a neighboring house. "Don't you dare get out of this car. I'm warning you, Delaney."

"Cody, look around. What do you see?"

"A nice, quiet neighborhood. Some place I'd eventually like to live."

Catherine scanned the two-story houses on both sides of the street. "These houses look expensive."

"They look like most of the newer communities that were built for families."

"Exactly! They're all two-story houses that have three or four bedrooms in them. I'd say they probably cost four or five-hundred-thousand dollars, so I'm wondering why Erickson would buy a fairly expensive house in a family neighborhood. He's single and attractive. Why didn't he buy a place in Delray, where it's jumping?"

"How do you know he's single?"

"He wasn't wearing a wedding ring."

"Not wearing a ring doesn't mean anything. But even if he is single, maybe he likes being around children… Where are you going with this?" he asked, glancing over at her.

She turned to him. "First of all, I'd like to know how he can afford this house on a custodian's salary. And more importantly, why does he have a lock on his gate? What is he hiding?"

"Okay. You got me there. But it's late, and I'm starving. Can we please get some dinner, before I take a bite out of these leather seats?"

Cody's cell phone rang. "O'Dell," he answered. "Yes.… Yes.… Who's with him?… We'll be there as soon as we grab a quick burger." He clicked off, and shifted the car into drive.

"What's up?"

"The Dixon boy's at the station with his father."

"Randy Dixon?"

"Yup! Looks like it's going to be another long night."

CHAPTER EIGHTEEN

"I don't know why we have to see that pimp tonight," Ricardo grumbled. "I told the redhead I'd be at her place early, and if I piss her off again, I won't score tonight."

"You'll get to her a little later," Dexter said, turning the corner onto Glades Road. "Chico's our pipeline to the street talk. Maybe he's heard something about the abduction."

Ricardo slumped down on his seat. "I doubt that. He's into gangs, whores and drugs, not stupid little teenagers who go out in a storm."

"He still may have heard something. It's worth a try," Dexter said.

"Fine. Where are we heading?"

"We'll hit the Town Center Mall first."

"Dex, the mall is still open. It's too early for him to be collecting his money from the hookers. They're still screwing in the side hallways, or jacking off some jerk in his car."

"Nope! He's here. I see his silver-gray Caddy parked over to the right," Dexter said, making a left into the large parking lot.

Ricardo straightened as soon as his partner parked their car beside the pimp's. When the motor was shut off, they both got out of the car, and he rapped on the Caddy's closed window. "Chico, wake up! We need to talk to you."

"Aw, shit. You two again," Chico said, opening his eyes and staring straight ahead through the windshield. "Whadaya want this time?"

"Don't be a fuckin' smartass," Dexter said, leaning forward and resting his arm on top of the roof.

Chico rolled down the window and turned to them. "So whadaya want? Let's hear it already. I need to get some shut eye."

"Have you heard anything on the street about the Blackstone girl?" Dexter asked, looking at the swarthy Latino who was wearing an expensive designer suit, and half-a-dozen thick, gold chains around his neck.

"Why do you always come to me? Why don't you bother someone else? You two are going to get me killed some day."

Ricardo smiled. "Then be sure you put us in your will, dickhead, 'cause we'd hate to miss out on all the money you're not reporting to the IRS."

Chico's eyes narrowed, and his long, finely-manicured fingers wound tightly around the steering wheel. "I didn't hear nothin' about that girl. No one is talkin' bout her."

When Dexter leaned into the car, Chico released the wheel and quickly slid over to the far side of the seat.

Dexter reached in and grabbed his arm. "Chico, look at me."

Instead of looking at the detective, he stared at the hand that was holding onto his arm.

"Okay. Sorry. I shouldn't have done that," Dexter said, removing his hand and taking a step back. "Chico, I'm going to let you in on a little secret."

Chico peered across at him.

"This is something you can't tell anyone. If you do, I'll make sure your ass is locked in a cell for more years than you can count. Understand, Buddy?"

"I understand," he mumbled.

"We think this guy is going to grab another girl, and very soon."

Chico's eyes wandered from one detective to the other. "So whadaya want me to do? You're the cops. Get him before he does that."

"Listen, you little shit. I want you to ask around. See if anyone has heard any rumors about the Blackstone girl, or who may have snatched her."

"Okay. I'll try. Now can I take my nap?"

"There's one other thing."

'Yeah. What is it this time?"

"We think this guy likes snakes."

Chico cringed. "You gotta be kidding."

"That's what we were told. Ask around. Find out if someone collects snakes. Another girl's life is on the line, and the clock is ticking."

Chico was on his phone when they drove away.

CHAPTER NINETEEN

Randy Dixon was a slim, handsome young man with shoulder-length brown hair and hazel eyes that were accentuated by long, dark lashes. His father, a prominent, middle-aged attorney who owned a large law firm in Boca Raton, was sitting at the table beside his son when Cody and Catherine entered the interrogation room.

"Mr. Dixon, Randy, thanks for coming in," Cody said. "I'm Detective O'Dell and this is my partner Detective Delaney." He sat down across the table from the father and son, and Catherine took a seat near the door.

"What is this about?" Mr. Dixon asked.

Cody sucked in a deep breath and released it before he began. "Mr. Dixon, we've been told that your son was a friend of Hillary Blackstone."

"Are you accusing my son—"

"No, we're not accusing your boy of anything," Cody said, cutting him off. "We'd just like to ask him some questions, because we believe he was the last person to see Hillary before she disappeared."

"And when was that?"

"Mr. Dixon, we have the store's security video. Randy was seen with Hillary before she left the Target store."

He looked at his son. "Is that right?"

The boy's hands were shaking, and his feet nervously bobbed up and down beneath the table. "She was shopping, and I said hello to her."

Catherine pulled her chair closer to Cody. "Randy, anything you say might help us to find Hillary," she said softly, looking directly at him. "You had your arm around Hillary."

"So what?" the father interrupted. "Boys and girls do that."

"Mr. Dixon, please understand that we're just trying to find a missing girl. We're not accusing your son of anything."

"Fine. Then go ahead."

"Randy, when you saw Hillary, did she say she was meeting someone when she left the store, or that someone was waiting for her in her car?"

"No," he answered, glancing up at his father. "I like Hillary. I asked her out a few times, and even to the prom, but she always turned me down. When she was in the store that night, I asked her why she came out on such a miserable night. She laughed and said she needed some cream for her hands."

"Randy, how come you were in that store on such a terrible night?" Catherine asked, noticing how the boy's bottom lip trembled.

"I've been working part-time in that Target since I was sixteen. My father said I had to save up for the extras at college."

"And that night?"

"I worked overtime, because the store was getting ready for the storm. I was told to make sure that none of the stock was close to the floor in case we got flooded, so I was piling stuff on the upper shelves."

Catherine nodded. "I'd like to ask you some questions about your ex-girlfriend. What was her name?"

"My son has lots of girlfriends," his father jumped in. "Randy is very popular. Girls call him at home non-stop to invite him to parties."

"I'm sure your son is very popular, Mr. Dixon. He's a handsome boy, and I understand he was the star of the football team."

That brought a smile to the man's face.

"Randy, I'm talking about the girl who was brought to the principal's office, because she was bullying Hillary."

"That was Sonny. She's a hot head. She thought Hillary was the reason I stopped taking her out, but Hillary had nothing to do with it. I just couldn't stand Sonny following me around wherever I went. She even came to Target and almost got me fired."

"What's Sonny's full name?"

"Sonia. She hated Sonia, and made everyone call her Sonny."

"What's Sonia's last name?"

"Same as mine, Dixon. But we're not related."

"Dixon," Catherine said with a smile.

"It's not funny. She always pestered me to marry her when we got out of school, and said that way she wouldn't have to change her last name."

"Isn't that the girl who told you she was pregnant?" his father asked, looking at him.

"She wasn't pregnant. She lied. I never laid a hand on her. I swear it, Dad."

"Randy, how do you know she wasn't pregnant?"

"If she was, it wasn't from me. I went out with her three times. We never did more than kiss, and she wasn't my girlfriend like she told everyone in school. She's just a whack job and big liar."

"Randy, did you see anyone following Hillary around the store while she was shopping?" Cody asked, taking over the questioning.

The boy shook his head.

"Did you notice anyone walking around that just didn't seem right? Perhaps someone who wasn't really shopping... just hanging around?"

Randy shook his head again. "There was only a few of us working that night. I did notice a couple of shoppers... men buying last-minute cases of bottled water. A couple of them also asked me if I had more batteries in the store room, because there were none left on the shelves."

"Nothing seemed odd to you?"

"I was very busy. I wasn't paying attention to who came or went, until I saw Hillary..."

"Go on," Cody prodded.

"She was dripping wet from the rain. I joked with her and asked why she didn't have an umbrella with her. She said the wind blew it away." He swallowed. "When she was ready to leave, I asked her if she wanted me to walk her out with an umbrella. She said she was so wet it didn't matter." He looked up at his father. "I shoulda walked her out. Maybe if I did, Dad..."

"It's not your fault," his father said, wrapping his arm around his son's shoulders. "The girl's parents never should have let her out in that weather."

Someone knocked on the door. Catherine walked to it, and stepped outside. When she returned, her face was pale. "We have a positive ID," she said, looking down at Cody.

The silence in the room was broken by the ringing of her cell phone. Catherine pulled it out of her pocket and answered, "Detective Delaney."

"It's Amanda. He's got another one. He's doing terrible things to her on a red bed."

CHAPTER TWENTY

It was drizzling outside when Catherine and Cody arrived at the Blackstones' residence.

"I think you should take this one," Cody told her when they reached the front door.

Catherine nodded. She hated having to tell someone that a loved one was dead, but if you were investigating that particular case, sometimes you were the one who had to do it.

A minute or two after Cody had knocked on the door, the outside lights went on, and Mrs. Blackstone opened it.

Catherine stepped forward. "Mrs. Blackstone, may we come in?"

Just one brief look at Catherine's face had Hillary's mother silently leading the way into the den. Mr. Blackstone, who was watching TV, rose when they entered. "Did you find her?" he burst out.

"I'm so sorry to have to tell you—"

Mrs. Blackstone crumbled to the floor in a dead faint. Cody immediately lifted the woman up, and carried her over to the sofa. While he was trying to revive her, Catherine was calling for an ambulance and watching Mr. Blackstone sink onto a chair and burst into sobs.

The paramedics arrived within a few minutes, and sprang into action. Mrs. Blackstone's vitals were checked, and then an oxygen mask was placed over her nose. "We're taking her to Delray Community Hospital," one of the medics told Cody. "Her pressure's too high. She needs to be closely monitored."

"Fine. We'll follow you, and bring her husband with us," Cody said. Then he turned to Catherine, who was kneeling in front of Mr. Blackstone, trying to soothe him.

"I don't want to know," the distraught father repeated over and over between sobs. "Don't tell me anything. I don't want to know. I don't want to know. My poor baby."

* * *

Amanda Plummer's face looked like she'd been crying when she opened the door to let the detectives in. Her eyes were red and swollen, and the front of her white blouse looked like it was wet from fallen tears.

Catherine peered down at her in the wheelchair. "I'm sorry we took so long to get here," she said, noticing how wild and unruly Amanda's unbraided hair was. "We had a hospital emergency. We couldn't help it."

"Come inside," Amanda whispered.

Cody and Catherine followed her wheelchair into the kitchen, and over to the table. Catherine sat opposite Amanda. Cody sat to right of Catherine.

"Amanda, what did you see?"

Amanda didn't answer at first. Her eyes stared at Catherine, but it was as though she was staring at some far-off place. Her chest rose and fell, and her mouth hung slightly open, drawing air into her lungs.

"Amanda, you must tell me what you saw. Please... We need your help."

Amanda's clenched hands came up on the table, and then she stared down at them. "It was terrible. I saw her on a red bed."

"Are you saying the bed was bloody?" Catherine asked.

"No. No, blood. A sheet or something was red, but no blood."

"Did you see him? Did you see his face?" Catherine said, reaching over the table and grasping Amanda's hands.

"I saw his back," she said, leaving her ice-cold hands within Catherine's. "He was just a dark shadow." She suddenly yanked her hands free, and started to rock back and forth in the wheelchair.

Catherine and Cody froze, watching her every move.

Amanda's eyelids flickered, then closed. The rocking went on, her chest hitting the table, her back hitting the wheelchair.

They waited and watched.

"I see them... I see that bedroom." Amanda rocked faster, deep in a trance. "It's a red sheet... a shiny, red sheet that she's lying on. There's red drapes... they're hanging from the ceiling around the bed." Amanda's breathing became labored. "She has curly, blonde hair. She's young... Frightened... She can't breathe... She can't breathe... His hand is pressing down on her throat... choking her..." Amanda's rocking increased, faster and faster. "He's over her... Raping her... Her face is turning blue... She can't breathe..."

Catherine gasped and grabbed onto Cody's arm.

"His blue aura is getting brighter. She can't catch her breath. He's still on top of her… Doing things to her… Terrible things… Making her cry."

"Where is she?" Cody pleaded. "Tell us, Amanda, so we can find her. Where is that place? Look at it. See it, and tell us where can find that girl."

"He's laughing now."

Cody rushed to the side of Amanda's wheelchair, knelt beside it, and grabbed one of her hands. "Amanda, where is that house? Look for it. Tell us where it is, so we can get to her before it's too late."

Suddenly Amanda jerked her hand away. Her eyes flew open and rolled up, until only the whites could be seen.

"Amanda, what's happening? What do you see," Cody pleaded.

"I see… I see him carrying her up to the snake room," Amanda answered, and then she passed out.

CHAPTER TWENTY-ONE

With their siren screaming and their red roof light flashing, Catherine and Cody made it back to their station in record time. Cody flew out of the car and Catherine raced into the station on his heels. The admitting office's mouth dropped open when he saw their panicked expressions.

"Mike, did a call come in about a missing girl?" Cody blurted out.

"No. Is another kid missing?"

"Don't know. If that call comes in, send it back to me immediately," he called back, rushing toward the interior door.

"No problem," Mike shouted to their retreating backs.

Cody sat down at his cluttered desk, and booted up his computer.

"Are you contacting the missing person's data base?"

Cody nodded, and pounded on the keyboard, ignoring the half dozen dirty Styrofoam coffee cups that could have tipped over.

"What are you two doing back here?"

"Uncle Steve, what the heck are you doing here?" Catherine said, eyeing his wrinkled shirt and rolled-up shirt sleeves. "It's almost midnight. Your doctor told you to take it easy for a couple of weeks."

"What's he doing?" he asked, staring at Cody and ignoring her question.

"Amanda just told us he has another girl."

"Aww, shit!"

"Uncle Steve, please sit down before you fall down."

"Well, what's going on?"

"Mike at the front desk said no one's called us to report a missing person, so Cody's checking the national data base to see what they have."

The chief sat down and stared at the computer screen as Cody typed: EAST COAST OF FLORIDA. POSSIBLE TEENAGER. FEMALE. BLOND HAIR. MISSING... He stopped and turned to look at the chief and Catherine. "Cathy, what do I type? How long can she be missing? Maybe he's keeping a whole slew of kids locked up someplace, until he picks one of them."

"Type in a week's time," Catherine said. "No! That can't be right. Amanda just warned us that he was making his plans to do it. He didn't already have her. He must have just snatched her. Put down within 48 hours. That should cover it."

Cody typed in the dates, and then hit the send key. Seconds later, the computer pinged that an email had come in. Cody clicked it open. It was a response confirming their request, and saying the information would be forwarded shortly.

The three of them just glanced at one another, not knowing what to say until Catherine broke the silence. "Uncle Steve, why are you here so late?"

"Had to clean up some paper work, and then I got more of the mayor's bullshit that I had to take care of."

"So what does he want now?"

"He invited me to one of his wife's charity events—"

"A charity event? That's a laugh," Catherine said. "I'm sure he'll make sure the press will be there, so he can show what a charitable person he is. The only thing that man is interested in is getting reelected and sitting in his fancy office. Charities, my ass."

"That's politics, my dear. Not only does he want me there in full uniform, but he wants a tableful of uniformed officers and their wives there to show that we also support his reelection."

"And just how much will our support cost each of us?" Cody asked.

"Five bills a plate," the chief answered. "But we don't have to worry about laying out the money. He says he's going to write our tickets off as another station expense."

"You're joking?" Catherine said. "That's got to be against the law."

"I told him that, and he said he'd sign the voucher and not to worry about it."

Catherine smiled.

"Cathy, why do you have that shit-eating grin on your puss?"

"Because, Uncle, I think we should let him sign that voucher for a phony expense, and then someone... someone should tip off Internal Affairs about a misuse of police funds."

A wide smile spread across Chief Delaney's face. "Mmm... what an interesting idea..."

The computer pinged again, and Cody clicked the incoming mail. "Nothing's come in within the last 48 hours. There's no hits. Nothing," he muttered with his shoulders drooping.

"If no one's called in, what do we do now?"

Cody turned to Catherine and shook his head. "We all go home."

Catherine's heart raced, and a vein throbbed in her neck. She'd been raped, terrified, and twenty years later still had nightmares, proof of the trauma she'd undergone. "Cody, we have to do something to help her. There must be—"

"There's nothing we can do, until we get that call," he said, looking at her stricken face and feeling helpless. "Only God can help that kid now."

CHAPTER TWENTY-TWO

While the officer's morning briefing was going on in the squad room, Catherine remained in her office glued to her computer screen. She hadn't slept well the previous night, because something about Amanda Plummer kept niggling in her mind most of the night. Giving up on getting any sleep, she made herself some herbal tea and carried the steaming mug into the living room.

Comfortable on the sofa with her bare feet stretched across the cocktail table, her thoughts focused on Amanda. *Why is her face scarred like that? And why is she a cripple? Was she involved in an accident, or does her physical disability and facial disfigurement have something to do with her psychic abilities?*

Catherine still hadn't come up with any answers by the time she'd finished the tea, but she'd spotted the telephone directory on a bookshelf across the room, and a new thought popped into her mind. Was Amanda married? Other than Amanda, Cody, and herself, no one else seemed to be in the house the two times they'd gone there to talk to her. But that didn't mean that a husband or other relative wasn't in another room. Sure enough, after looking through the book, she found a Michael and Amanda Plummer listed at the same address.

Out of sheer curiosity, Catherine entered his name in the criminal data base as soon as she got into her office, and there he was. Michael Plummer had been convicted of Aggravated Battery eight years earlier, after assaulting and almost killing his wife, Amanda. Since he'd had prior arrests for assaulting two other women, this third offense was listed as a class 3 felony. After checking his record further, Catherine discovered that he was still incarcerated in the Florida State Prison, serving out a fifteen-year sentence.

"Mmm," she mumbled aloud, clicking on the printer. A copy of Michael Plummer's criminal record slid out a moment later.

"What's up, Delaney," Cody asked when he walked into her office.

Catherine's chair swivelled around. "You first. Any missing person calls come in?"

"Nope. Dexter's contacting his snitch to see if he's heard anything. He'll let us know if he gets a lead. So what was so important that you didn't come to the briefing?"

"I couldn't sleep last night—"

"That's your fault. I told you to sleep over at my place."

She ignored his remark, rose from the chair, and started to pace around the small room. "Amanda's husband is the one who beat the shit out of her and left her paralyzed."

Cody said nothing.

"He's in Florida State Prison, serving a fifteen-year sentence."

"Okay."

She stopped pacing, and faced him. "He was charged with Aggravated Battery. He's up for parole in a few months."

"Okay," he repeated, walking over to her desk and sitting on the edge of it. "So what are you getting at?"

"I don't know if Amanda divorced him, or if they're still married. It doesn't matter either way. The question is: is that man still pissed at her for having to serve time, and if so, will he try to hurt her again or kill her?"

"Babe, you said it wasn't going to happen for a couple of months. Find out the exact date of his parole hearing and we'll monitor it. If the board approves his early release, I'll ride up to the prison and have a little chat with him."

"Cody, no one deserves to be beaten like that," she said, slamming her fist against the wall. "I don't want that bastard getting out for good behavior, or some other bullshit like he's suddenly found religion. I want that son-of-a-bitch to serve his full fifteen years, and not one day—one hour—or one minute less."

"Calm down, Delaney. That's not our decision to make."

"I don't give a shit if it's fair," she said, tightly wrapping her arms around her middle. "I don't want her hurt again. She's been through enough. Look what he's done to her. She won't be able to defend herself. She—"

"Babe, calm down," he said, rising and walking to her. He unfolded her arms and grabbed hold of her hands. "One way or another, we'll make sure nothing happens to her. Trust me. But for now, let's go and pay her a visit. I want to ask Amanda if this new girl is still alive, and hopefully... hopefully this time she'll be able to tell us where we can find that goddamn house."

CHAPTER TWENTY-THREE

Plainclothes detectives Stan Wilkins and Thomas "Hawk" Whitehall were on their way into the twelfth pet shop that carried snakes. There were 42 pet shops that sold them within a thirty-mile radius of the canal where the female victim's body had been found, but so far nothing was panning out.

"This is the second day we're on this fuckin' snake detail," Wilkins bitched, opening the shop's door and letting his partner enter before him. The interior of the well-lit store was spacious, and smelled of kitty litter. Puppies barked, and birds tweeted and squawked in different areas. Shelves were filled with bags and cans of animal food. Toys, and dog coats and collars hung on racks.

Hawk walked over to a young man who appeared to be in his mid-twenties, and tapped him on his shoulder. "Excuse me. Are you the owner of this store?"

"No, I'm not the owner," he answered, shutting the door of a cage that held a dozen or more colorful parakeets. He turned around. "I'm the manager. Can I help you?"

Hawk showed him his badge. "We'd like to ask you some questions," he said, peering at the multiple gold rings that pierced the man's nose, mouth, and ears.

"Sure. My help isn't in yet, but the store's not busy. Ask away?"

"Your ad says you carry snakes."

"We do. What kind are you looking for?"

Hawk glanced at Stan.

"Actually, we're looking for a person who buys a lot of snakes, possibly dangerous ones," Stan said.

"We don't carry poisonous snakes. Those you can buy on-line."

"Shit!" Stan exclaimed. "Are you saying anyone can order a poisonous snake on line?"

"Sure can," he answered, rubbing his heavily tattooed arm. "Most of them are shipped from foreign countries. If you'd like me to order one for you, I can do that, but I'd have to have the snake shipped directly to you and not to the store."

"Has anyone recently ordered one of those snakes? Say within the last couple of months?"

"No, I'd remember that. Mostly we get kids whose mothers won't let them have a dog, so they settle on a snake or lizard that won't grow too big or poop on the floor."

"Do you know if anyone else in this store placed that kind of order?"

"I'm the manager here. I'd be the person they'd have to come to. The others are part-timers, and they can't place any pet orders."

"What about someone who buys a lot of snakes and mice? Do you remember one of those customers?"

The manager tugged on his lip ring. "There was a man a while back… Yes, I remember him now. He bought every one of the snakes we had in stock that day. Mmm… There must have been at least six or nine of them, and he also bought some mice."

Stan and Hawk eyed one another.

"Do you remember his name? Do you have a record of that sale?" Hawk asked.

The door opened, and a woman with two little boys walked in.

"I'd have to check my records," he said, looking at the customers. "I'll be right with you folks. Have a look around."

"Mommy, look. There's a cute puppy over there," one of the youngsters said, running over to the wall that was lined with puppy-filled cages.

"I'm sorry. I've got to go and help them," he said, ready to walk away.

"Hold up! This is very important." Hawk handed him a card. "Please call me the minute you find his name."

"I'll call you, but it probably won't be until tonight, after the store closes," he said, looking at the boy who was sitting on the floor with his fingers reaching into one of the lower cages. "I can't spend too much time in the back of the store, but I will call you if I find something." He was just about to walk away again, but stopped and turned back. "There is another thing I can check out."

"What's that?" Hawk asked.

"I just remembered the old guy who bought a dozen mice and another snake yesterday."

"What's his name and where can we find him?"

"My sales help is coming in at noon. Soon as he gets here, I'll check yesterday's receipts and give you a ring."

CHAPTER TWENTY-FOUR

The engine in Cody and Catherine's unmarked car wouldn't turn over, so they borrowed a black-and-white patrol car from the station's motor pool, something they didn't like to do when they were dressed in civilian clothes.

"She's not home," an elderly gentleman called out from the neighboring yard as they were walking toward Amanda's house.

"Hi there," Catherine said. She and Cody changed course and headed over to him. "Would you happen to know where the lady went?"

"Yup! Helped her get into her van like I always do," he said, stroking his long, kinky-white beard. "She's visiting the orphanage, just like she does every week since I know her."

"Sounds like you know Amanda very well," Cody said, noting the man was wearing a knobby, gray sweater in the eighty-seven degree heat.

"Yup! For more than twenty years now."

"Mister…"

"It's Jake," he told Cody, glancing up at him. "Looks like you folks can use a cold drink."

"We'd love some cold water," Catherine said with a smile.

"Well then, come on in and sit a spell. I have some fresh lemonade I just made with lemons from my own trees."

Jake's house was almost as hot inside as it was outside. The furnishings were clean, but definitely had a woman's stamp on it. Every piece of upholstered furniture in the small living room had at least three crocheted doilies on it, and every table top was covered with framed family photographs and stacks of books and magazines.

"Here we are," Jake said, walking in a few minutes later with three glasses on a wooden tray. "Sit. Sit. Make yourselves comfortable." After they sat down on the green velvet sofa, he handed Catherine and Cody tall, cold glasses that were filled to the top. Jake sat across from them in a dainty Victorian ladies' chair, and then took a long sip of lemonade.

"Mmm. This is really delicious," Catherine said.

"That's what Amanda always says every time I bring her a pitcher. Are you here about the missing girls?"

Catherine choked on her mouthful.

Cody leaned forward, the sweating glass clutched in his hands. "Amanda told you what she saw? The girls, and—"

"Amanda and I are good friends. Very good friends. She's almost like a daughter to me."

"Tell us about Amanda," Cody said, softly.

The old man carefully set his glass on the side table, and turned back to them. "She's a sweet thing. Used to be real pretty. Uhh... Not that she's not pretty now," he said, quickly correcting himself. "Amanda told me she grew up in an orphanage. She didn't tell me what happened to her folks or why she didn't live with a relative, and I didn't ask her. She worked hard at a local McDonalds when she got out of that place, and after a spell she got promoted to manager. Then she met *him*," he said, frowning. "I told her not to marry that man. Didn't like him from the start, because he had shifty eyes. But Amanda was young and looking for someone to love her, so she did what she did, and it was trouble from day one."

Catherine set her empty glass on the table. "Jake, what do you mean trouble from day one."

Jake sighed and settled back against the chair. "You being police, I guess it's all right if I talk about her. It's not that I like to gossip about people, but—"

"No, no. we understand you're talking to us, because you're Amanda's friend."

"I am her friend, and I'm afraid she's going to get hurt again."

"Hurt? How's she going to get hurt?" Catherine asked.

"It's her husband. He's getting out of prison soon, and Amanda's scared to death he's going to come after her for having him locked away."

Catherine glanced at Cody. "She told you that?"

The old man nodded. "That man is dangerous. From the day she introduced him to me, I knew he was a drinker, because he reeked of hard liquor. I warned her about him, but Amanda laughed and said they had just come from a party. Party, my butt! As soon as they got married and he moved in with her, I could hear him shouting and cursing her all the way into my house. I also saw the black and blue marks on her face and arms," he said, with his eyes growing teary. "I called the cops a few times when I heard them fighting, but Amanda would never press charges."

"Go on," Catherine prodded.

Jake sniffed, took a handkerchief out of his sweater pocket, and blew his nose before he went on. "She got pregnant," he finally said in a whisper.

"Amanda had a baby?" Catherine blurted out.

"She would have had a baby if he didn't nearly kill her that night. It was horrible. She was so excited about having it. Sometimes she'd put my hand on her stomach so I could feel the baby kicking. It would have been a little girl…" Jake swallowed hard, and wiped the tears that were now running down his wrinkled face. "Such a shame. Amanda would have been a wonderful mother. She had a beautiful little nursery set up, a white crib and dresser, and a pretty pink chair for her to sit in while she nursed her baby. She gave everything away to the orphanage."

Catherine's eyes teared up, and she tried to blink them away. "Jake, tell us about the night her husband was arrested. Did it happen at her house?"

"Yes. It was awful. I still have nightmares about it. That night I could hear him shouting at her, and I could hear her screaming for help for the very first time ever. I called 911, but didn't wait for the police to come. I ran over to her house to help her, but the door was locked and I couldn't get in. When I ran around to the side of the house to break a window, I saw Amanda on the floor. Her body was twisted, and her face was bleeding. He was standing over her with a bloody knife…"Jake's hands were trembling, and tears streamed down his face. "They tried to save her baby, but they couldn't. The baby girl died a few days after the doctors operated on Amanda's broken back, and I… I was the one who had to bury that little…" He dried his face, and blew his nose again. "Poor Amanda couldn't bury her own child, because she was in the hospital for months."

"Oh, my God," Catherine mumbled. "And now he may be getting out."

"I've been trying to get her to move away from here, before he gets loose," Jake said, twisting his handkerchief. "But she says she won't leave me."

"Jake, do you know if Amanda always had visions," Cody asked. "I mean, has she always seen people and things happening, or did it start after she'd been hurt?"

The man's lips twisted in a wry smile. "Amanda told me that she has always been able to see things happening to other people, even when she was very young." He looked at them, his wrinkled face masked in pain. "Isn't it sad that she couldn't foretell what would happen to her that terrible night?"

CHAPTER TWENTY-FIVE

On the way back to the station, Catherine got a phone call from her friend Susan. "Cathy, Lillian was supposed to show up two days ago to clean my place, but she didn't come and she didn't call and that's not like her. I tried to call her, but the recording said her phone was not in service."

"The same thing happened to me, Sue. She didn't show up at my place last Wednesday, and she didn't call to change the date." Catherine said. "Maybe she's sick."

"That's what I thought, so this morning before I came to work I drove over to her house. Her brother, whatever-his-name is, answered the door. My God, the man was filthy and he stunk so bad, I had to back away from him and his filthy dog"

"So, what did he say?"

"He didn't talk; he just motioned with his hand that Lillian had gone away."

"Maybe she's taking a little vacation."

"You think so?"

"Could be, or maybe she finally got the accounting job she's been searching for. I've got to go. We just parked at the station, and I've got to get inside and clean up the mess on my desk, before my ass gets demoted to street patrol."

"Okay, but let's get together soon. I miss you."

"Miss you, too." Catherine clicked off. Her hand was just about to open the car's door when a dispatcher's call came in saying body parts had been found, and then giving the location of the find.

Three patrol cars and a white CSI van were already lined up in front of the Banana Boat Restaurant when Cody and Catherine pulled up. Officer Ramos from the Boynton Beach station met them at the door.

"What are you two doing here?" the stocky cop asked.

"Making sure you guys do a good job," Cody teased. "What's going on? I hear you did a little fishing."

"Fish isn't how I would describe what was found," he said, grinning. "Seems one of the customers who moored his boat to the pier, saw a plastic, bubble-wrapped package floating in the water. He said he pulled it up thinking it was drugs, but then nearly shit in his pants after he opened it up and saw a rotting, black leg."

"Thanks," Cody said. "We'll check it out."

"The scuba team's here," the officer called after them.

"Shit," Catherine said, following Cody through the door, and into the busy and noisy restaurant. "Do you think it could be the girl Amanda told us about?"

Cody didn't reply. He wound his way around the tables that had plates of half-eaten lunches on top of them, passed the people who were standing three-deep in front of the window, trying to get a glimpse of what the police were doing on the pier, and then onto the pier where the police were gathered. On the floor of the bleached wooden pier were six bubble-wrapped, large packages, and an open one with the remains of a putrid leg.

Cody walked over to one of the Crime Scene Investigators that he knew. "Steve, what's going on?"

"Ah, Cody. What brings you to my neck of the woods?"

Cody looked down at the bloated, severed leg. "We got another missing girl, so I'm checking this out."

"Yeah, I heard about the canal girl. You think the same guy cut this one up and dumped her in the Intercostal this time?"

Cody shrugged. "Did you call the ME?"

"He's on his way."

Cody looked at Catherine, who seemed to be studying the leg. "Why are you staring at that leg?"

"I don't think this is our gal. The leg is too decomposed and according to…" She hesitated, not wanting to mention Amanda's name, and then have to explain they're working with a psychic. "She thinks the next one was just killed, or is still dying. This looks too decomposed."

"It could be another kid that we don't know about."

"It could be," Catherine said. "I'll call the ME's office later, and have him fax a copy of his report to us as soon as it's ready."

Cody nodded. Later, as they were leaving the restaurant, he said: "I think we have to pay another visit to your friend to ask her about this latest development."

"Cody, I don't want to put Amanda through this ordeal again. Let's leave her alone for a while."

He stopped walking. "Why? She's the only thing we've got on our plate to stop this maniac. We have to talk to her."

"She's fragile and hurting," Catherine said, looking up at him. "Let's wait for the ME's report, before we put her through anymore."

Cody's jaw clenched. "No! We can't wait. I'm going to get a piece of the plastic that the leg was wrapped in, and have her touch it like you wanted her to touch the Blackstone girl's blouse."

"But, Amanda's—"

"Catherine, I'm sorry, but Amanda is not important right now. We have to catch this killer, and touching that plastic may give her a clear image of the monster we're looking for. You wanted to do it. Now I do."

"Cody, I—"

"Catherine, stop arguing with me. You're the one who convinced me that Amanda's abilities are for real, so we have to try this approach. We can't wait."

"Cody O'Dell, you're an insensitive bastard. I hate you!"

CHAPTER TWENTY-SIX

Frank Dembeck wasn't what Stan Wilkins and Thomas Whitehall expected to see when his front door opened later that afternoon. Not only did the man who had purchased all of those snakes and mice at the pet shop look 80 years old, but he was a dwarf who stood about four-feet tall and had a larger than usual head.

Hawk was the first one to recover from his shock. "Sir, are you Frank Dembeck?" he asked, peering down.

"Yes, I'm Frank Dembeck," the man answered in a full-timbered, gravelly voice.

"Mr. Dembeck, I'm Detective Whitehall, and this is my partner, Detective Wilkins. Can we come in and ask you a few questions?"

"What about?" he said, his hand shading his eyes from the glare of the sun, and not budging an inch.

"We're wasting our time," Wilkins mumbled, swiping sweat off his forehead. "He's not the one. He can't be."

Dembeck looked puzzled. "What's this about?"

Hawk cleared his throat. "It's about your snakes."

"My snakes? What about them?"

"We understand you collect them."

"Come on, Hawk. We're wasting our time."

Hawk glared at his partner, then turned back to Dembeck. "Do you collect them?"

"Yeah, I collect them. So what?"

"As a reptile collector, can you tell us if there's a club, or a group that meets to discuss your snakes."

"I have friends on Facebook that collect snakes," he said, shifting from one short, thick leg to the other. "Sometimes we chat about what we just bought, and sometimes we meet to trade them if we live near one another."

Wilkins eyes widened, but he kept his mouth shut.

"Are you saying that you meet people around here who also collect snakes?"

"Detective, I'm not going to answer any more of your questions, until you tell me what this is about."

This time Stan spoke up, and his voice had an angry edge to it. "We're questioning *you*, because we believe someone who collects snakes may have abducted a young woman, and we're trying to find her."

"What… I…" the man sputtered. "Are you saying you think I grabbed a girl?"

"No, Sir, but we sure could use your help," Hawk said, to calm the man down.

"Well then, how can I help you? What do you want me to do?"

"Tell us your Facebook link, so we can become a friend and follow your conversations. Will you do that?"

"Yes, certainly. I'm listed as Frank Dembeck, but I'm not sure you can become a friend because I've already reached my 5000 friend limit."

Wilkins groaned. "See, I told you this was a waste of time."

"Wait! I've got an idea," Dembeck said, glancing up from one detective to the other.

"Go on," Hawk said. "What is it?"

"I've been meaning to go through my list of Facebook friends and get rid of a few of them, so I could accept some more interesting ones. Give me a day to work on it, and then try to log onto me tomorrow."

"Mr. Dembeck… Can I call you Frank?"

He nodded.

"Frank, we'd appreciate it if you would work on that as soon as we leave here. It's urgent that you do it right away, because a girl's life is at stake. It's also very important that you don't let on that we're following you. Do you understand?"

"Are you saying that one of my friends may be the person who—"

"Yes. It is possible that one of the people you've been corresponding with may be the one who's abducted a young girl, and even killed another one."

Frank gasped and stumbled back in shock.

"Frank, listen to me," Hawk said, "We need you to keep writing to those snake collectors the same exact way you've always done. Don't change your wording or shortcuts. Do you understand?" He reached in his pocket for a business card, and then handed it to Frank. "Call me the minute I can get on your page."

Frank nodded, then stood at the door watching the detectives walk back to their car.

Wilkins looked at this partner as they were driving down the road. "Do you really think that son-of-a-bitch is stupid enough to go on the internet and chat about his snakes?"

"Let's hope so, Stan. Another girl's life may depend on it, if Delaney's psychic friend is right."

CHAPTER TWENTY-SEVEN

Cody ignored Catherine's silent treatment on the drive from the Banana Boat to Sonia Dixon's house, but once he'd stopped the patrol car and shut off the engine, that changed. "Delaney quit giving me that infantile pissed-off act, and grow up! Like it or not, we have a job to do. If you want to sit in the car and brood, fine." He turned, opened the door, and quickly got out of the car.

It took only moments for Catherine to follow him up to the Dixons' house.

Cody rapped on the front door. No one answered after repeated knocks, but hearing laughter coming from the rear of the house, he took off for the back yard with Catherine trailing him.

"Here I come," a bikini-clad young girl said as she dove into the pool.

"Hey, you two! What are you doing back here?" a tall, slim, brunette called out when she spotted Cody and Catherine walking across the lawn. She and two other oil-slicked teenagers, who'd been sunning themselves, got up from their lounge chairs.

Catherine showed the girls her badge. "Which one of you is Sonia?"

"I'm Sonny," the same brunette snipped. "Is my bitchy neighbor complaining about the noise again? Tell the old fart it's light outside, and we have a right to be out here during the day."

The girl who had dived into the pool climbed out, and joined her friends. "Sonny, what's happening? Why are the cops here?"

Cody gave Catherine a nod, his sign that she should take over the questioning.

"Sonny, is your mother or father at home?" Catherine asked, even though no one had come to the door.

"No. My mom's shopping for a change, and my dad's working."

"Sonny, we'd like to talk to you privately. Can we go inside?"

The teen tossed her long, wet hair over her shoulder and jutted out her chin. "I have nothing to hide from my friends. Whatever you want to talk about, you can do it in front of them."

Catherine wanted to slap the smug look off her face, but controlled the urge. "I want to ask you about Hillary Blackstone."

Sonny glanced at her friends. "What about her?"

"We were told you two didn't get along. Is that true?"

"She wasn't part of my circle. So what? Why are you asking me about that lesbo?"

"Why are you calling her that?"

"Because that's what I heard about her," Sonny answered, smirking at her friends, who were listening to her every word.

"Sonny, why were you called into the principal's office? What was the problem between you and Hillary?"

The smile dropped off Sonny's face.

"Sonny, I asked you what the problem was."

"I didn't know then that she was a lesbo, so I thought she was trying to steal my boyfriend. I had some words with her, and the next thing I knew, I was called into David's office—"

"David? Who's David?" Catherine asked, glancing from Sonny to the other girls.

"David Spencer is… was my principal."

Catherine eyed her up and down, lingering a moment on her large rounded breasts that were barely covered by the bikini top. "Do all of the students call him David, or just you?"

Sonny's face reddened.

"Most of the girls in our senior class called him David," a shapely blonde said, giggling and glancing at the other girls as though they were all in on a juicy secret.

Cody's nostrils flared. "What about the boys?" he asked, staring at Sonny. "Did they also call him David?"

The girls looked at one another, but no one answered.

Cody took his time looking from one girl to another. "Young ladies, I don't like what I'm hearing here. I'm going to ask each of you a question, and your answers had better be truthful, or else. Got me?"

The girls glanced at Sonny, before looking at Cody.

"You're first, Sonia Dixon. Has your principal ever laid his hands on you?"

Sonia bit her bottom lip and said nothing. Her friends edged back.

Cody's dark brown eyes bore into Sonia's blue ones. "Ms. Dixon, how old are you?"

"Seventeen. I'll be eighteen in a couple of months."

"Seventeen... Hmm... Ms. Dixon... Sonia... I'm going to ask you again. Did David... Mr. Spencer ever put his hands on you in an inappropriate way?"

Sonia's hands seductively rubbed the sides of her thighs. She looked at her friends, and smiled coyly.

"For the third time, Sonia. Did your principal ever touch you in an inappropriate way?"

Sonny's smile widened. "Mmm. Yes, I guess you could call it that."

The blonde's hand quickly covered her mouth, and the other two girl's faces paled.

Cody's lips thinned. "Did that happen in school?"

"Sure. Lots of times in David's office."

Catherine saw Cody's shoulders pull back, and his jaw tighten. "What about out of the school?" she asked.

"Yes. David would pick me up in our special place," she said with her long lashes fluttering. "David and I were lovers for a while, but then I decided he was too old for me, and I wouldn't see him again no matter how many times he called me."

Catherine looked at the other girls. "What about the three of you? Did Mr. Spencer ever try anything on you, in or out of the high school?"

The girls immediately shook their heads.

"Are you sure?"

There were three adamant verbal denials.

Cody glanced at Catherine after taking in a deep breath and releasing it, then back at the girls. "Girls, Detective Delaney is going to accompany you into Sonia's house and wait while you change into dry clothes. Then all of you will call a parent and tell them to meet you at the Boca Raton Police Station. Understand?"

"Why?" Sonia snapped. "We haven't done anything wrong."

Cody's eyes narrowed to slits, and his finger pointed directly at Sonny. "Don't give me any lip, young lady. Just do as I say, or we'll take all of you to the police station dressed as you are. Now, move it and make it fast. I don't want to hear another word out of any of you! Get going."

After Catherine and the girls had gone into the house, Cody called the station and asked to be put through to Detective Betancourt.

"Cody, what's happening, man?"

"Dex, I want you and Ricardo to pull Spencer in for questioning."

"Really? How come?"

"I have a seventeen-year-old who claims she's been having an affair with him."

"Statutory rape? We'll get on it. What about a search warrant for his house?"

"Not yet. I'm bringing the girl and her friends in for questioning. When I have their written statements, we'll get a warrant for his house, car, and that barn you told us about. Also, get a couple of cars over here to help me transport these girls."

After Cody gave Dexter Sonia's address, he answered a waiting call. "Yes, Chief."

"Cody, Madeline Kefler has just been reported missing."

CHAPTER TWENTY-EIGHT

Sonia Dixon and her friends were detained in four separate rooms when they arrived at the police station, and that made Sonia furious.

"Why can't we be together?" she shouted as she was being led into a padded interrogation room. "We're not criminals. I demand you put us together immediately!"

"Sonia, calm down. Have a seat," Catherine said. "I'll bring you a drink if you'd like something."

"Fuck your lousy drink! I'll have my parents sue you and this whole fuckin' police department for false arrest."

"You haven't been arrested," Catherine said, trying to control her own temper. "Would you like a drink while you wait for your mother to arrive?"

Sonia balled her fists at her sides and glared at Catherine, refusing to sit down.

"Fine. Have it your way. If you change your mind about that drink, knock on the door." After leaving the room and locking the door behind her, Catherine stopped beside Detective Feinstein's desk. "What a pain in the ass," she mumbled, peering over his shoulder at the video that was being taken of Sonia.

"What's with that kid?" he said, watching Sonia repeatedly kick the padded wall while she cursed out loud. "She's got a mouth like a drunken truck driver."

"Lou, keep your eyes on her, and call me if she starts bashing her head on that wall, instead of her foot."

"Why is she in there?"

"We're waiting for her mother, so we can question her about being raped."

"Rape? No wonder the kid's freaking out. Don't worry. I'll call if there's a problem."

Catherine headed to her uncle's office, where she knew her partner was being briefed on the new missing person. She passed Cody, who was leaning against the doorframe with his arms crossed over his chest, and walked over to her uncle, who was sitting behind his desk with a cigar stub dangling out of his mouth.

"Okay, you two. Who's the missing girl?"

Her uncle took the stub out of his mouth and set it in the overflowing ashtray. "Her name is Madeline Kefler," he said, looking down at a small pad. "She's twenty-four, petite, and has blonde hair. According to the manager of the Sassy Woman Boutique in the Delray Marketplace, her assistant didn't show up at the store for the last three days, and that was unlike her."

"And the manager's name is?"

He glanced at his notes again. "Levine. She called this morning, and is on her way in to fill out a missing person's report."

"Maybe Kefler isn't missing. Maybe she went on a vacation, or took off with a boyfriend," Catherine said, sitting across from him.

"Cathy, one of our men mentioned that possibility to her, but she insisted Madeline Kefler would have called if she was going to take some time off. The woman said she was so worried about Kefler that she drove over to her house this morning to see if she was sick or had had an accident. No one was at home, and her car wasn't on the driveway."

"So she took off. That's what I just said."

"Well if she took off for three whole days, then why'd she leave her dog at home? Levine said she saw a small dog scratching on the kitchen window, and the pooch didn't look too good."

Catherine watched her uncle get up from his chair, walk around to the front of his desk, and then perch on the corner of it. "Levine said she called Kefler's sister in Utah," he went on. "Seems she also hadn't spoken to her sister for days, so she told the manager to contact us immediately."

"So what do we do now?" Catherine asked, looking over at Cody, who hadn't moved an inch, and hadn't joined the discussion.

"I sent a couple of men over to the girl's apartment complex. They're going to find the superintendent or manager, and get him to let them into her apartment."

"Can we do that? Is it legal?"

"Her sister gave us permission. Soon as I hear something from our men, I'll fill you and Cody in, and we'll go from there."

"Tell them to look for a picture of Ms. Kefler, and have the photo verified by her sister in case we have to make an announcement on TV. I also want a copy to show Amanda as soon as possible."

"I'll send it over to you soon as I get it. Now tell me why you brought those girls in," he said, looking first at his niece, and then over at Cody.

Catherine got up. "We questioned David Spencer, the principal at the high school Hillary Blackstone attended. He said he resolved a bullying squabble between Hillary and this kid, Sonia Dixon. She's one of the four girls we just pulled in. We also learned Spencer had the custodian set rodent traps in the girls' locker room."

"Cathy, I don't understand. What do rodents have to do with any of this?"

"Snakes eat rodents, Uncle Steve. The custodian told us that Spencer removed one of them from a trap. Was that rat thrown away, or did he feed it to a room full of snakes?"

"Are you saying this principal is a person of interest in the Blackstone case?"

"He's more than that now. Cody and I went to Sonia Dixon's house to learn more about him, and that seventeen-year-old dropped a bomb on us. She claims she's had an affair with him, and she brazenly made that statement in front of her three girlfriends."

"Seventeen? That's statutory rape," the chief sputtered.

Cody nodded.

"That may be so, but only if it's true."

Cody lifted away from the wall. "Delaney, what do you mean, if it's true?"

"I've got mixed feelings about Sonia."

"Okay. Go on. Let's hear what you have to say, before I add my thoughts to the mix."

Catherine shoved her hands into her pants pockets. "Think about this. First, we find out Sonia was stalking Randy Dixon, the boy we saw with Hillary in the Target. While we questioned him, his father let on that Sonia claimed Randy made her pregnant. But his son swore to us that he never did more than kiss her. And now, Sonia claims she's had an affair with her principal. Does this seem normal to you guys?"

"So the girl tells lies," the chief said. "So what? Teenagers are known to fabricate whoppers."

"No, it's more than whoppers. I think this girl has a problem. A sociopathic problem. Psychopaths distort the truth. They lie with a straight face to get what they want. They don't care about other people's feelings. It's all about what they need, and what they want. They manipulate people."

"What about Hillary Blackstone?" he asked, getting off the desk. "Do you think Sonia had anything to do with her disappearance or—"

"I just got another thought," Cody said, cutting in. "And it's a chilling one. Sonia Dixon referred to Hillary as 'that lesbo', meaning she knew Hillary was a lesbian. Other than Hillary's lover, Cathy, and me, the only other person who was aware of that fact was the principal. Did he tell Sonia? If so, why? Was he so obsessed with Sonia that he'd kill for her to keep their affair going on?"

Catherine tugged her fingers through her long, dark hair. "You think Sonia may have put him up to it for sex?"

Cody said nothing. He just left that thought hanging in the room.

CHAPTER TWENTY-NINE

Sandra Parker's mother was the first to arrive at the police station. "Sandra, Mrs. Parker," Catherine said, when she entered their room. "I'm Detective Delaney."

"Why was my daughter brought to this police station?" Mrs. Parker quickly asked, as Catherine sat down on the opposite side of the table. "What did she do wrong?"

Catherine looked across at the petite, blonde-haired teenager. Her eyes were red-rimmed from crying, and her face was as pale as a porcelain doll's. "Mrs. Parker, your daughter was at the Dixon residence this afternoon when her friend Sonia made a very disturbing statement."

"What has that got to do with my daughter?"

"Your daughter witnessed her friend's statement. I believe you should be made aware of what was said, because it might involve your daughter as well as some of her girlfriends."

After placing her clasped hands on top of the table, the woman looked at her daughter, and then back at Catherine. "All right, Detective. What did my daughter's friend say that was so terrible?"

"Sonia Dixon told us that she had a sexual affair with her high school principal."

"What?"

Sandra was trembling, and her eyes were fixed on the table. "Sandra, this is very important," Catherine said softly, looking at her. "Please don't be afraid to answer truthfully. You won't get in trouble. Did Mr. Spencer ever put his hands on you where he shouldn't have?"

Mrs. Parker's eyes bulged, and her chest heaved. She looked at her daughter, and waited for her answer.

"No," the girl said in a whisper. "He never did anything to me."

"Did Sonia ever mention what he did to her before this afternoon?"

Sondra shook her head. "No. She told us she had sex with a lot of boys, but she never said she did it with him."

"I can't believe what I'm hearing," Mrs. Parker sputtered, looking from Catherine to her daughter and then back to Catherine again.

"Mrs. Parker, Sonia's accusation is very serious. Criminal charges are pressed on adults who engage in this kind of behavior with a minor."

"I'm stunned. I've met that man on many occasions. He goes to my church. I can't believe this. He seemed so nice, so respectful, so caring for all the students."

"Mrs. Parker, these charges haven't been substantiated. We're checking into the allegation, and we're going to question Mr. Spencer."

"What's going to happen now? Are you going to arrest him?"

"Not at this time. We can only arrest someone if we have positive proof that a crime has been committed. There is a chance that Sonia has made up the whole story, and this man is innocent."

"Good heavens... why would a child make up this kind of story?"

"Sometimes children make up stories to become more popular. Let's hope it's only that, and not true. In any case, we'll be in touch with you when we know more. Until then, please keep this matter quiet, because we wouldn't want to ruin a man's reputation if he's innocent."

The questioning of Sarah Douglas and Marcy Western before their mothers had similar results. The girls cried and said they'd never been abused by their principal, and their mothers went from being stunned, to being furious, and at other times they were left speechless.

Catherine was exhausted by the time she entered the room where Sonia and her mother waited. "I'm Detective Delaney," she said, walking in.

Sonia glared at her. Her mother, a stunning redhead who could have been a model, was busy examining her long, polished-red fingernails.

"Mrs. Dixon."

The woman looked up. "It's Ms. Dixon. My husband and I are no longer married."

Catherine hesitated a moment. When questioned, Sonia had said that her father was at work, implying he still resided in their house. "Ms. Dixon," she finally said. "Has your daughter told you why she's here?"

She sighed, as though sitting in a police station was nothing more than a waste of her precious time. "Yes, Sonia said she made up some silly story to impress her friends, and you took her seriously and brought her here."

Catherine leaned back against her chair. "Hmmm. Did she tell you what the story was?"

"Look, Detective, it was just a silly story." She rose, ready to leave.

"Sit down!" Catherine snapped, jerking forward and slapping her hand on the table.

The woman dropped down on the chair like she'd been struck.

"Your precious Sonia accused the principal of her school of having sex with her."

The woman actually smiled.

"You think it's funny?"

"Yes. It's hilarious! My daughter makes up stories all the time. No one takes her seriously. It's a game she plays. Everyone ignores her."

"Sonia," Catherine said, staring directly at the girl. "Did you have an affair with David Spencer like you told us, or was it just a made-up story?"

Sonia's smile was wider than her mother's. "You heard my mother. I tell stories. It's a game. Like my mother says, just ignore me."

Catherine's hands clenched. She had to get out of that room. "I'll be right back," she said, then left the room and locked the door. Once outside, she drew in a deep breath to calm down. "What the fuck is wrong with those two?"

"Cathy, what's wrong," Cody asked when he reached her. "You look like you're ready to explode."

She straightened. "You're right. I am furious. Cody, for once in my life I'm totally stumped, and don't know what to do next."

CHAPTER THIRTY

"I'm not hungry," Catherine mumbled, sitting in a booth at a Chili's restaurant.

"Your stomach's growling, Delaney. So quit the bullshit, and decide what you want to order before the waitress comes back."

She looked down at the menu for a moment, then back at him. "We should have kept Sonia at the station, until we questioned Spencer."

Cody drummed his fingers on the table. "You know we couldn't do that. We had nothing to hold her on. Besides, Spencer wasn't home, and who knows when we'll get him."

The young waitress who had given them the menus, returned with a basket of chips and a cup of salsa. "Have you decided what you want to order?"

Cody peered over at Catherine.

"The ribs. And I want them well done."

"What about a drink?"

"I'll have the two-for-one Margarita special, and tell the bartender to make them extra strong."

Cody smiled and ordered the same things.

When the waitress had removed the menus and left, Catherine leaned back against the upholstered seat and stared at him.

"Okay, Babe, why are you frowning? What's eatin' you?"

"We should have had a BOLO issued for Spencer."

"Come on," he said. "A 'Be-On-The-Look-Out' would have half of our force looking for him, instead of the missing girl. We'll get him when he returns to his house."

"Tell me why his house is still shuttered? He's not a part-time resident who goes away for the summer. Why couldn't we get a warrant to search his house to see if the girl is in there?"

"A judge would never give us a search warrant. We have nothing on him. Our hands are tied. We don't have a choice. We have to wait."

Catherine leaned forward. "No, we don't have to wait. You and I could go over to his house, and—"

"Breaking and entering is against the law. We—"

Cody shut up when the waitress returned with their drinks, and set them down on the table. "Your food will be ready soon." She was about to walk away, but stopped and turned back. "Aren't you the detectives I saw on TV when the mayor was talking about the missing beauty queen?"

"Yes," Catherine replied. "Do you know Hillary Blackstone?"

The waitress's head bobbed up and down. "Yes, I went to school with her. Hillary's very nice. I used to sit with her at lunch sometimes. Once I took her to the nurse when she was having a bad asthma attack."

"I didn't know Hillary had an allergy," Catherine said.

"No one knew. She kept it a secret, because she worried about being disqualified from the pageants if they found out about it."

"Susan," Catherine said, seeing the name tag on her shirt. "Why are you telling me this?"

"Because I just remembered Hillary used to have an inhaler with her, and I'm wondering if she has one with her now."

"Thanks for sharing that with us," Catherine said, nodding and picturing Hillary as she lay on the morgue's stainless-steel table. "We'll be sure to check it out. And, Susan, if you think of anything else, please call the Boca Police Station and ask to speak to Detective Delaney. Anything else you can tell me might be very helpful."

Susan smiled, said she would, and then walked away.

"Cody, how come the Blackstones didn't tell us about Hillary's asthma?"

He shrugged. "Lots of people have asthma. It's treatable, so it's no big deal to some. I was just surprised to hear the waitress say that pageant officials might disqualify contestants who have a disability, or a non-serious medical condition. It doesn't sound right. I remember a few years ago, there was a deaf contestant who won one of the big titles, and later went on to become a famous actress. No, I think she got it wrong."

Catherine stared at the chip she was crumbling onto the table.

"Why are you biting your lip? What are you thinking?"

"Amanda kept telling us that this new girl couldn't breathe."

"I remember her saying that," Cody said. "She said he was pressing his hand down on her throat."

"Exactly. He was strangling her. Could it be that this monster gets more excited when he sees his victim struggling to breathe?"

"Who knows why sickos do what they do?"

"Cody, as soon as we get back to the station, I want to have another look at Hillary Blackstone's autopsy report, to see if the hyoid bone in her neck was broken."

"Come on, Delaney. Can't that wait until morning? I thought we'd go back to my place to have some dessert."

"Dessert? Sorry, O'Dell."

He grinned. "Call it whatever you want to call it, Babe, I need you in my arms."

"Sorry, but that dessert will have to wait. I need to see if Hillary was strangled. If she was, I'm going to check the National Criminal data base to see if a convicted strangler was recently set free, or another strangling bastard recently got away with his crime."

CHAPTER THIRTY-ONE

Catherine knew Cody was royally pissed off when he dropped her in front of her condo to get her car, but she couldn't help it. As soon as she learned that Hillary Blackstone had been raped before being murdered, the nightmares of her own rape started in again. They worsened for her after Amanda described the second rape, so she desperately needed to find the strangler before he could rape and kill again.

"Where's your side kick?" the admitting officer asked as soon as she walked into the station.

"At home, taking a bubble bath," she flippantly answered, heading to the inner door. When she pulled the door open, she was startled to find her uncle standing there."

"Cathy, you're back?"

"I have something I have to do."

"Where's Cody?"

"He's at home, taking a bubble bath," that same officer called out with a chuckle.

The chief smiled. "Do you need me to help you?"

Catherine shook her head. "It won't take long. I just want to check out a hunch I have."

"Want to share it?"

"No, it may be nothing. Go home. Get some rest. If I find something important, I'll give you a buzz."

Her uncle gave her a quick hug and headed to the door, but then changed his mind. "Cathy, I have some good news for a change."

"The missing girl has been found," she said, hope shining in her eyes.

"I wish. No, it's not that. We caught two guys who robbed the CVS where the mayor's son works."

"Oh, well… I guess that's better than nothing. How did it go down?"

"Our lab guys were the ones who actually solved that case. I spoke with Stu. He said as soon as he saw the photographs of the pharmacy's concrete floor; he knew the clawed markings had been made by a heavy-duty construction excavator. And sure enough, he was right. Two miles down from the shopping strip, RJ Construction Company was putting up an office building. The two men were working at that site."

"An excavator? You mean one of those big things with the bucket at the end of its long arm?"

"That piece of equipment actually weighs more that eighty thousand pounds. That's why it wasn't blown over by the high winds. According to Stu, the arm is what tore off that part of CVS's roof, not the wind. And then the bucket was lowered, and they chopped the safe out of the floor. Bits of concrete were still stuck between the claws, when our men examined it. Amazing, isn't it?"

"What about the drugs?"

"Gone," her uncle said. "They're on the streets, feeding another addiction."

"Well, at least the two who were caught will be off the streets."

"All right, enough. I'm going home," he said, patting her arm. "Try not to stay too late."

"I won't." She reached over and kissed his cheek, then walked through the door to the inner office space.

"I put some messages on your desk," an officer said as she was passing his cubicle.

"Thank you." Catherine kept walking, and with each step she took toward her office, her anxiety grew. Had she received another call from Amanda? Had another girl been snatched? Did the ME find out who the dismembered body parts belonged to? By the time she had reached her desk, her heart was pounding and a pulse was throbbing in her neck.

I can't do this tonight, she thought, staring at the tall pile of folders on top of her desk, and the half-dozen pink message slips that were tucked under the corner of her phone. "Cody is right," she mumbled, backing out of the room. She reached into her pants pocket, pulled out her cell phone, and called him.

He answered on the first ring. "What, Delaney?"

"I changed my mind about having dessert, O'Dell. Get ready, I'm coming over."

CHAPTER THIRTY-TWO

Catherine smelled the fresh-brewed coffee before she opened her eyes. She smiled, and listened to Cody as he warbled a song in off-key notes. It felt right, lying in his king-size bed. Catherine stretched her legs beneath the sheet, then tossed it off, and went to join him in the shower.

"Well, well, well. Sleeping beauty has finally gotten her luscious body out of my bed," he said, pulling her in beneath the warm spray. He took his time soaping one of her breasts, then did the same to the other leaving both nipples hard, pink, and protruding.

Cathy leapt up a bit, and wrapped her legs around his waist so that her curly mound was pressed against his rising penis.

Cody's kiss was urgent. It sent sparks of fire down her spine. She kissed him back hungrily, her need growing almost as fast as her lover's erection.

"Catherine, I love you," he moaned between kisses.

She inserted his hardness into her core, and moaned as she moved forward and back in a slow, steady rhythm.

"Tell me you love me," he said, grabbing her buttocks and ramming himself in deeper.

"I love you, Cody O'Dell. I love you. Harder. Faster. I need you, now."

Cody grunted, and quickened his thrusts. It didn't take long after that. They climaxed together like they always did, and ended the interlude with another soul-searching kiss.

They didn't bother to dress when they got out of the shower. With bath towels wrapped around their dripping-wet bodies, they walked into the kitchen.

"How many eggs should I make you," he asked with his head in the refrigerator.

"Four. I'm starving after all the exercise I've gotten," she said with a little giggle. She poured steaming-hot coffee into two mugs, and then brought the mugs to the table. "Can I help you?"

He shut the refrigerator door, then turned to her, holding a carton of eggs in one hand and a loaf of bread in the other. He stood there, looked over at her, and said nothing.

"Cody…"

"Cathy, this is silly," he said, his arms swinging out. "We love each other. I want us to be together, not going from my place to your place or your place to my place, like a couple who are first getting to know one another."

She smiled at his obvious frustration, and the fact that his towel was about to drop off him.

"Damn you, woman. Why are you smiling?"

"Because you look so cute swinging that bread and carton of eggs around."

"What?" he said in a squeak.

"Why don't you ask me if I'll move in with you?"

His mouth flew open.

Her smile widened. "Yes, I will move in with you, Cody O'Dell."

"You will?" he muttered as his towel dropped down to the floor.

"Only if we can have more dessert after breakfast."

CHAPTER THIRTY-THREE

Three standing microphones had already been set up outside the Boca Raton Police Station, when Catherine and Cody arrived. Chief Delaney, who was dressed in his ceremonial navy uniform adorned with his service medals, was conferring with two other uniformed officers. A horde of sweating news reporters from the local radio and television stations were gathered in front of them, shouting out questions that were left unanswered. The stations' videographers, who were shouldering heavy cameras, were filming them and the local residents who had joined the throng.

Catherine walked up to her uncle's side, and tapped his arm.

"Cathy," he said, acknowledging her. His face was wet with perspiration, and droplets of sweat dripped down to his jacket. "Here's the copy of that picture you wanted," he said, pulling a folded sheet of paper out of his inner jacket pocket, and handing it to her.

Catherine opened it, and then looked down at the image of a smiling young woman who was cuddling a shaggy-haired, small dog. A lump formed in her throat. She passed the picture to Cody. He studied it a few moments, and passed it back to her.

"Chief, who are we waiting for?" Cody asked.

He didn't have to answer, because Mayor Clarkston's sleek, black limo had just double-parked at the curb. The reporters quickly rushed toward him, shouting out questions as he extracted his plump body from the lush interior. Clarkston gave them a wide mayoral smile, shook some of their hands, and stopped to praise others for the wonderful articles they'd written endorsing his bid for reelection.

Catherine glanced at her uncle, saw him swallow, then draw in a deep breath, trying to keep his dislike of the pompous mayor hidden.

"Mayor Clarkston," said the chief, extending his hand. The mayor nodded and ignored his hand.

Catherine only took one step forward before Cody grabbed her arm and pulled her back. "Cool it, Delaney."

"I'd like to punch the lights out of that ass," she whispered.

"Me, too." He squeezed her arm.

"Ladies and gentlemen," Clarkston bellowed, his head held high, and his stubby nose in the air. "It is with great sadness that I have to come before you today to announce that another young lady has been reported missing." He adjusted his designer, silk tie. "The young lady…"

He bent down to whisper something in the chief's ear, and then righted himself after the chief whispered something back. "The young lady, Miss Madeline Kefler has been missing for three days."

Soft murmurs spilled out of the crowd.

"He didn't even know her name," Catherine mumbled. Cody squeezed her arm harder.

"Chief Delaney, would you please tell the public how they can help us find Mrs. … Mrs. Hoffer."

"That moron's got Alzheimer's," Catherine mumbled. Cody elbowed her ribs this time.

"Ladies and gentlemen," the chief said somberly, gazing at the large crowd before him. "Miss Madeline Kefler, has been missing for three days. Madeline is 24 years old, stands five feet, two inches tall, and has blue eyes and short, curly-blonde hair. We urgently need your help to find her. Miss Kefler's picture will be handed out to all of you. Please broadcast this information and her picture as soon as this interview is over. Please… I urge everyone to be on the lookout for this young lady. She was last seen coming out of a Shell gas station on Congress Road in Boynton Beach. Her car is a gray, 2012 Honda Accord. The rear bumper is missing, and her license plate is SHOPPER. If you've seen this young lady or her vehicle within the last few days, or you see it in the future, please call the Boca Raton Police Station immediately. An award of five thousand dollars has been posted for the safe return of Miss Kefler. Thank you.

"Let's go," Catherine's uncle said, grabbing her arm as soon as he'd finished his speech. They headed into the police station, not bothering to bid the mayor farewell, and walked quickly into the briefing room that was filled with police officers and lab technicians.

"Everyone take a seat and let's get started," the chief called out from the front of the room.

The room quickly quieted, and seats were taken.

"Twenty-four-year-old Madeline Kefler has been reported missing. Her picture is taped on the board behind me, next to Hillary Blackstone's," he said, still looking out at the crowd. "Due to information we received, we believe both abductions have been perpetrated by the same man."

"Why are you saying that?" an officer called out from the back of the room.

The chief nodded at Catherine. She rose and walked up to his side.

"Did your psychic friend tell you that," another officer shouted.

Comments and snide remarks filtered through the room. Catherine raised her palms high for them to be quiet. When the room was still again, she lowered her hands. "I know that many of you are skeptics and don't believe in psychics. I can't blame you for feeling that way, because I didn't believe in them either. That is, until I saw and heard one of them go into her trance. What she said shook me, because her vision was so vivid and horrifying. She saw Hillary being raped, then saw her being carried up to a snake-filled room. She even told me that we'd find her body in a canal. We did…" She hesitated to catch her breath, and wiped her sweating palms on her pants. "And now this same person said she saw a curly, blonde-haired woman being raped, and then being carried up to that very same snake-filled room. Look at the new picture on the board."

Whispered words flittered around the room, and chairs creaked.

"It's the same man," Catherine said, "but she says she can't see his face."

"Is this new girl still alive?" a female officer sitting in the front row asked.

Catherine peered down at her. "I don't know."

"You said this woman saw the guy carrying her up a flight of stairs," Betancourt said from the side of the room.

Catherine nodded. "Yes, that's what she said. Wherever that house is, it's a two-story structure. That's all I know for now. If I get something else, I'll tape a memo on this board, so check out the board." She returned to her chair.

"What about those body parts that were fished out of the Intercostal?" one of the crime scene investigators called out. "Do we know who that victim is?"

"No, Greg, not at this time. We're still waiting for the Medical Examiner's report." The chief turned to Betancourt again. "Dexter, have you located that high school principal?"

"No, we're trying to trace his cell phone. I'll let you know as soon as I get a hit."

"What about your informant?"

"The pimp's asking around, but so far, he hasn't heard any rumors on the streets."

The chief looked over at Cody. "I don't see Wilkins and Hawk. Where are they, and what are they looking into?"

Cody stood up. "They're following up on the snake theory. They've questioned a lot of pet shop owners to find out if any of their customers are large snake collectors. One of the managers gave them a lead, and they're on their computers checking it out." He sat down.

The chief looked out at his audience. "Anyone have something to add?" When there was no response, he dismissed the meeting and quickly exited the room.

"I want to talk to the manager of that boutique," Catherine said, rising.

"Give me a few minutes to check the messages on my desk, and I'll be with you."

"Cody, after that, I want to see Amanda again."

"To show her the picture?"

"I have to be sure that the girl she saw in her vision is—"

"Madeline," he added for her. "I understand. As soon as I get a snippet of plastic that was wrapped around that floating leg, I want her to touch it and tell me what she sees."

"It can't be Madeline. I told you, the timing is all wrong. That leg part was too decomposed to be her."

"You're probably right about that, but maybe she'll be able to tell us who this new victim is."

CHAPTER THIRTY-FOUR

Cody was more impressed with the clothing carried at the Sassy Woman Boutique than Catherine was. Not only did he stop to stare at the display in the front window, but once in the store, he actually touched a couple of slinky and beaded garments that were on the mannequins.

"Cathy, you've got to try on that red gown that's in the window," he said, while they were waiting for the manager.

She eyed him and said nothing.

"It would be perfect for you to wear to the mayor's charity event."

"I don't wear red," she mumbled. "And the neckline is cut far too low."

"No it's not. You'd look great in it."

She cocked her head to the side, and gave him one of her leave-me-alone looks.

"Sorry to keep you waiting. I'm Mrs. Levine. You asked to see me?"

"Mrs. Levine, I'm Detective Delaney, and this is my partner Detective O'Dell. Is there some place we can talk privately?"

"The stockroom," she answered, fingering one of the rhinestone buttons on the front of her finely tailored black dress. "Please, follow me."

"Sorry, it's such a mess back here," she said, after they entered the well-stocked room that was lined with racks of expensive clothing. "You must be here about Madeline. I'm absolutely sick with worry about her."

"Can you tell us a little about Miss Kefler," Catherine said. "What were her hobbies? Did she have a boyfriend?"

The frown on the attractive, middle-aged woman's face deepened. "Madeline took fashion merchandising in college. She wanted to eventually become a buyer. Clothing, fabrics, accessories, were all she ever talked about. She loved her job here, and our regular customers always asked for her."

"What about a boyfriend? Did Madeline have one?"

"Yes, yes, she had one up until a couple of months ago, and then I heard her telling one of the salesgirls she was friendly with, that they'd broken up."

"Do you hear why they broke up? Was there an argument?"

"I'm not sure," Levine said, toying with that same button. "I think she said something about him wanting to relocate to Texas for a new job, and his asking her to go with him. Like I said, I'm not positive about that. The store got very busy at that point, and I had to take care of the customers. I could ask that salesgirl about their break up, but she won't be in until tomorrow."

"What's the salesgirl's name," Catherine asked.

"Michelle Pollard. She's off today, I could speak—"

"Don't bother," Catherine said. "I'll stop in tomorrow. Mrs. Levine, do you know if Madeline had any hobbies or belonged to any clubs or a gym?"

"I don't know about her going to a gym or belonging to any clubs. The only thing I do know is that Madeline liked to take long walks with her dog early in the morning, and after she got home from work. It's a shame about her dog. I couldn't take it, because I have two cats at home and they'd probably tear the poor thing apart."

"What happened to her dog?" Cody asked.

"He's in the pound. I feel terrible about that. Madeline will be horrified when she finds out where he's been."

Catherine cringed when she heard her say "when she finds out." "Mrs. Levine, do you remember the name of Madeline's boyfriend?"

"Joseph, but I don't remember his last name."

"Here's my card," Catherine said, handing her one. "If you do remember his name, please call me."

"I will. I'll also ask some of the girls if they know his name, and get back to you if I hear something. Is there anything else?"

"Yes," Cody said, grinning. "What size is that red gown in the front window?"

"Cody!" Catherine burst out.

"A size six," the manager said, returning Cody's smile.

"Wrap it up. We're taking it."

"Cody, no!"

"Oh! And if you have a fancy wrap to go with it, throw it in the box and add it onto my bill."

CHAPTER THIRTY-FIVE

As soon as Catherine and Cody stepped out of the boutique's glass door, the clouds burst open and a gray sheet of rain poured down. They dashed to the car, but were soaked to their skin by the time they'd climbed inside. Cody tossed the shopping bag onto the back seat, then turned to the front and mopped his face dry with his hand.

"You didn't have to buy me that," Catherine said, securing her seatbelt. "I won't wear it to that event, so you've wasted your money, O'Dell."

He started the engine and turned on the windshield wipers.

"Did you hear me?"

He reversed the car out of the parking spot, then put his foot on the gas and drove off.

"Are we going to Amanda's?"

"No."

"Why not?"

"We're going to the pound to get her dog."

The wire-haired, gray and black mutt was curled in Catherine's lap as they traveled to the psychic's house. To keep him from tumbling off should the car stop short, Catherine kept her hand on his back. "So now that you got...whatever-his-name-is out of that awful place," she said, feeling the dog's heart pounding beneath her palm. "What are you going to do with whatever-his-name-is?"

"Take him home with us."

"With us?"

"Yup, with us. You're moving in, remember? He'll be our watch dog."

"You're joking. He's ugly, and he's too small to be a watch dog."

"He'll grow on you. Give the poor little guy a chance."

Catherine groaned and glanced down at the dog. He'd obviously heard her, because his soft brown eyes looked up at her. "Shit!"

"That's not a good name for a dog, Delaney. Think of something else."

Catherine gave in and started to laugh, but her laughter was cut short when the radio crackled with the dispatcher notifying them that another body had been discovered in a canal.

As Cody pulled the car off Route 7 and onto the shoulder behind a line of police and first response vehicles, the dog suddenly lurched up, and started to bark and howl. Catherine could hardly hang onto him as he scratched on the window and jumped up and down in her lap, trying to get out of the car.

Looking out of the side window, through the fine drizzle that was still coming down, Catherine saw a ring of officers surrounding a nude body that was lying on a grassy embankment. The victim had short, blond hair. Catherine's stomach lurched. She looked at Cody, and hung onto the dog. "It's got to be her."

Cody's eyes were hard with anger. "Make sure the dog doesn't get out of the car. Let's get this over with. That bastard has to be stopped."

Keeping the dog within the car while trying to climb out and close the door had sweat glistening on Catherine's face. As she followed Cody towards the body, the overwhelming stench of death brought acid bile up to her throat and tears to her eyes. The blue, bloated victim's body was lying face down, exposing maggot-infested lacerations on her back and legs. Cody tried to hand Catherine a pair of latex gloves that he'd taken out of his pocket; she shook her head and refused them.

"Who found the body," he asked the four crime scene detectives.

"A homeless guy who was fishing in the canal. He accidentally snared her, and pulled her to shore."

"Where is he now?"

The same man answered. "On the way to the station."

"Have all the pictures been taken of the surroundings, and the corpse?"

"Yes. Soon as the Medical Examiner shows up, we'll search the area for evidence, although I don't think we'll find anything close by. I think your guy dumps them upstream and they float down here."

Cody nodded, then looked over at Catherine, who was still staring down at the body. "Delaney?"

"I'm not an ME, but I'd say her neck has been broken. Look at the way her head is tilted. That's not normal."

"It could have happened in the water if something hit her."

"Cody, I'm going back to the station. Get a lift back when you're done."

"Why are you leaving?"

"I need to check out my strangler theory. I should have done it yesterday. It can't wait."

CHAPTER THIRTY-SIX

"I don't have much time," he mumbled, walking over to one of the many different-sized glass fish tanks that were filled with squirming mice or fat rats that he specifically bred for his collection of snakes. His gloved hand reached into one of the larger tanks. He selected two plump mice from the dozen that were running around, grabbed them by their long tails and then pulled them out. He made short work of chopping off their heads with the small ax, then chopping their bodies up and adding the bloody bits to the metal pail that was almost filled to the top.

After wiping the table top off with a blood-stained rag, he picked up the pail and headed toward the stairs. His grin was broad and his eyes glistened with excitement by the time he reached the special bedroom door. He knew they were hungry—very hungry—waiting for their master to feed them. It gave him great pleasure, watching their bodies slither toward the food. He loved the sound of their hissing–loved to watch them glide over one another to snatch a morsel of flesh. When he'd watch them, he'd picture himself on the downstairs bed—felt himself grow more powerful—and then the need to seduce another helpless beauty would almost overwhelm him.

He finally opened the door and stepped into the hissing, squirming, tangled mess. "There you go," he said, tossing the contents of the pail to the far side of the room. He watched for a few moments, enjoying the spectacle, then left the room and relocked the door.

Once downstairs, he rinsed out the pail, set it aside, then walked over to a very large glass tank that was covered by a heavy wire lid. He looked at the heavy-coiled viper that he'd just imported from the southern Mexican border. This rattlesnake—unlike the other poisonous snakes in his collection—was almost six feet long, and had sharply defined dark diamonds on its back in combination with a pair of broad, dark-brown stripes that ran from the top of its head down its entire body.

"Are you hungry, my precious?"

The snake lifted its head.

"Ahh… you recognize your master's voice. You've been good. I got almost a whole vile of venom when I milked you."

He walked back to a mouse tank, selected one, and then brought it over to the rattler. This time he didn't bother to kill the mouse. He lifted a corner of the lid, and dropped it in live. A split second later, the snake's head darted out, and his fangs sank into the gray creature's back. The small rodent's legs kick up twice, and then it lay still, gasping for breath.

The man smiled. "Good. You're just like me. You like to watch them struggle and kick. I'm sorry, but I have to leave all of you for a while," he cooed, glancing around at all the filled tanks. "There's plans to be made." His smile widened. "Not like grandpa's plans to pick up those black, slutty girls. I'm going to get me another pretty, white one." He tapped on the rattler's glass cage, saw it snatch the mouse and swallow it whole, then left the room laughing hard and loud.

CHAPTER THIRTY-SEVEN

All eyes were on Catherine as she led the mutt through the police station and into her small office.

"Want water?" she asked the dog, looking down at him.

He woofed, and wagged his tail.

"Great. Now I'm talking to a dog," she mumbled. "Okay. Let's go, but don't get too used to me, because I'm not keeping you."

The dog woofed again, and circled around her feet.

Catherine took her coffee mug off the cluttered desk, and headed to the bathroom to rinse the leftover coffee out of it. The dog followed with its leash dragging on the floor behind him, until it snagged on a chair leg. "What now," she mumbled, stooping to unhook his leash. "Stay out of trouble, Pal, or else." She shoved the leash in her pants pocket, and then walked on with him prancing beside her.

Back at her desk, with the dog lapping up the cold water, Catherine browsed through her stack of messages. She was just about to dial Ms. Levine's number at the Sassy Woman Boutique, when a call came through from the admitting officer.

"Catherine, there's a young man out here who's asking to speak to a detective. I think you'll want to talk to him. Should I send him back?"

"No. I'll be right there."

Catherine headed back out to the reception area, and again the dog followed her. As soon as she opened the door, the dog dashed out and ran over to a tall, well-dressed young man.

"Harry," the man said, kneeling and petting the squirming dog. He lifted the dog into his arms and stood up.

"His name is Harry?" Catherine said, wincing and walking to him.

He placed the dog back on the floor. "Madeline gave him that name."

"Madeline who?"

"My girlfriend, Madeline Kefler. I'm Joe Raganno. Maddie and I have been dating for more than two years."

Catherine led him into one of the interrogation rooms, and told him to have a seat. Once he was seated, Harry jumped onto his lap. "I'm Detective Delaney. May I call you Joe?" she asked, setting a pad and pen on the table.

He nodded. "Did you find Maddie?"

"I'm sorry," she said, eyeing his clean-shaven face and his business suit and tie. "Not yet. Joe, I was told you went to Texas to start a new job. How come you're in Florida?"

"I just went for a second interview. Nothing's definite yet. I have to wait to hear back from the firm, because they're interviewing other applicants."

"I see. Have you spoken to your girlfriend in the last few days?"

He shook his head. "I thought she was angry with me for considering the relocation and just not answering her phone. When I arrived at the PBI airport and heard her name coming from on one of the overhead TV's, I listened to the reporter, then got my car out of the lot and drove right over here."

"When you spoke to Maddie last, did she mention going to meet someone?"

He shook his head again. "The last time we spoke, she was getting dressed to go to work. I told her I'd call back later that evening. I called a few times, but she never answered, and the message machine was turned off."

"How long were you in Texas?"

"I stayed a couple of extra days to visit family and friends." He glanced down at the dog, then back at Catherine. "I wanted Maddie to come with me on this trip. I thought if she met my folks, it might persuade her to move with me if I got the job. I love her. Before I left, I asked her to marry me."

"What was her answer?"

He loosened his tie. "She said she loved me, but didn't know if she was ready to leave Florida, because her career was just getting started."

"So she didn't give you a yes."

"She said we'd talk about it when I knew more about getting the job. I figured I had time, so I dropped it," he said, growing teary eyed.

Catherine noticed it, and moved on. "Could Maddie be visiting friends, or have taken a trip?"

He pulled a handkerchief out of his jacket pocket and dabbed his eyes before answering. "No. Maddie loves her job," he said, his lips tightening slightly. "I asked her a couple of times to take a weekend off so we could go hiking or visit Disneyland. Her answer was always: 'the store is too busy on a Saturday to take any time off.' Something must have happened to her. That job means everything to Maddie."

"Joe, do you know if she ever got any threatening phone calls?"

"She never mentioned any."

"What about someone following her. Did she ever mention that?"

"No, never. I know she always walks the dog at night, but if something happened to her on one of those walks, why is Harry here?"

Catherine scribbled a few words on the pad. "Joe, I'd like your flight information and the name of the hotel that you stayed in."

"Why? Do you think… I don't understand."

"I'm sure you have nothing to do with Madeline's disappearance. This information is only for our records. We're checking everyone who knows Ms. Kefler, so please don't concern yourself."

After writing down what he told her, Catherine hooked the leash on Harry, and she and the dog walked him out to the reception area.

"Here you go," she said, trying to hand him the leash.

"What? I can't take him. They don't let dogs in my complex."

"Well, what am I supposed to do with him?"

Joe shrugged. "I don't know. He's not my problem. I have to go, or my car might get ticketed." He turned and rushed out of the station.

Catherine stared after him. The voices of officers who were talking in the background faded, and she paid no attention to those who walked around her. *Your car might get ticketed? How? We don't have meters in front of the station*, she thought, watching him climb into a brand new Lincoln Navigator that had a roof rack and top of the line polished-aluminum wheels. *Why didn't you take your girlfriend's dog until she got back, or do you already know she's never coming back for him? You bet I'm going to check out your air flights and where you stayed, you son-of-a-bitch.*

When Catherine was back at her desk, her mind went into overdrive. *Maybe his tears were bullshit. Maybe he was royally pissed that she'd turn down his proposal. And maybe the Blackstone girl's disappearance had nothing to do with Kefler's. Our finding both bodies in a canal might be a coincidence—a copycat thinking he can throw us off his trail.*

CHAPTER THIRTY-EIGHT

For the next hour Catherine was busy reviewing Hillary Blackstone's file, and her notes on Madeline Kefler. She reread the medical examiner's autopsy report a couple of times, and just as she suspected, Hillary hadn't drowned, she'd been strangled.

Next she checked the National Criminal data base for known stranglers who were living within a twenty-five mile radius of where the two bodies had been found. There were two men who had been convicted of aggravated assault. Hernandez Ramos, a tall, sturdy, heavily tattooed, forty-seven-year-old Latino was the first on the list. His current address was in Lantana. He had strangled his girlfriend until she was almost dead. The second one was William Stockwood, black, twenty-seven, accused of robbery with the intent to kill by strangulation. His victim was an 82-year-old woman. Stockwood was also big enough to lift a young woman, and he had just been released after serving ten years in Florida State Prison. Catherine opened a file on each of them, and was about to go into the chief's office to ask for the two of them to be picked up for questioning, when Dexter walked in.

"We nabbed the principal. He just got home. He's in room one when you're ready."

Catherine rose. "Great. Come in with me." She grabbed his file from the pile on her desk, and a yellow pad and pen, and followed him into the interrogation room. David Spencer was sitting when they entered, looking very annoyed. His khaki slacks were creased and soiled, and his white T-shirt had a few dark, brown stains on it.

"Why am I here?" he asked, his voice low and velvety smooth.

"I'm Detective Delaney, and this is Detective Betancourt," she said, as they both sat down opposite him. "I'd like to ask you some questions."

"Is this about the Blackstone girl? I already told the police everything I know about her."

"Mr. Spencer, can you tell me where you've been for the last two days?"

"I went deep sea fishing up in Port St. Lucie. Is this about the Blackstone girl? You didn't answer me."

"What are all these stains on your shirt?" Catherine asked, deliberately ignoring his question.

"I fillet a few fish. It's their blood." He looked at Dexter. "I wasn't allowed to change my clothes when I got home." He turned back to Catherine. "So, what is this about?"

"This is about Sonia Dixon."

"Who?"

"Sonia Dixon. Her nickname is Sonny."

"I still don't know who you're talking about."

"She just graduated from your school."

He sighed. "Lots of kids graduated this year."

"She's the girl who was bullying Hillary Blackstone. I understand you called both girls into your office to resolve the problem."

He nodded. "Ahh. Now I remember her. It was about a boy. I told her that she wouldn't graduate if she continued to bother the other girl. The threat worked, and that was the end of it."

"Can you tell me why Sonia calls you David?"

"What?"

"Some of her friends say all the girls called you David."

The principal's back straightened. "Not to my face they didn't."

"Sonia also said the two of you were having an affair."

He lurched up off the chair. "What the fuck are you talking about?"

"Please sit down."

"I will not. This accusation is preposterous! I never laid a hand on that girl—or any other girl in that school—ever!"

His anger, and closed fists didn't convince Catherine. "Why would she lie about it? She said it happened in school, and you also met with her after school."

The man's mouth moved, but nothing came out. He stared at them wide-eyed, and his face flushed red.

"Having sex with a minor is a criminal offense called statutory rape."

His head wagged from side to side. "I didn't do it. The girl's lying. Give me a lie detector test. It'll prove I'm not lying to you."

Catherine rose, and so did Dexter. "As soon as we get a swab of those stains on your shirt, you can leave. We'll be in touch when the test can be arranged. In the meantime, please don't leave town."

Spencer looked stunned and said nothing.

After Catherine and Dexter left the room and locked the door, she said: "I don't think that schmuck did anything to Sonia, but we'll give him the lie detector test anyway, and throw in a few questions about Hillary."

CHAPTER THIRTY-NINE

Catherine heard Cody's heavy footsteps approach her office, and stop at the door. She swiveled around in her chair. He said nothing, just looked at her and leaned against the doorframe. His face and hair were wet with sweat, his clothes were a wrinkled mess, and the bottom of his pants and shoes were caked with mud. But it was the utter bleakness that stared out of his dark eyes that got her pulse racing.

"I was able to see her teeth when her body was turned over," he said, stepping away from the door and then sinking onto a nearby chair. "The two top ones are slightly crossed over like I saw in her picture. It's Kefler. No doubt about it."

"Did the ME confirm a broken neck?"

"He didn't say. He collected his usual evidence, and bagged her hands to save what might be under her nails. Our team searched the perimeter for evidence. They found nothing. My conclusion," he said, shoving his fingers through his hair, "she was dumped in the canal at another location and floated down stream. Burt will fax his report to us as soon as he finishes it. The lab reports will come in later."

As the round wall clock ticked its metallic cadence above Catherine's desk, the two of them sat there saying nothing. While Cody peered down at his clasped hands that dangled between his knees, she looked at the frown lines etched on his forehead. Catherine finally broke the silence. First she told him about her conversation with Kefler's boyfriend. Next, the interview she'd had with David Spencer and his impending lie detector test.

He looked at her, but still said nothing.

Catherine swiveled around to her desk, then turned back holding two folders out to him.

"What are these?"

"Files I just opened on two rapists. Their names were listed on the National Criminal data base. Both of them live within a twenty-five mile radius of where we found the two girl's bodies. We need to pull them in for questioning."

"Sounds good. How's your snake theory panning out?"

She got up. "Wilkins and Whitehall are handling that. The little man they're working with—"

"Little man?"

"The guy has Achondroplasia. It's a growth disorder that causes dwarfism." She walked over to her desk, and pulled another folder out of the pile. "His name's Frank Dembeck," she said, after glancing at the tab. "They connected with him through a pet shop manager who said the man bought a lot of snakes at his store. Seems the little guy is on Facebook with other snake collectors. He told Whitehall and Wilkins that he sometimes meets other collectors to trade snakes."

"Sounds like lots of fun," Cody said, rising. "So what's happening with it now?"

"They were able to get onto Dembecks' Facebook page."

"And?"

"They're in their office monitoring Dembeck's friends' messages on their computer. Anything that comes in from one of his snake buddies will be checked out. If one of them wants to do a trade, Dembeck agreed they could join him. That's it. All we can do now is wait for that hit."

"Have you spoken to Amanda?"

"No." She shoved her hands into her pants pockets. "I was waiting for you to get back, so we could drive over together."

"Still want to show her Kefler's picture?"

"We have to show it to her. What if the girl she saw in her last vision wasn't Madeline? What if it's a different girl who hasn't been reported missing?" She tossed Dembeck's folder onto her desk, then turned back to Cody. "Did you get that piece of plastic that you wanted her to touch?"

"Not yet. Burt says they're still doing DNA testing on all of it. If we're lucky, they'll get a profile off a piece that was wrapped around one of those body parts. Come on, Delaney. Let's give this to your uncle. I want to stop off for a burger, before we see Amanda."

"You drop it off. I'll wait in here."

He eyed her.

"My uncle's got Harry in there, and he won't leave me alone."

"Harry? Who the hell is Harry?"

Catherine's hands came out of her pockets and onto her hips. "Harry," she said, glaring at him. "Is the name of that ugly-looking mutt you insisted we bail out of the pound, the miserable beast that gobbled up my whole slice of pepperoni pizza. That's who."

Cody walked out of her office laughing.

CHAPTER FORTY

The first words out of Amanda's mouth after opening the front door and seeing the two detectives and the dog was: "You poor baby." Her arms reached out. Harry jumped right onto her lap, snuggled against her middle, and then whimpered and whined like he was in pain.

Amanda rolled herself into the kitchen with the dog still in her lap, but didn't pull the wheelchair too close to the table.

"Want me to put him down on the floor," Catherine asked her.

"No, he needs to be comforted."

"Why do you say that?"

"Because, he's her dog. He knows she's not coming back, and he's hurting. When I heard that girl crying that last time, she said something about her dog and I saw him." She looked down at her lap. "Yes, he was her dog."

Catherine pulled the folded picture of Madeline out of her pants pocket, unfolded the white sheet, and slid it across the table top. "Is this who you saw the last time we were here?"

Amanda didn't touch it. She peered at the image for only a moment before she nodded.

"Amanda, have you had any other visions since we last saw you?" Cody asked. "Were you able to see where that house is? We need to find it."

Amanda stared down at the dog, and drew in a deep breath. "It's very painful... I mean when I see those terrible images. I took a sleeping pill last night, because I didn't want to see anything, but this morning... this morning when I was just waking up, I heard voices. Many voices. Women's voices. Some of them were crying, so with my eyes still closed, I looked for them." She shivered and drew her knitted shoulder wrap tighter. "They... they were under the ground and their hands were clawing, trying to get up, out of the earth."

Catherine glanced at Cody.

"You saw them buried in a cemetery?" he asked.

"I don't know where they were. I didn't see gravestones or markers, just fields... fields of flattened grass or reeds above those hands. It was tall stuff... flattened close to the ground." Her voice had grown lower. "It wasn't clear. The image was hazy. All I really saw were their boney, dirty, black hands... broken nails on those hands that were clawing... clawing hard to get out of the dirt."

"Did you see any trees, or houses, or any kind of store by those fields?"

She looked at Cody. "Only fields of flattened grass... and... and deep tire tracks... deep, long tire tracks that ran into the long field... and ran over those hands."

"Tire tracks going where?" Cody prodded, placing his hand on her arm. "Think Amanda. Try to remember everything you saw."

Amanda closed her eyes and started rocking and rocking, back and forth, back and forth. The dog jumped off her lap and sat on the floor looking up at her, his tail not wagging, his brown eyes fixed on her.

Amanda's breathing became labored. She started to moan.

The dog whimpered softly.

Catherine and Cody silently waited and watched her.

"She's in the trunk... curled in the trunk... he's driving through the fields... tires in the ruts... the car's shaking... her body's bumping in the trunk... her eyes are open... her face is blue... he's stopping the car... getting out... it's raining hard... very hard... very hard... he's... he's a blur... I see his back... he's carrying her now... her yellow hair is wet... it's covering her eyes... It's raining harder... I hear... I hear a splash... She's gone. It's over."

"It can't be over," Cody pleaded. "Amanda, keep looking. Where is he going? Is he back in the car? Is he driving? See where the car's going. Please... Please keep looking. Tell me what you see."

Amanda's eyes flew open, then rolled up until only the whites could be seen. A moment later, her head hit the table and she was out. Catherine quickly tilted her head back and patted her cheeks. When Cody brought a cold, wet towel over, she pressed it against Amanda's forehead until she became conscious.

"Amanda, I'm so sorry we have to put you through this," Catherine said to the pallid-faced woman. "We're just frightened there's going to be another girl."

Amanda shuddered. "I wish I could help you more, but I can only tell you what I see when I see it." She looked down at the dog, who was still sitting on the floor looking up at her. "What are you going to do with him?"

Catherine looked at Cody as she answered. "I don't know. We both work long hours. The dog would be a prisoner in an empty house if we kept him."

"Then let me have him? I'd love to have some company."

Catherine continued to look at Cody.

"Are you sure he wouldn't be too much for you to handle?" Cody said, glancing at the wheelchair, then back at her.

"I have a good neighbor friend who helps me out. Between the two of us, we'll manage. Please, I'd love to have him."

"Sure," Cody said. "We met your neighbor the other day. He seems like a nice gent. Listen Amanda, Catherine and I have—"

"Cody didn't do anything," Catherine said, cutting him off. "I was curious about… well about your scar, so I looked into a few things."

Amanda's mouth dropped open.

"I know about your ex-husband," Catherine said. "And what he did to you. I also found out that he's up for a parole hearing."

Amanda kept staring at Catherine.

"Cody and I want you to know that we're going to that meeting. If we can't keep him in that place to serve out his full sentence, we'll make sure that he never bothers you again. Do you hear me? You needn't worry about him. He's done, finished, out of your life."

But Michael Plummer wasn't waiting for his parole hearing. Two hours earlier, unknown to all who were sitting in that kitchen and the guards at the Florida State Prison, he had hidden himself in a large, burlap laundry bag, and was transported by truck through the prison's open steel gates.

CHAPTER FORTY-ONE

"God, am I stuffed," Catherine moaned, as she and Cody walked through the filled lot to get to where their car was parked. "I shouldn't have eaten all that garlic bread."

"And the second bowl of salad that was smothered in dressing," he added, smiling and opening the door for her.

Catherine climbed in and pulled the door shut. As she was fastening her seatbelt, Cody got in.

He started the engine, and shifted into drive. "I can't wait to get under a hot shower."

"Cody, I want to make a quick stop."

"Cathy, please. Let's call it a night. I'm hot, full, and ready to fall off my feet."

She looked over at him. "It's just a quick stop. It will only take a few minutes, and it's not far away from my place."

"Why your place?" He pressed his foot on the gas pedal. "I thought we agreed you were moving in with me."

"I need my clothes. I can't keep washing out two outfits like I was a homeless person. Cody, please. I want to drop by my cleaning lady's house to see how she is, and also to ask her to help me get my place ready to sell."

"In that case, give me her address. The sooner you move in, sweetheart, the happier and more satisfied I'm going to be."

When they arrived at Lillian's small, shabby house, Cody was still smiling.

"It doesn't look like anyone's home. The lights are out."

"Well, as long as you got me here, go and ring the bell. Maybe they're in the back of the house where you wouldn't see any lights."

When Catherine got out of the car and saw the knee-high grass that hadn't been cut, she drew in a breath and headed up the uneven brick path toward the house. The white paint on the door was dingy and peeling, and a black shutter on the right window was hanging by a screw. After knocking on the door a few times and hearing nothing, she frowned. Lillian was a perfectionist. Why wasn't her lawn mowed? Why was her home looking in such disrepair? To make sure she was at the right house, Catherine stepped back to check the numbers over the door. It was Lillian's place, and although she'd never been there before, her gut feeling told her that something was very wrong.

After knocking again and still getting no reply, she decided to walk around the house and look through the back windows to see if anyone was inside. Getting to the back yard was even harder, because it was totally dark and all sorts of junk littered the side yard. A small light filtered out of the kitchen window when she climbed up on the small wooden porch. She knocked on the back door, while peering through the window. A fat, balding, middle-aged man looked up from the table where a small candle flickered. He motioned with his hand for her to go away. She knocked again, harder this time. He waved his hand again, and then blew out the candle.

"What the fuck?"

Catherine returned to the car, and told Cody what had happened. "Drive around the corner. I want to talk to the neighbor who lives directly behind Lillian's house."

For once, Cody didn't argue with her. After he parked the car, he offered to come in with her, but she declined his offer.

The neighbor's door was answered after only two knocks. "Yes," a slim, jean-clad teenager said.

Catherine showed the girl her badge.

"What now? Is she back and complaining again? We're not in the pool, and we're not even in the back yard."

"Are you talking about the lady who lives in the house behind you?"

"Rosa, who's at the door?" a woman called out.

"The police, Mom."

The woman quickly came to the door in her pink bathrobe. Her feet were bare, and her hair was up in pink curlers. "What's the problem?"

"I'm a friend of your back yard neighbor, and I'm worried about her."

"She's away," the woman said. "We haven't seen her in the yard since before the hurricane."

"What about the man in her house?"

"That's her weirdo brother," the girl said. "He used to have a big, white dog, but it's also gone. Maybe his sister took the dog with her when she left."

"Listen, I don't like to cause any trouble, but…" The woman hesitated and Catherine waited. "I think his electricity has been turned off, because at night I see him roaming around the house and the back yard with a candle."

"I just saw him with a candle," Catherine said.

"He's going to start a fire. I just know it. You're the police. Can't you have some… some government agency check him out?"

Catherine pulled one of her cards out of her pocket. "Please call me if you see the lady again."

"But what about—"

"If his sister doesn't show up in a week or so, I'll have someone talk to her brother. Thank you. I'm sorry to have bothered you."

"Tell them to look in that metal shed," the girl called out when Catherine was almost at the car. "He's always in there, and the smell coming from it stinks."

"So?" Cody said as she was settling herself in the car.

She looked at him. "The neighbors said they haven't seen Lillian since before the hurricane, and the brother is a weirdo who walks around with a candle."

"Well, you got your answer," he said, starting the engine. "Her brother drove her away. Good for her."

CHAPTER FORTY-TWO

Detectives Stan Wilkins and Thomas Whitehall had been sitting at their computers all day, monitoring Frank Dembeck's Facebook page. They had spoken with the little man early that morning and asked for his help, by staying on line all day. They'd reminded him to act and write like he always did, and when one of his snake collector friends came on, to engage them in a longer than usual conversation or initiate an IM (instant messaging conversation) so they'd have time to check that person's profile.

For more than five hours, the two detectives scanned the usual chatter about who did what and when. Lots of cartoons and written jokes were displayed, along with pictures of friend's cats, dogs, family outings, and people who were struggling with an illness and asking for prayers.

"I can't believe people are so stupid they'd announce to the world they and their families are leaving for vacation," Stan said. "What if I was a burglar? I'd know where they live and exactly when they're going to be away. It's so stupid of them. I can't believe they do it."

"Yeah, I know," Hawk said, sitting at his desk and looking at the same message on his computer. "The pedophiles love the morons who post their kiddie's pictures." He got up and stretched his back. "Want to call in for some Chinese food?"

"Sit down. We got a hit."

Hawk quickly sat down, and read Dembeck's last message from J. H. Higgins.

MY BOA JUST HAD 60 LIVE BABIES. THEY'RE A MIX OF RED & YELLOW. WILL GROW UP TO 13 FT. & 100 LBS. WILL LIVE UP TO 30 YRS. FOR SALE REASONABLE.

Hawk clicked on J.H. Higgin's picture, and his profile page opened. "It can't be him, Stan. It says he lives in Georgia. We're looking for someone in Florida."

"Gotcha. Make the call, and order me a combination dish and a wonton soup. Looks like it's going to be a long night."

"What kind of combo?"

"Shrimp in Chinese vegetables. Wait! Hold on. We got another hit from Snake Lover. He says he just bought a beautiful 10 foot Burmese Python."

Hawk clicked on Snake Lover's picture. His profile came up, and it said he resided in Florida. Dembeck was immediately called.

"Hello."

"Frank, this is Detective Whitehall. Try to IM Snake Lover. Ask him if he wants to trade or sell his snake. If he agrees, set up a meeting place. Do it now, before he gets off line."

Dembeck immediately opened an IM.

DO YOU WANT TO TRADE OR SELL THAT PYTHON? WOULD LOVE TO HAVE IT IN MY COLLECTION.

Snake Lover didn't reply, but R. Johnson joined in the conversation and wrote:

HAVE 14-FT BLACK MAMBAS. MOVING. MUST SELL. ANY OFFER. WILL TRAVEL TO DELIVER.

"He's no good," Hawk said. "He lives in Mexico."

"Make a note on him," Stan said. "He may be looking to sneak into the U.S. We'll pass his name onto immigration."

"Stan, we're barking up the wrong tree, checking out the ones who are dealing with venomous snakes."

Stan looked over at him. "Why? What's your reasoning?"

"Delaney said her woo-woo friend saw the girls in a room filled with snakes. They have to be non-venomous snakes, otherwise the guy would have to be nuts to walk around them."

"He is nuts. Why else would he murder people?"

"Here's another one," Hawk said, staring at his screen.

NON-POISONOUS SNAKES 4 SALE. CALIF. KINGS, MILK & RAT SNAKES. WILL MAKE GOOD PETS 4 KIDS. CHEAP.

Hawk quickly dialed Dembeck. "Frank, IM that last guy. He lives in West Palm. Set up a meeting for tomorrow if possible. Hurry."

Frank Dembeck followed directions and started an IM.

HOOVER, I'M INTERESTED IN BUYING 3-KINGS, ETC. 4 MY COLLECTION. CAN U MEET TOMORROW TO BUY OR TRADE?

Hoover replied.

SALE ONLY—NO TRADES. 3:00 P.M. TOMORROW. LK 4 GREEN/ SPARK/CHEVY WILL B PARKED AT OFFICE DEPOT/CONGRESS AVE/ BOYNTON. CASH ONLY.

By ten o'clock. that evening, Stan and Hawk were calling it a night, and turning off their computers. They were not only famished, they were totally exhausted and bleary-eyed from staring at their screens for so many hours.

"We did good," Stan said, getting up and arching his back. "We got three appointments for tomorrow."

"I'll give Delaney a call right after we chow down. We'll let her and O'Dell go to those meet-ups, and we'll stick to our computers."

"Why do we have to be at our computers?" Stan asked, rubbing the back of his neck. "Dembeck will be off his so he can go to those meetings."

"We can't let him go to them. We need him to keep chatting on his Facebook page. Other snake nuts may contact him. Maybe the one we're looking for didn't get online today. If that's the case, none of the guys that we set up for tomorrow is our killer."

"You're right, Buddy," Stan said, slapping Hawk on his back. "What do you say we get out of this hell hole and sit down in a restaurant like normal human beings?"

Hawk had just shut off the lights in their office, when Frank Dembeck received a message from Grandpa's Boy.

FOUND ANOTHER PRETTY ONE. CAN'T WAIT TO PICK UP MY NEW PLAYMATE.

CHAPTER FORTY-THREE

At 6:45 A.M., Catherine heard her cell phone ringing in Cody's kitchen, where she'd plugged it in to recharge the battery. By the time she got herself out of bed and half dragged herself in to answer the call, the person had hung up.

"Shit!" She hit the call button. The phone rang twice and was picked up. "Amanda, did you call just me?"

"Yes. I'm sorry to call you so early, but… but I saw something I'm not sure about."

"It's all right. Don't worry about it," Catherine said, bending and taking a bottle of orange juice out of the refrigerator. "What did you see?"

"It was strange. I saw a double image."

"What do you mean, a double image?" She sat down at the table with the bottle held on her lap.

"It was like a split screen. There were two faces, two girls, and both images looked exactly the same."

Catherine's pulse raced. "Amanda, let's go over this slowly. Start from the beginning."

Cody walked into the kitchen, took the juice bottle off her lap and went to the cabinet for glasses.

"I was sleeping soundly, then woke up with a jolt. The room was dark. Catherine, my visions sometimes start like that, but when I closed my eyes again, nothing happened. Since the dog was lying in bed with me, I thought he must have poked me to go outside."

Cody placed two filled glasses of juice on the table, and pulled a chair close to hear what Amanda was saying.

"I got in my wheelchair, and let him outside. It was when he came back to the kitchen door, that I saw them standing in my back yard. The girls looked exactly the same."

"Are you saying they were standing in your yard?"

There was no reply.

"Amanda, are you there?"

"I was trying to remember it. I'm not sure where they were standing. They were surrounded by darkness. Kinda like floating in a black space."

"What did the girls look like? What were they wearing? Did you see anyone with them?"

"Catherine, it could be only one girl, not two. I don't know how to explain it. I've never envisioned anything like this before. It was like looking at a reflection in a mirror. Like seeing the same thing twice."

"What was she wearing? What did she look like?" Catherine repeated. "How old did she look?"

There was a pause, before Amanda answered. "I can't remember."

Cody took the phone out of Catherine's hand. "Amanda, it's Cody. Would it be all right if we came over to see you?"

"You mean right now?"

"Yes. Please. Maybe this new girl that you've just seen is about to be abducted. Maybe with our help, you can have a better vision and we can get to her before she's taken."

"All right, but I won't be dressed. My aide doesn't come this early."

"Amanda…"

"Yes."

"Please don't do anything that might get you seeing things before we get there."

"I can't promise that. I can't control when I see things that are going to happen, or what's happening at that time. But I will try. I'll make myself some breakfast to keep my mind occupied."

"Thank you. We'll be there as soon as we can." He hung up and turned to Catherine. "If she's right, something is about to happen, or has already happened to another girl… or girls."

Both glasses of juice were left untouched on the table.

CHAPTER FORTY-FOUR

A fine, misty rain was coming down as the two of them walked up the path toward Amanda's house. Halfway to her front door, the dog started to bark furiously. Cody knocked on the door softly, and as he did, Catherine watched the sparkling droplets of rain drip off his dark, unruly hair. She was just about to reach up and wipe his wet cheek, when the door opened and the dog charged out.

"Harry, get in here," Amanda ordered, as the dog circled around their feet.

Harry immediately quit his barking, and jumped up on top of her lap.

"Good boy," she said, patting his head. "Mama's going to give you a cookie as soon as we get inside."

The kitchen smelled of bacon and some kind of toasted garlic-spiced bread when they entered. Catherine's mouth watered. She waited for Amanda to take a dog treat out of a box and give it to Harry, and then said, "I see you've already gotten doggie treats."

Amanda smiled. "My friend went to the supermarket for me late last night." Her smile grew wider. "It was a waste. Harry ate half of my breakfast and left his bowl of dog food untouched." She wheeled herself over to the table with Harry still sitting on her lap.

Catherine and Cody joined her at the table.

"Amanda, have you had another vision?" Catherine asked.

Amanda drew in a deep breath and then released it. She rubbed her fingers over the dog's back, and chewed on her bottom lip. "I couldn't help it." She looked across the table at Catherine. "When I saw the brown toast… the brown… the color made me see those hands again."

"You mean the hands that were trying to dig their way out from beneath the earth?"

Amanda swallowed. "I started to count them."

"The hands?"

She nodded. "I counted twenty-six of them, and then I stopped because their frantic clawing and scratching was making me sick to my stomach."

Catherine glanced at Cody. Her heart missed a beat and then charged on. "Cody, do you think there are other girls that he's killed that we haven't found out about?"

"I don't know what to think," he said, rubbing the back of his neck. "Maybe those hands have nothing to do with these killings. Maybe those hands are from years ago, in an entirely different location. Amanda," he said, turning to her. "Have some of your visions taken place in other locations... locations outside of Florida."

"Sometimes, but they always happen to people who are close to me."

"Close to you," Catherine repeated. "What do you mean by that? Close to your body? Close to your house? Exactly how close to what?"

Amanda stopped petting the dog. She stared first at Catherine, and then at Cody. It was obvious that she was trying to figure out how to explain what she'd just said.

"Catherine, when I have these visions, they always come true."

"I know, Amanda. You've already told us that."

"I know they come true, because I always read about it in the papers or hear about it on the news within a few days of it happening... It always... always happens fairly near to where I am at the time."

Catherine gasped. "Amanda, are you saying that these killings are taking place close to your home?"

"It always happens within twenty to forty miles of where I am. Like when I was flown up to a trauma center in North Carolina for my injuries. I also had visions there, and they also came true. I hate it. I wish these visions would stop coming to me, because they leave me sick for days. I can see accidents before they happen and murders when they're being committed. I feel the horror of the injured and dying in my bones, and see the events playing out in my mind until I want to scream at the top of my lungs."

"Amanda," Cody said softly. "Are you saying that these murders... the murders of these last two girls who were found in the canal took place close to where you live?"

She nodded. "These things... these happenings that I see always take place within twenty to forty miles of where I'm at, whether it's in Florida or another state. I don't know why it's only within a limited area. It just is what it is, and I can't explain it."

"What about this new image? The two girls? Are they still alive?" he probed.

"I didn't see a killing," she said, her breath becoming short. "I still don't know if there was one or two of them. The only thing I remember seeing is a double image of long, dark hair and green eyes… And also, very long, polished red nails as they held their hands out toward me."

CHAPTER FORTY-FIVE

After Dexter got a call from Chico's number one girl, he and Ricardo drove over to visit him in the Boca Raton Regional Hospital. The reception lobby was crowded and busy. People were streaming in and out of the place, a couple of babies were howling in their strollers, and other children were playing tag, almost tripping some of the adults.

"He's in ICU," a gray-haired volunteer who was sitting behind the receptionist's desk told Dexter. "Only family members can visit him."

Dexter flipped open his badge. "Ma'am, will this do?"

"He's up on the second floor, officer. Ask one of the nurses what room he's in."

"Didn't she tell you why he was in here?" Ricardo asked, when they reached the bank of elevators.

"She just said he was in the hospital, and then hung up."

When the elevator door directly in front of them slid open, a horde of people pushed past them and into the elevator, leaving no room for them. "What?" Ricardo stuck his foot against the door's edge so it wouldn't close. "Everyone out," he said, showing them his badge.

The occupants, many of them holding flowers or balloons, mumbled and complained, but got out, leaving a young woman and a redheaded boy inside. Ricardo kept his foot by the door, waiting for them to leave.

"Why you standing there?" the olive-skinned kid who was about seven or eight years old asked.

"Did you hear me tell you to get out of the elevator?"

"Yeah, but I'm not getting out. Make me," the boy said, crossing his thin arms over his chest and glaring at the detectives.

Ricardo looked at the woman. She was gorgeous, had to be in her early thirties, and had the kind of body that would drive any red-blooded man wild. "Does your kid always talk back?"

"My mother can't hear. You have to sign."

Dexter slipped past his partner and got into the elevator. "Ricardo, get in. We're wasting time."

The boy smiled. He'd won. The elevator door closed, and when it reopened on the second floor they all got out, and they all walked over to the nurse's station.

"What room is my dad in?"

"What's your father's name," a nurse asked, staring down at him.

"Chico."

Both detectives' eyes popped open.

"It's really Camacho Montoya," the boy said, as his mother placed her hand on his shoulder.

"I'm sorry, son, but only your mother can go into your father's room."

Once again, Ricardo flipped open his badge. "The kid has to go in. His mother is deaf and he signs for her."

The boy turned around and gave Ricardo a wide smile that exposed a couple of missing teeth.

Ricardo tried not to smile back, but lost the fight. "What's your name, kid?"

"Chico Junior."

Dexter groaned.

"Tell you what, Chico Junior. My partner and I are going inside to talk to your dad first, and then we'll come and get you. Okay, Partner?"

The boy seemed to mull it over for a few moments, and then nodded.

"Good. We won't be long."

Room 2013A was at the very end of the long corridor. "Dex, do you think that woman knows what kind of business her husband's in?"

Dexter didn't bother to answer.

The room they entered had two beds in it, and reeked of disinfectant and urine. The one closest to the door was empty and had fresh linens on it. Chico was lying on the bed close to the window. A light over his bed was lit, but his eyes were closed. He was hooked to all sorts of machines that bleeped and blinked in a steady rhythm, and an intravenous line that was connected to his hand was pumping a clear fluid into it.

"Chico," Dexter whispered at his bedside.

His eyes blinked open. "Shit! Not you two again."

"What happened?" Ricardo asked from the other side of the bed.

"Docs said I had a heart attack."

"Sorry to hear that," Dexter said. "You gonna' be all right?"

"Yeah, if you guys leave me alone and stop putting pressure on me."

Ricardo and Dexter glanced at one another.

"I still didn't hear anything from my people on the street." Chico's hand grabbed his chest, and then he coughed. "Your guy's got to be someone important with a shit load of money. No one's heard of him, and no one's sold him any drugs or weed. He's upper-crust. Doesn't hang in our neighborhood. I can't help you, man. I tried." He coughed again. "That's it. I just want out of here."

Ricardo shifted from one foot to the other. "Your wife and son are waiting to see you."

Chico's hand grasped the bed sheet, and his face registered panic. "You didn't tell them what I do. Did you?"

"No," Ricardo answered. "He's a cute kid. Every kid deserves to think his dad's a hero."

Chico breathed out a sigh of relief. "Thanks. I appreciate that. Soon as I get out of this place, I'm retiring."

"Really?" Dexter said, flipping some dreadlocks off his shoulder.

"It's time. I've saved some money. Enough to take my family, and move to St. Thomas. Fellers, be sure to come and visit me sometime." When Chico saw Ricardo's smile, he quickly said: "I didn't mean that. No way do I ever want to see you two again."

After wishing Chico good luck, they walked out of his room. "That guy must have a fuckin' bundle," Ricardo said. "He can't be more than forty, or forty-two years old. I wonder if his wife was one—"

"Shut up. The kid's walking over here."

"Can we go in now?" Junior asked, holding onto his mother's hand.

"He's waiting for you," Dexter said, patting him on the head.

"Dex, what do you think's going to happen to Chico's business now that he's retiring?"

"Get in the elevator," Dexter said.

"What? What's the matter?"

"Retire, my ass. No way is he walking away from that money."

Shortly before reaching their car, Dexter's cell phone rang. He pulled it out of his pocket. "Betancourt," he said. "Yes, Chief, hold on a sec." He shouldered the phone, then pulled a small pad and pen out of his pocket. "Okay, let me have it."

Ricardo watched him scribble on the pad and then end the call. "What's up?"

"We have to pick up a William Stockwood for questioning."

"What's his story?"

"He's a sexual offender who lives close to the canal where the two bodies were found."

CHAPTER FORTY-SIX

"You two look like drowned rats," Chief Delaney said when Catherine and Cody entered his office, every inch of their clothing drenched, and their wet hair dripping onto their faces.

"The hurricane wasn't enough. Now it's pouring outside for a change," Catherine said, sitting in front of her uncle's desk.

Cody sat beside her and leaned forward with his elbows on his knees, his hands steepled under his chin. "Chief, we just came back from talking to Amanda Plummer. It's not good."

"Please don't tell me she saw another kid being abducted."

"Uncle Steve, Amanda said she saw a double image this time."

"What the hell does that mean? Is she saying two kids have been abducted this time?"

"She doesn't understand the vision," Catherine said. "She's not sure if it's one girl or two that she saw. Also, she says she hasn't seen a killing, so that girl may still be alive."

The chief sighed and leaned back against his chair.

"There's more," Cody said. "She's seen hands clawing their way up from the earth. Twenty-six hands," she said, "but there may be more, and she doesn't think they're buried in a cemetery."

"Twenty-six hands? They're underground, and not in a cemetery? My God, you two! What's that supposed to mean? Is this woman crazy, and giving us a line of bullshit?"

Catherine slid forward on her seat. "Amanda's not crazy. She really does see things, and she's proven it to us with these last two murders. Her vision of hands could mean there are other victims. Victims that may or may not have anything to do with these last two girls who were dumped in the canal. Uncle Steve, Amanda told us that she only has visions if it happens within twenty to forty miles of where she physically is."

The chief's chair tilted forward with a squeak. He grabbed a cigar butt out of his filled ashtray, but didn't stick it into his mouth. "Are you telling me that these murders were committed within forty miles of where she lives? That means—"

"Exactly! Wherever that place is, Amanda said she sees no buildings or structures in sight. She told Cody and me the ground has flattened vegetation on it, and deep tire ruts that lead to a canal."

"That means its farmland, or vacant, underdeveloped acreage," Cody added, rising and tugging his fingers through his hair. "Chief, we need a helicopter to start searching the open land within forty miles of Plummer's home. Locating those ruts—"

"Cody, those ruts could have been made by any damn piece of farm equipment. It's a wild goose chase, because whatever ruts there may have been, have probably been washed away by this rain."

"Chief, you may be right, but we have to give it a shot."

"There's no way I can get a copter up there while it's pouring outside. Besides, if the copter actually got close to the killer's location, the racket might warn him that we're onto him. Then the bastard might take off, and we'd never catch him."

"Uncle, we have to try something," Catherine said. "We can't just sit here and wait for another kid to be murdered."

"Cathy, honey, it's a risk. If he takes off, he'll keep on killing, but who knows where. I say we hold off on the copter for a couple of days, so we don't spook him into running. What do the two of you say? Should we give it a couple of days?"

"No! I don't agree," Catherine said, staring directly at her uncle. "We can't wait. If Amanda envisioned another girl, he may already have her. We can't hold off. We need to find that house before he murders her."

CHAPTER FORTY-SEVEN

After adjusting the water to warm, he stepped into the stall shower, closed his eyes, and let the water pour over his heated body. He'd had a very restless night filled with the same recurring dreams that he had had since childhood. Those dreams always ended with his initiation—a dream that made his heart pound so hard and quick, that he always awoke in a panic, not knowing if he was twelve years old again—and not knowing if he was back in his grandfather's secret place.

His father and mother were always too busy with this or that to find time for him. He didn't play sports, because he wasn't as big and sturdy as the other boys in his class. He liked to sit by himself and read books—lots of books on different subjects—books that transported him out of his sterile, unhappy home to foreign lands and exciting adventures.

It was Grandpa who forced him out of his shell when he was nine years old. It was Grandpa who showed him how to raise snakes. The old man loved the feel of them winding themselves around his neck and arms. At first he was afraid and wouldn't touch them.

Grandpa had called him a sissy, so he had to prove that he wasn't. That was the beginning—the start of a unique relationship—a bond that no other grandfather and grandson could ever dream of, no less have. He was taught how to raise the rodents that would feed the snakes, and eventually —when he was comfortable handling the various species—Grandpa taught him how to carefully milk the venomous ones.

As the memories began to unfold, he slid down to the tile floor and placed his hand on his limp penis. He loved remembering his twelfth birthday—the day he was initiated. Grandpa was waiting for him when he got out of school.

"I have a surprise for you, boy."

"Really?"

Grandpa smiled. "It's your birthday. You're going to become a man. I have a special treat for you, but you have to promise you won't tell anyone what it is, because it's got to be our special secret."

He remembered sitting in that old, battered truck with a wide grin on his face. He couldn't wait to get his present. When they got to Grandpa's house, his grandfather unlocked the front door. He followed him upstairs to another locked door, his excitement growing until he thought his heart would burst right out of his chest.

"Now, I don't want you to be shocked when I open the door," Grandpa said when they got upstairs.

But he was shocked. The room he was taken into this time wasn't the snake room that he was always limited to. The door Grandpa opened was to one of the bedrooms, and lying upon a bed that was covered by a bright, red sheet lay a beautiful nude, black girl. Her hands and feet were tied to the metal head and foot boards, and her eyes were half open and dreamy like.

"Grandpa, what's she doing here?"

"She's your present. Let me show you what I want you to do to her. Come closer. Stand by the side of the bed and watch me, boy, so you know what to do when I'm done with her."

He smiled as the shower poured over his head, his raised nipples, and his hardening penis, remembering every detail of his initiation into manhood. He saw his grandpa take off his pants. Saw the old man's stiff erection sticking out like a flag pole. He grew harder picturing how the old man straddled the girl. He could still see her eyes open in shock, and the soft moan that escaped her full, red lips.

"This is what you do," Grandpa said, ramming his dick into the girl's black, hairy vagina. "Did you see that boy?"

He remembered nodding, feeling his own rod grow bigger and harder by the moment, until he thought it would explode like a volcano.

"And then you keep doing this," Grandpa said, plunging in and out, in and out, "until you get soft again. Understand, boy?"

He'd nodded his head vigorously, and could barely catch his breath he was so excited.

"Well, what are you waiting for? Get undressed and get over here."

And he did undress—and he did go over to that bed and straddle her— and he did pump back and forth until his seed spurted inside of her just like it was doing now as he sat on the tile floor with the water flowing over him.

And then he remembered watching Grandpa give the black girl the final injection of venom that left her gasping for air, and her body heaving until she finally shut her eyes and died.

"I'm proud of you, boy," Grandpa had said, patting his back.

He was thrilled that Grandpa was pleased with him. So pleased, that he'd do anything the old man asked him to do. Later that evening, before he was taken back to his empty home, he helped Grandpa dig the hole in the field, and then dump the girl's limp body into it.

He smiled. He loved the memory of his initiation. When it played back in his mind, it always made him ejaculate, and always had him making plans to continue doing what his grandpa had taught him to do.

When he rose from the floor to shower off, his mind automatically switched over to the plan that he'd made for that evening.

You're so lovely, he thought, fondling himself. *I can hardly wait to see your long, black hair splayed across the red sheet as I ram myself into you.*

CHAPTER FORTY-EIGHT

The chief was standing behind his desk, and Catherine and Cody were standing before it, when Wilkins tapped on the doorframe.

"Come in, you two, and join the party in this sauna," the chief called out. "The air conditioner is on the blink for a change."

Wilkins and Whitehall stepped into the stifling-hot office that smelled of stale cigar smoke.

"Good morning, Sir,"

"So far, there's nothing good about it, Wilkins," the chief grumbled. "What can I do for you?"

"Actually, we were looking for Cody and Catherine, because we've got a problem."

"See. I told you it wasn't a good morning," the chief said, plunking down in his chair and staring up at the sweating detective. "What's this latest problem?"

"Hawk and I need Cody and Catherine's help with something."

Wilkins and Whitehall looked as wet and tired as Cody was. He knew the overtime hours these guys were putting in, and how these senseless murders were dragging them down. "What do you need us to do?" he asked.

Stan turned to Cody. "Hawk and I told you we found this little man who collects snakes. We—"

"Are you talking about Dembeck? You told me that you'd follow up on the premise that our killer collects snakes," Catherine said.

"Yes, Dembeck's the one I'm referring to, Catherine, and we are following up on your theory. Yesterday, the little guy let us get onto his Facebook page so we could see who he was chatting with. A few local guys who got online said they were looking to sell some snakes, so we had him set up three different appointments for today."

"That's great. So what's the problem?" she asked. "Hopefully one of them will turn out to be who we're looking for."

"The problem is twofold," Hawk answered. "First, we were going to ask you and Cody to keep those appointments, so we could stay online with Dembeck. We need to keep monitoring his Facebook and Twitter pages, because the collectors that we set up for today's meetings might turn out to be duds. If your hunch is right, Catherine, it's important we keep searching."

"Cody and I can handle those meetings. What else?"

Hawk shoved his hands in his pants pockets. "Unfortunately, the little man is not online, so we can't get onto his Team Viewer which lets us get onto his Facebook page. The second problem," he added, sounding frustrated. "The man's not answering his phone, so we don't know if he's home, or if he's gone to meet those people without us."

"Do you have the info where you're supposed to meet those collectors?" Cody asked.

"Right here in my pocket."

"I'll tell you what. Hawk, you and I will keep those appointments, and Stan, you keep calling the little man and checking to see if he's turned on his computer."

"Sounds like a plan to me," the chief said.

"Hey, what about me? What am I, chopped liver or something?" Catherine snapped.

Her uncle shook his head and sighed. "Catherine Delaney, cool it. Much as I don't like it, you're going to be interviewing William Stockwood when he arrives at the station."

"Great. You got one of the rapists I asked you to pull in. What about the other one?"

"He's—"

"Forget it, Chief," Cody cut in. "Let someone else question him."

"O'Dell, knock that macho bullshit off. I don't need you to tell me what I can or can't do." She turned from him to her uncle. "I have some things to do in my office. Give me a heads-up when he gets here."

Cody let it drop. He didn't want to embarrass her in front of the others. The nightmares would come, and he'd handle them like he always did. "Stan, let's get out of here. We've got snake people to meet."

The chief's phone rang. He lifted the receiver

Everyone froze where they were.

"Chief Delaney here.… Who?… Sorry, I have nothing to tell you at this time… What?… Snakes?… I know nothing about snakes, so please don't print unsubstantiated rumors." He hung up.

"Uncle Steve, what was that about?"

"That was a reporter from the *Sun Sentinel*. She heard we're looking for someone who collects snakes, and asked if it was the person who murdered the two girls. She wanted me to verify what she heard, before her story is printed in tomorrow's newspaper. Even though I gave her nothing, I'm sure that story is going to be tomorrow's headline."

"Oh, crap!" Catherine muttered. "If she prints that story, she'll tip off our killer and scare him away, before we can get our hands on him."

"Actually, it may not be bad," Cody said. "Snakeman might like the notoriety. Sometimes those madmen contact reporters to give them a clue about their next plan. It's a form of bragging. Them saying, 'I'm smarter than you are.' Chief, let's get a warrant to tap her phone, and then send one of our guys over to record the conversation if he does call."

"You're right," Catherine said, excited. "The serial killer profiles that I read said many of those lunatics either called or wrote to the reporter. And, in all of those cases, they made a mistake which led to their capture."

"I'll give Mary Kaye a call and tell her what we're planning to do," the chief said.

"Mary Kaye," Catherine repeated, looking at her uncle. "Was she the one who just called from the *Sentinel*?"

He nodded. "She's the attractive brunette that's always calling and busting my chops for a scoop."

CHAPTER FORTY-NINE

When Catherine's telephone rang, she rushed over to her desk and picked up the receiver.

"Catherine, William Stockwood is waiting to be questioned in interrogation room two," Officer Riley said.

Just the name of the rapist had Catherine's heart racing and sweat rolling down both sides of her face and between her breasts. *You can do it,* she told herself, sucking a deep breath into her lungs. *Your rapist is dead. Uncle Steve shot him. It's over with. This is your job, Catherine Delaney. Get your shit together, and do what you've been trained to do.*

Catherine's inner voice was still in turmoil when she reached the closed door to room two. She was just about to pull it open when she heard Dexter Betancourt call her. She turned around and waited until he reached her. "What's up?"

"I'm goin' in with you."

Her eyebrows lifted.

"Cody asked me to."

"That figures." She turned and opened the door. Dexter followed her inside, but stood by the door.

Six-foot, two-inch William Stockwood was leaning against the padded wall. His well-defined muscular arms were folded across his chest, and a menacing scowl was plastered on his ebony face.

"Please have a seat, Mr. Stockwood," Catherine said, sitting down.

"Why am I in here?" he asked in a gravelly voice, staying where he was.

Dexter took two steps forward. "The detective asked you nicely to sit down."

The two men eyed each other for a few moments, and then Stockwood sat in the chair across the table from Catherine.

He glared at her. "Why am I in here?"

"My name is Detective Delaney," she said, keeping her voice low and even. "I want to ask you some questions."

"I served my time," he said. "You're not my parole officer. Why am I in here?"

"I want to know where you've been for these last few days."

"It's none of your fuckin' business, lady."

Three steps were all it took for Dexter to reach Stockwood. He grabbed him by the neck of his T-shirt, pulled him up onto his feet, and then smashed him against the wall. "You may not respect 80-year-old ladies, you cocksucker, but you most definitely are going to show some respect to Detective Delaney. You hear me?"

"I'm not going to let you pin something else on me like you did the last time," Stockwood said, his large hands fisted at his sides. "I didn't rape that old hag. She was half blind, and any tall, black man would do."

Catherine got up. "Let him go, Dex."

Dexter turned to her, but held onto Stockwood.

"I said let him go. He's not our guy."

Dexter blinked, then released his grip and stepped back.

"You're free to go, Mr. Stockwood. I'm sorry to have inconvenienced you."

Stockwood stood there looking stunned.

Dexter stepped to the side, to let him pass.

When he reached the door, Stockwood turned to Catherine. "I didn't rape her."

"I believe you."

As he stood there looking at Catherine, his face softened.

"I was raped as a kid," she said softly, not caring that Dexter now knew her secret. "I know you don't have it in you to do that to anyone, so good luck, William. Start a new life."

There were tears in William Stockwood's dark eyes when he walked away.

"Dexter, you are not to repeat what you just heard in here."

"I don't understand," he said, flipping some dreadlocks off his shoulder. "Why didn't you question him? The old woman ID'd him."

"Dexter, if Stockwood had enough money to hire a decent lawyer who bothered to check out the DNA on the rape kit, I don't think that young man would have spent a day in jail."

"I still can't believe what you just did, Catherine Delaney."

"Dex, you're the same exact color, height, and built as Stockwood. I bet if you were in that line up, that old lady might have fingered you. Think about it, pal."

"But how do you know he had nothing to do with these girls?"

She placed her hand on his arm and looked up at him. "Only a female whose been raped can know the essence of a rapist. That man doesn't have it in him. Let me know when they bring in Hernandez Ramos. I'll be in my office making some calls."

"Fine. I've got to check on that principal. He's inside getting his lie detector test."

CHAPTER FIFTY

The phone in Catherine's office rang as soon as she took one step into it. She rushed over to her desk, and snatched up the receiver. "Hello. This Detective Delaney," she said, not recognizing the caller's phone number. "Who am I talking to?"

"Detective, this is Emily Patel, the manager of the CVS that was robbed. I'm sorry I've taken so many days to call you, but Sheldon... I mean, Mr. Clarkston just gave me your message."

"Thank you for calling, Ms. Patel," Catherine said, surprised that she'd even gotten the call, since her card had been deliberately dropped on the floor. "I wanted to question you about the robbery, but it's not necessary now that we've caught the two suspects."

"Did you get the drugs that were stolen?"

"I'm afraid not."

"That's a shame. I asked Mr. Clarkston about it, but he said he didn't know."

"Ms. Patel, as long as I have you on the phone, can I ask you a few questions?"

"Sure. I'm calling from the store, so I might have to cut it short if I'm paged."

"Fine. I'll try to make it brief. How long have you been working in that store?"

"A long time now. About eight years. I started as soon as my second son started his freshman year in college."

"College is expensive."

"It sure is. And every year his tuition goes up."

Catherine couldn't help herself. She had to know more about the mayor's son, and if everyone else also thought he was an asshole. "What about Mr. Clarkston? Has he been working in that store as long as you have?"

"Sheldon? Oh, I'm sorry, but we're friends, and I always call him that. Yes, he's worked here since I started and even longer, although I don't actually know how long he's been working here or at the other stores."

"What do you mean about the other stores? Wait! Ms. Patel, hold on a minute. Someone just walked into my office." She put her hand over the phone.

"Catherine, the ME's report just came in on the body parts," her uncle said, dropping the fax on her desk.

Catherine nodded and he left. "Ms. Patel, are you still there."

"Yes, I'm still here."

"What did you mean about the other stores?"

"Sheldon is a trouble shooter."

"What's a trouble shooter?"

"He mainly works in this store, but if another CVS is short a pharmacist for some reason, he fills in at that place."

"Really?"

"He's wonderful," the woman gushed.

"How so?"

"He personally takes an interest in our senior customers. They like him and trust him, because many times he tells them that he won't fill a particular prescription, because the drug will interact badly with other drugs that they're taking. And sure enough, when they contact their doctor, they come back with a new prescription."

"Well, that certainly sounds commendable," Catherine said, still not convinced the man was likeable.

"Listen, I have to go. I'm being paged at the front counter."

"I appreciate your calling. Thanks," Catherine said, and then hung up.

"He passed the test," Betancourt said, poking his head into her office.

Catherine swiveled her chair around.

"The principal passed the lie detector test, but…" He stepped inside.

"But what?"

"Spencer lawyered up for the test. Seems he never touched that Sonia kid or any other kid sexually, but when the examiner asked him about the Blackstone girl, the lawyer shut him up real fast."

"His lawyer wouldn't let him answer the question?"

"Nope! He said he had to confer with his client, because he didn't know what it was about."

"Shit!" She rose and started to pace.

"I'll tell you one thing, Catherine. Spencer's face got so red when that girl's name was brought up, that it almost turned purple."

"We need to get him back."

"We sure do. The sooner the better."

CHAPTER FIFTY-ONE

It was still pouring outside when Cody parked the unmarked car in the strip mall's parking lot.

"No one's standing in front of the Bed and Bath shop, or in front of any of the other places." Hawk said, scanning the long sidewalk in front of the row of stores.

"Maybe he's waiting for the rain to let up. We're early for this appointment. Let's give it a few minutes."

Hawk unbuckled his seat belt. "You know, Cody, I raised pigeons on a tenement rooftop when I was growing up in the Bronx, but for the life of me, I can't understand why anyone would raise slimy snakes."

"You got me there. I always wanted a dog when I was growing up, but never got one."

Hawk looked over at him. "How come?"

"My mother said it would dirty the house. She got me goldfish instead. Eventually, I think they went swimming in the toilet when she tried to clean their bowl, but she never admitted it," Cody said, smiling. "After that, I decided girls were more fun to play with."

"How old were you when—"

"Hold it! That may be him running across the lot."

They watched a long-haired, young man who appeared to be in his early twenties dash through the rain toward the shopping mall, then stop in front of the Bed and Bath store and look around.

"Looks like he's waiting for someone," Hawk said, noticing how his wet, clingy clothes emphasized how skinny he was.

"Let's go."

"Cody, hold on a sec. He's pulling something out of his pants pocket. Huh. It's a plastic bag."

"You think he's selling?"

"Looks like he's lighting a hand rolled job, but the bag isn't full enough to sell any of it."

"Come on. We're wasting time," Cody said, opening the door.

The kid was still dragging on the cigarette when they reached him.

"Are you Martin?" Hawk asked, catching the smell of weed that wafted about him.

He expelled a mouthful of smoke. "I didn't expect two of you."

"I'm Detective O'Dell," Cody said, showing him his badge.

The cigarette was quickly flipped into the street. "I'm not doing anything wrong, man. There's no law saying I can't sell snakes."

"That may be so," Hawk said, stepping closer so that he towered over him. "But smoking weed in Florida is. Let me see your license, wise guy."

Martin pulled a billfold out of his back pocket and handed it to him.

"Martin Leader, this says you live in Port St. Lucie," Hawk said, still holding onto the wallet. "What are you doing around here?"

Cody's eyes widened. Port St. Lucie was only ten to fifteen miles away from where Amanda Plummer lived.

"I raise snakes," Martin answered. "I drive all over to sell them."

"How'd you get that shiner and cut on your nose?" Cody asked.

"I picked the wrong guy to shoot pool with last night."

"Is that so? Where's your car, Martin?" Cody asked, standing taller.

The kid swallowed. "Hey, give me a break, man. I'm just trying to make a few bucks to feed my old lady and kid."

"Yeah, I heard that one before. I asked you where your car is."

Martin turned and pointed to a beat up, red, Ford pickup truck.

"Let's go," Hawk said, grabbing hold of Martin's arm, then leading him through the deluge toward his vehicle.

When the three of them reached the truck, Cody took over again. "Martin, turn around. Put your hands on top of the hood, and spread your legs. Hawk, frisk him."

When Martin didn't move fast enough, Hawk spun him around and shoved face forward against the truck. "Well, well, well," Hawk said, after the first feel of his back. "Look at what you shoved under your belt. It's a nice, shiny, black Smith and Wesson."

"I've got a license to carry that."

Hawk ignored him, tucked the hand gun in his own pants pocket, then continued with the pat down. "Let's see what else you got... Whoa, and an illegal switchblade in your pocket. Looks like you're comin' to the station with us, Mr. Martin Leader who raises snakes to feed his old lady and kid."

"Hawk, cuff him and turn him around."

After Martin's hands were restrained in a handcuff tie, he was turned to Cody.

"Martin, where do you breed your snakes?" Cody asked.

"At home. In my basement."

"Hawk, before we take him in, we're going to drive this gentleman home, so he can show us where he raises his snakes," Cody said, staring directly into Martin's light blue eyes. "Do you have any objection to us looking around your house Mr. Leader?"

Martin shook his head, then stared down at his flip flops.

Hawk caught on and nodded. "What about the other two appointments?"

"Call the chief. Fill him in on our travel plans, and then tell him to get someone to cover those meetings for us."

CHAPTER FIFTY-TWO

The smaller of the two conference rooms in the station was hot and crowded when Cody joined the chief and other detectives who were standing around and talking to one another. Catherine was across the room, her back leaning against the gray, cinder block wall, talking on her cell phone. She eyed him up and down and gave him a half wave, while going on with her conversation.

"You look like you just came out of a clothes dryer, my boy. You're a wrinkled mess," Chief Delaney said when Cody reached him.

"Chief, I'm too tired to give a damn what I look or smell like."

"It's too bad that Martin appointment didn't pan out. I was hoping he was the one, and we could wrap up this mess."

"Me, too. He's just a screwed-up kid, married to a screwed-up kid, who have a baby with cancer of the eye. I thought I'd start some sort of fund up for the baby. She's going to need lots of medical care."

"Sure. Whatever you do, you can count me in,"

Catherine joined them. "You look like hell, O'Dell."

"Thanks." He sneezed. "You're the second person who's told me that in less than two minutes." He sneezed again, pulled a handkerchief out of his pocket, and blew his nose.

"You're catching a cold."

"No kidding. I'm hoping you'll sweat it out of me later."

"Everyone ready to start this briefing?" the chief called out, leaving the two of them and walking over to the head of a long oval table. He sat down, and then rapped hard on the table top. "Let's go! Get a move on guys. It's eight P.M. I want to be out of here in less than an hour."

Conversations quickly stopped, and seats around the table were quickly filled.

"Good. Who wants to start?"

"I will, Chief."

"Go ahead, Catherine."

Catherine glanced around the table before beginning. "My source had another vision. This time, she saw a double image. It may be one girl, or two girls who have, or may have been, abducted."

Murmurs and groans flittered around the room.

Catherine went on. "This woman… our psychic has been right so far, and I'm fearful that she might be right again. Also…" she glanced at Cody, "Ms. Plummer told Cody and me this morning that she only has these visions of accidents or killings, when they take place within twenty to forty miles of where she physically is."

"That's crazy," Ricardo Alvarez called out.

"Ricardo, Amanda swears it's true, and I believe her. The proof is, whatever she's told us so far has come true. I'm taking what she just told me seriously, and so should all of you."

"Where does she live?"

"Delray Beach."

Eyes darted everywhere, and the room grew silent.

"Delaney, are you saying this guy's knocking his victims off within forty miles of Delray Beach?" Alvarez asked.

"Yes, that's what I'm saying. Amanda sees fields with flattened vegetation, no houses or structures anywhere, and tire ruts leading to a canal. Cody and I believe the place he's murdering these girls is on farmland or undeveloped acreage." She turned to her uncle. "What about the copter that Cody and I asked for?"

"I put in an order with the Sheriff's Department. They said some time tomorrow, after the rain lets up. Anything else, Cathy?"

"Yes. Joseph Raganno, Madeline Kefler's boyfriend's alibi checked out. He was in Texas when she was abducted and murdered. One other thing, David Spencer, the high school principal who was accused of sexually molesting a minor took his lie detector test. The results said he didn't abuse any of his students, but when he was asked about Hillary Blackstone, his lawyer wouldn't let him answer. Obviously, we'll have to bring him in again for questioning, because he's still a suspect in this case. Also, the school custodian needs to be checked into. He's living in an expensive house in a family neighborhood, and when we spoke to him, he referred to Hillary Blackstone in the past tense when her body hadn't been discovered. We need to bring him in tomorrow, and we need to find out more about him. Someone needs to talk to his neighbors. That's it for me."

"Cody, why don't you go next," the chief said.

"Dexter and I met with a young man who sells snakes. He was young and fit. We thought he was a possible suspect. We drove him back to his house in Port St. Lucie, because it's within the forty-mile radius of Ms. Plummer, and also because of his interest in snakes. His house was a dump and he was raising a hundred or so snakes in his basement. With a little persuasion, he let us search the place. There was no sign of any foul play, restraints, blood stains, or splatters anywhere in the entire house. He's not the one. I got a call from Angelo. He and his partner Nick met with the two other individuals who sell snakes. Both have been crossed off. One can barely walk, no less lift a young woman, and the other one was a frail senior." He looked over at Stan Wilkins. "Stan, did the little man get back on line?"

"No, and I couldn't get Dembeck on the phone. Maybe we've scared him. I'll drive over to his place before I come in."

Cody turned to Catherine. He was afraid to ask her, but he knew he had to. "Catherine, what happened with your interview?"

"You mean with William Stockwood?"

He nodded.

"He's not the one!"

"What?" Cody said, puzzled by her clipped response.

"I said he's not the one. I'll talk to you about it later. I'm waiting for Hernandez Ramos to be found. We're you able to talk to Burt about that autopsy report?"

"I had to wait until he got back to the lab, and then he tried to explain it to me. I can't say that I fully understand everything he said. I was tired, wet, and half listening. I'll reread the report later, but here's the gist of it. Hold on a sec." He reached into his pants pocket and pulled out a small pad. "Based on the pelvic bone and two x chromosomes found in the blood cell," he said, looking at what he'd written. "The ME says the body parts belong to a Caucasian female. She's probably in her late-forties to mid-fifties. He got her fingerprints. She has no criminal record; therefore he can't identify her. Also, since we haven't recovered her head, he's unable to get any dental records." He stopped reading and looked at the group. "What I did find interesting was him telling me that after he studied a piece of leg bone under the microscope, he came to the conclusion that her body had been cut up with a crude, hand saw because the bone and flesh were jagged. He also x-rayed that leg, and found flakes of rust metal embedded in the flesh. So we have to find a rusted-old fashioned saw, and a strong, pissed-off guy who spent hours and hours cutting a woman into pieces."

"That sounds like it's going to be lots of fun," Betancourt said, not smiling.

There were a few chuckles around the room.

"Anyway," Cody said, starting again with a tired sigh. "Burt also said that while he was examining that piece of leg bone, he saw signs of cell damage which indicated that leg had been frozen, then thawed, before it was dumped in the water."

"Terrific," Catherine mumbled. "Did he say how long she was dead, before we fished her out of the water?"

Cody shook his head. "No. This is just his preliminary report. Burt's waiting to get back extensive lab results, and a DNA profile. It could take a while. He said he'll get back to us as soon as he has more information. In the meantime, we'll have to keep searching the national missing person's data base for a missing middle-aged woman. She could be from anywhere, or a foreign visitor on vacation."

"Cody, do you think this murder and the murders of two girls are related? All of them were dumped in a waterway."

"I don't think so, Chief. I believe these murders were committed by two different individuals, and I don't know which one of them is more vicious."

CHAPTER FIFTY-THREE

"Hi, mom. Lizzy and I got everything ready."

"Thanks, Honey. I'll just change my clothes, and be right in to help you."

"Don't take too long. Amber worked all day to get this lasagna just right, and she even baked a chocolate cake for desert."

"Where is your sister?"

"In her room, talking to Randy for a change."

Stacy walked over to the sink where her daughter was standing, and kissed the top of her head. "I love you."

"Stop with the mushy stuff and get out of that suit," Amber giggled. "Get a move on. We're eating in the dining room tonight."

Stacy had started toward the kitchen door, but abruptly stopped and turned around. "In the dining room? How come? What are you and your sister up to?"

Amber stepped over to the stove, lifted the lid off a pot, and started to stir the string beans.

"Amber Jamison, you answer me right this minute, young lady."

The twin turned to her mother, the wooden spoon still in her hand and dripping butter onto the floor.

"Who have you invited to dinner?"

Amber sighed. "Dad called to say he was in town, and—"

"Your father! It's not going to happen. Your dad and I are not getting together. I told you that, so let it be and stop trying to interfere."

"Mom, we're not trying anything, I swear. Lizzy and I haven't seen him in a month, and he said he was only going to be in town for two days."

"He's got a girlfriend. Is she coming, too?"

Amber's eyes filled with tears. "No, only dad's coming. Please, Mom. Just this once, please try and not yell at him or be snarky. It's only for a couple of hours, and then he'll be gone again."

"Hey! What's going on in here?" Lizzy said, stepping into the kitchen and flipping her long ponytail off her shoulder.

Stacy turned to her other daughter. "Did you know that your sister invited your father to dinner?"

"Really? Cool. I just invited Randy to come over."

"I give up. You're both impossible."

The identical twins eyed each other and tried to hide their smiles.

"I'm going inside to change. Make sure you don't use my holiday china and Grandma's silver. Understand me? This isn't a party." She groaned, and walked out of the room swearing under her breath.

"What a pleasant little family scene," he mumbled, sitting in his car and peering through the Jamisons' kitchen window. "Tomorrow night, Sweetie. On the way home from your dance lesson."

CHAPTER FIFTY-FOUR

The phones weren't ringing and the entire police station was remarkably quiet when Catherine and Cody arrived. As they passed by the detectives who were working in their cubicles and headed toward the chief's office, everyone's eyes followed them, but no one said a word. Neither Catherine nor Cody knocked on his door, they just walked in and over to the front of his desk.

"Did you see this?" she said, laying the newspaper on top of his desk. The headline read: PSYCHIC WORKING WITH POLICE TO CATCH SNAKEMAN KILLER.

Her uncle sighed. "I not only saw it, I just got off the phone with the royally pissed-off mayor."

"So what did the asshole have to say this time," Catherine asked, sinking onto a chair.

Her uncle smiled. "'If you don't catch the fucking madman and stop advertising our department is working with a witch doctor, Delaney, you're going to be putting in for a retirement check.'"

"Why, the—"

"Calm down, Honey. He doesn't scare me in the least."

"Uncle Steve, what about that copter? Are we going to get it today?"

He shook his head.

"Why the hell not?"

"Clarkston found out about my request and nixed it."

"But—"

"Catherine Delaney, you don't think I'm going to let that moron stop me, do you? I'm calling in a favor from a friend of mine who owns a small plane and helicopter company. Grant's daughter was shot by her boyfriend a few years back, and I nailed him within hours. His manager promised he'd have him call me, as soon as he gets back in town this evening."

"Chief, I don't like how slow this case is going," Cody said, still standing. "Another kid's life might be on the line."

"What do you suggest we do at this point? We're covering every lead we get."

"Maybe we should ask the Feds for their help."

"We can't call them in. The mayor also warned me not to do that."

"That asshole doesn't give a shit that another kid might get murdered," Catherine said angrily, getting up. She walked over to the bookcase and slammed her hand against it. "I say screw him! I'm making a call to someone I know."

Cody and her uncle watched her pace.

"I don't care what Clarkston says," Catherine snapped, ramming her hands into her pants pockets. She stopped pacing and looked at them, "We need their help. Amanda saw hands. Lot of hands. It can only mean multiple murders. We need the Feds to check their data base for similar killings. What if this guy went to an out of state college? What if he started killing while he was there?"

"You're right," her uncle said. "Make that call. Fuck the little shit!"

CHAPTER FIFTY-FIVE

Catherine had just gotten off the phone with Jason Pollack, and had a smile on her face when Cody walked into her office and sat down on the edge of her desk.

"What's up, Babe?"

"My Fed friend promised to help us."

"Great. We can use that help."

"Why the visit?"

Cody rose. "Got an interesting call from a buddy of mine."

Catherine peered up at him.

"He's a fire chief." Cody hesitated.

"So? What the hell did your fire friend tell you?"

He looked down at her. "He said there was a fire at your cleaning lady's house last night."

"Lillian's house?"

"I'm afraid so. The whole house went up, before they got to it."

"What about her brother?"

"He didn't make it out."

"That's terrible."

"It's worse than terrible. When they were sifting through the debris, they found a decomposed head in the refrigerator."

Catherine's mouth dropped open and her eyes bulged.

"They sent the head to the medical examiner's office. I already called Burt. He's checking the DNA to see if it's a match with the body parts that were dumped in the Intercostal."

Catherine sat there stunned, just staring up at him.

"Are you all right? I didn't know how to break it to you…"

"Cody, I can't believe it. Lillian took care of that man since he was a little kid. She told me that she did everything for him. How could he do that to her?… To his own sister?" Her eyes filled with tears, and she let them run down her face.

Cody pulled her up from her chair, and wrapped his arms around her.

"Catherine, oh… I'm sorry. I'll come back later."

Catherine stepped out of Cody's embrace, and swiped her eyes dry. "Come in, Dex. What is it?"

"Hernandez is waiting for you in room three, but if you want me to take it…"

"Thanks. Cody and I will go in, in a couple of minutes."

"Everything okay?" Dexter asked.

"No," Cody answered. "We found the missing head that we were searching for, and we believe Catherine knew the women."

"I'm sorry, Catherine. If there's anything I can do, let me know."

"Thanks." She turned to Cody. "I'm ready. Let's get this interview over with. I need to call Susan and let her know what's happened to Lillian, before she hears about it on the news."

"But it hasn't been confirmed. Don't you think you should wait until it is?"

"Cody, it is Lillian. I'm positive of that. Susan called this morning and said she was driving over to her house again. I have to stop her. I have to be the one to tell her, not some CSI on the scene."

Hernandez Ramos was still cuffed and sitting at the table when they stepped into the interrogation room. He glared at Catherine first and then Cody, and remained silent as they joined him at the table.

Catherine set her folder on top of the table, then looked across at the stocky man whose face and arms were totally covered with multi-colored tattoos.

As they'd agreed before entering the room, Cody was going to handle the questioning while she took notes. Before starting, he folded his arms across his chest, and boldly stared at the man. Finally, he leaned forward and said: "You were in possession of a firearm when you were picked up, Ramos. That's a violation of your parole."

"I hadda' protect myself," Ramos answered with a brazen smirk.

"Too bad you won't have that gun with you when you go back to prison."

The smile stayed on Ramos's face, and he tilted the chair back, until it rested against the wall.

"I hear they don't like snitches in there."

The smile slid off Ramos's face, and his chair quickly righted itself. "What the fuck are you talking about?"

"I'll tell you what I'm talking about, after you answer a few questions."

"I don't know nothing. I'm clean. Been trying to start over, and keep out of trouble."

"Really? What about the little girls we found in the canal? After you raped them, did you throw both of them in the canal so they could also get clean?"

"Shut the fuck up!" Ramos shouted, jumping up from his chair.

"Sit down!"

"It's those two girls—the ones that were reported on television. You're trying to pin those murders on me. Fuck you! I had nothing to do with them! Nothing!" he shouted.

"I told you to sit down," Cody warned, getting up and leaning across the table.

"I want a lawyer," Ramos said, breathing hard and not budging. "I'm not saying a fuckin' thing. I have a right to a lawyer. That's it. I'm finished with you."

After they left the interrogation room, and collected their weapons, Catherine let out a sigh. "Cody, I think he's a shit, but he's not the one. I've got to go back to the data base, and start all over again to see if I missed someone."

"You're right. He's not the one, but he screwed himself carrying that concealed gun."

"What are you going to be doing now?"

"I want to check in with Hawk and Stan, to see if they were able to contact the little man. After that, I'll take a ride over to the custodian's house to talk to some of his neighbors. Want to come with me?"

"Absolutely. Give me an hour to print out some stuff." He was about to walk away when she added: "Maybe this time I'll be able to peek in Erickson's windows if he's not in there."

CHAPTER FIFTY-SIX

After stopping off and sharing a large pepperoni pizza, Catherine and Cody rode over to Anton Erickson's house to question him further.

"His garbage cans and recycling bins are all over the sidewalk," Catherine said, as she unbuckled her seatbelt. "Either he's lazy, or not at home."

Cody unfastened his belt and got out of the car with her. When they reached the locked chain-link gate, a shapely blonde in a bathing suit called out from the neighboring yard that he wasn't at home.

"Shit," Catherine mumbled. "Now I can't do my commando act, because she'll see me." She headed over to the woman and flipped open her badge. "Ma'am, I'm Homicide Detective Delaney, and this is my partner, Detective O'Dell. Do you know where Mr. Erickson is, by any chance?"

The woman dropped her garbage can lid, and stepped back like the two of them had infectious diseases. "Homicide detectives? I saw Anton driving away a little while ago. Why are you looking for him?"

"We'd like to ask him some questions," Catherine said, giving the woman a quick once over. "Are you a friend of his?"

"No, just a neighbor… Unfortunately."

"Do you have a problem with him?"

She didn't answer at first. "What is this about?"

"Mr. Erickson works in a high school. We want to talk to him about some of the students."

"He's a teacher? God help those kids."

"Listen, Miss…"

"It's Mrs. Gleason."

"Mrs. Gleason, it's obvious that you're not particularly fond of your neighbor. Perhaps you'd like to tell us why."

She glanced up and down the street to make sure no one would see her talking to cops.

"Mrs. Gleason," Catherine said, growing impatient. "A couple of girls from the high school he works in have been murdered, so if you know something that might be helpful, please talk to us. What seems to be the problem?"

"Murdered? Are you talking about those two girls on the news? He works in that school? You think he has…"

"We're not implying Mr. Erickson had anything to do with those girls; we just want to ask him some questions," Cody said. "Since you've seen him drive away, I'd like to ask you a few questions, if I may."

"Detective, I… I have two little girls," she said, struggling to get her words out. "Is he dangerous?"

Cody shook his head. "No, Mrs. Gleason. We just want to have a few words with him, but since he—"

"But, is he a suspect? The detectives I see on the TV always call the person they're questioning a suspect."

Although the police had no proof that Erickson had committed a crime, Catherine didn't want to lie in case anything happened to one of her daughters. "Mrs. Gleason, Mr. Erickson is one of many people we refer to as a Person of Interest. That doesn't mean that he or any of the other people we may question are guilty of a crime. Right now, we're questioning a lot of people. So, let me ask you: Have you seen Mr. Erickson with any teenage girls around his property?"

"I've never seen him with females of any age, and that's the problem."

"What do you mean?" Cody probed.

"I don't want what I tell you to get back to him, because I have enough problems with him as it is."

"We won't say anything," Catherine assured her. "Go on."

"You'd never know it to look at that strapping man, but he's gay. I'm not against gays. Believe me. My best friend's son is gay, and he's my godson. It's just that we both have pools in our back yards."

"What about your pools? "Catherine asked.

"He has pool parties. Lots of pool parties with naked men playing with each other. It's disgusting, absolutely disgusting, what grown men do to one another. And it doesn't just happen at night. Sometimes it happens during the day, and then I can't let my girls outside to play, or they might see what's going on."

Cody and Catherine were speechless.

Finally, Cody managed to ask: "Would you like to file a complaint?"

"I did. Twice! But when the police showed up, the bunch of them were already in the house. Then I got his lawyer's letter saying that if I continued to harass his client for enjoying his private property, I'd be sued for harassment. See that realtor sign on my lawn," she said pointing to the For Sale sign. "I'm selling the home I love, moving away from my friends and everything I love about this neighborhood, because that man is immoral. Is there anything else you want to know about Anton Erickson?"

Catherine shook her head. "No. Thanks for your time, and good luck with your move."

"I hope you find that killer."

"Mrs. Gleason, we're going to take a quick peek around your neighbor's property. We'd appreciate you not mentioning it to him."

"You'll be wasting your time going over there," she said, stooping down for the garbage can lid. "He never opens the shutters on his windows, so you won't see anything."

Catherine halted. "He never opens them?"

"Never. A box was accidentally delivered to me a while back. Before I dropped it on his doorstep, I looked up the company it came from." She smirked. "They sell whips and chains and all sorts of fetish, sicko stuff. That's probably why he keeps those shutters locked tight."

"I never would have thought he was gay," Catherine said, fastening her seat belt.

Cody started the motor.

"Where are we going now?"

"Home. Back to my place." He pressed his foot down on the gas pedal, and took off.

"Why do you have that gleam in your eyes, O'Dell?"

"All that talk about fetish stuff has made me horny, Delaney."

She smiled, and watched the road ahead.

CHAPTER FIFTY-SEVEN

When Detectives Stan Wilkins and Thomas Whitehall entered the chief's smoky office, he quickly placed his lit cigar down in an ashtray.

"If either of you tell Catherine you saw me smoking," the chief said, smiling and waving the smoke away from his face. "I'll have both of your badges."

Stan sat down in front of his desk. Hawk remained standing beside him.

"What can I do for you gentlemen?"

"We have a problem," Stan said, drumming his fingers on his knees.

"We all have problems. So what else is new?"

"Chief, we still can't reach Dembeck. We kept calling him, and we even rode over to his house. Hawk and I need a warrant to enter his home, so we can confiscate his computer."

"Whoa there! First of all, who the hell is Dembeck?"

"He's the little man we told you about who collects snakes. We got on his Facebook page to monitor the messages he was getting from his snake friends, and now we can't reach him," Hawk answered.

The chief scratched the back of his neck. "I don't know if I can get you a warrant. Did he commit a crime? Is he a suspect? Give me something to work with."

Stan got up. "Chief, this is serious. We have to get into the little fuck's house. Catherine said the killer collects snakes. You heard her at the briefing. We can't get on his computer any other way."

"I can't help you. I'm sorry. A judge will never issue a warrant on that kind of flimsy premise. Your man would have had to commit a crime, or be suspected of committing one."

Stan glanced over at his partner.

"Well, he is a suspect," Hawk stated firmly. "We believe he may be an accomplice in the abduction and murder of those two girls."

"The little man is an accomplice? Really? Rethink that, gentlemen," the chief said. "That bullshit won't fly with any judge."

"Chief, he has a big strong partner that helps him," Hawk tacked on. "The little man is the ruse that lures the girls. Right, Stan?"

"Absolutely! He tells the girls that he's hurt or lost or something like that, and they fall for it. Then his partner snatches the kid."

The chief lifted his cigar out of the ashtray, and then took a very long drag on it. "Mmm. Very interesting," he finally said with a gleam in his eyes." Write up the request, gentlemen, and I'll make that call."

It was growing dark by the time Wilkins and Whitehall were able to get to the little man's house with their warrant. Fortunately for them, they didn't have to use the battering ram they'd brought with them, because the front door to his house was suddenly pulled open when they were halfway up the path.

"Police! Don't shut that door," Hawk shouted, picking up his pace.

The young man froze and waited with his hand on the doorknob.

Hawk displayed his badge. "Who are you?"

"Frank's neighbor."

"What's your name?"

"Greg. I live next door."

Although the boy was dressed like a typical teenager, in a T-shirt and jeans, he had the muscular body of a mature, heavy-set man. "What were you doing in Mr. Dembeck's house?" Hawk asked.

"I was doing Frank a favor. He asked me to take care of his snakes while he was away."

"Do you know where he went?" Hawk asked.

Stan stood aside and let him do the questioning.

"I think he went to an out-of-town hospital. He's gone there a few other times. I don't know that for sure, but I think that's where he must have gone."

"And each time he goes away, he asks you to take care of his snakes?"

He nodded. "Yes. We both collect them, so it's no big deal. Sometimes Frank gives me a few of his snakes, so I don't mind doing him the favor."

"Tell you what, Greg. My partner and I have a warrant to enter Mr. Dembeck's house," Hawk said, staring directly into the boy's light blue eyes. "We'd like you to accompany us, and witness what we're going to do. Do you have a problem with that?"

The boy swallowed. "No, I guess not. It's just that my girlfriend is waiting for me to pick her up."

"I guess she'll have to wait a little bit longer. Let's go. Lead the way."

Stan cringed after taking one step into Dembeck's living room. The only piece of furniture inside the space was a single burgundy-colored leather recliner. He glanced around at the walls that were lined with metal shelves. On them were large, glass tanks that were filled with squirming, colorful snakes.

"There are more tanks in his bedroom," Greg said from the doorway. "Do you want to see them?"

"No," Stan answered, backing out of the room, until he bumped into him.

"Are any of these poisonous?" Hawk asked, peering into the tanks as he walked past them.

"No. Frank got bitten once. He doesn't like the poisonous ones."

Hawk turned to him. "Does he have an office? We need his computer."

"It's in one of his back bedrooms. Follow me."

As the three of them were heading down the hallway, Stan noticed another room that had glass tanks in it. He stopped walking. "What's in those tanks?" he said, pointing into the room.

The boy stopped and turned back. "Mice. Frank raises them as feed for the snakes. He makes a lot of money on them."

"How so?" Stan asked, turning to him.

"He's got someone who can't raise enough for his large collection, so he buys dozens of them from Frank at a very good price."

"Do you know who that guy is?" Hawk asked.

"No. I never met him or heard his name, but Frank once told me that this guy raises all kinds of snakes, even the poisonous ones."

CHAPTER FIFTY–EIGHT

"That pea soup was pretty good for canned soup. Too bad we didn't have a little ham to add to it," Catherine said, picking up her soup bowl, and then carrying it and the spoon over to the stainless steel sink.

"I'll pick up some more, the next time I go shopping."

When Catherine walked back to the table to collect Cody's plate, he grabbed her around her waist and pulled her onto his lap. "O'Dell, you're amazing. I don't know if I have the strength for you," she said, wiggling her backside on top of his erection.

"Babe, if you keep doing that, we won't make it back to the bedroom for another round." He lifted up her hair, and kissed the side of her neck in the sensitive spot that was just below her ear. She shivered in his arms, then leaned in close and kissed him hungrily. Cody's hand slid under the white T-shirt she'd borrowed. Her nipples were hard when he squeezed them. Catherine moaned and dug her nails into his shoulder when his fingers began to probe the wetness between her legs.

Cody was just about to lift her off his lap and carry her to the bedroom when her cell phone rang. "Let it ring, Delaney," he mumbled in her ear. "We're taking the rest of the evening off."

"It may be Amanda… about the girl." she said, slipping out of his embrace. She rushed over to the far counter, but the phone stopped ringing the second her hand reached for it.

"Come back here, my luscious, delectable, wild woman. We need to finish what you started."

Catherine laughed and took one step toward him, when the phone rang again. She turned back and grabbed it. "Hello, Delaney here… Who?… What did he say?… Yes, give me his number… What hospital?… Thanks, Mike." She hung up, and turned back to Cody. "That was from the station. Amanda's been shot!"

He quickly rose. "What did you say?"

"Her neighbor Jake called the station and left a message for me. Amanda's in Bethesda West. It's the new hospital that just opened on

Route 441. He didn't say anything else, only that she'd been shot. We have to go."

"Right! Get dressed. I'll be with you in a minute. I want to call in a BOLO for her ex-husband."

Bethesda West Hospital's huge, round lobby looked like the entry into an expensive spa, not a local hospital. The white marble floors shined, the leather seating added to its elegance, and on top of all that, a baby grand piano sat in the center of the towering space.

Jake Turner was seated near the reception desk, facing the entrance. When he spotted Catherine and Cody, he got up and hobbled to them.

"Jake, how is she?" Catherine asked.

"I don't know. The paramedics let me ride with her in the ambulance, but when they wheeled her into the emergency room, they wouldn't let me go in with her."

"Let me see what I can find out, "Cody said. He headed over to the reception desk on the right side of the lobby. Catherine saw him showing the plump receptionist his badge, but couldn't hear what he was saying. Moments later, the woman picked up her phone and made a call. Cody waited. She told him something after hanging up, and then he walked back to them.

"She's in surgery. We can go into the patient's waiting room, and the surgeon will see us when he's finished. Jake, what happened?"

The old man's wrinkled face was almost white. His hands were shaking, and tears filled his eyes.

"Why don't we sit down for a few minutes, before we go inside," Catherine said, taking hold of Jake's arm and leading him over to the nearest chair. Once he was seated, she sat beside him, and took one of his shaking hands into hers. "Jake, tell us exactly what happened. How did you find Amanda?"

Jake drew a deep breath into his frail body before beginning. "I was watching television," he said softly, looking down at their joined hands. "I thought I heard the dog howling, but wasn't sure, so I just sat there and kept watching the silly show. After a while, when the dog was still carrying on, I realized something must be wrong at Amanda's house, so I tried to call her on the phone. When she didn't answer after three tries, I put my clothes back on and went over there." He shook his head, and rubbed his free hand over his nubby sweater. "I should have gone over when I first heard the dog's howls. I'm so stupid. She could die, because of my stupidity."

Catherine squeezed his hand. "Jake, you didn't do anything wrong. Amanda's lucky that you found her." Tears were trickling down the old man's face when he looked up at Catherine. She reached up and wiped them away with her fingertips.

"She's like a daughter to me. If anything happens to that sweet girl, I'll never forgive myself."

"Shush... Nothing's going to happen to her," Catherine said, praying inwardly that she was right. "Amanda's strong. She'll pull through this."

"Jake," Cody said, kneeling in front of him. "What happened when you got to Amanda's house?"

Jake left his hand in Catherine's when he turned to Cody. "She didn't answer the door, so I used my key to get into the house. I kept calling out to her, but she didn't answer me. I looked for her then and... and then I found her lying on the kitchen floor in a puddle of blood. The back door was wide open. The wheelchair was tipped over. The dog was standing by her side, poking her bleeding arm and yowling for her to wake up. I called 911. Told them to send an ambulance right away." He stopped to catch his breath. "When they asked if she was alive, I didn't know what to tell them, because her eyes were shut, and her chest wasn't moving up and down like she was breathing. I can't believe what's happened to that girl. Why her? Hasn't she had enough?"

When Cody stood up, Catherine saw the frustration and anger on his face. She knew if the distraught old man wasn't sitting there, he'd be ranting and raving to let off steam.

"Jake, did you see anyone in the yard?" Cody finally asked.

"It was dark outside. I didn't see anyone."

"Jake, think hard," Cody said, "When you first went over to Amanda's house, did you see a car parked in front of it, or one driving away?"

Jake's lips quivered as he mulled the question over in his mind. Then he looked back up at Cody. "I'm not sure. I wasn't paying attention to cars or people. I just wanted to get to Amanda as fast as I could. That was the only thing on my mind. I'm sorry. I wish to God I could tell you more, so you could catch... It has to be her ex. He's the only one who would hurt that poor girl."

"Cody, the prison got a BOLO out after his escape, right?"

"Yeah, they got right on it," he said. "But we're not going to have much luck, unless someone reports a stolen car and we find it."

"What about Amanda's house?"

"A team should be at her house now, searching for evidence. That's all we can do right now. Come on; let's go to that waiting room. The doctor may be looking for us."

CHAPTER FIFTY-NINE

"Dembeck's calendar says he has an appointment at Boston's Children's Hospital tomorrow at 4:00 P.M.," Stan Wilkins said, after riffling through a stack of papers on top of the little man's desk. "It doesn't have the doctor's name, just the time and a note to bring his scans and X-rays with him."

Hawk had pulled the lower drawer out of the desk, and was searching through the files. "Maybe I can find some insurance papers that'll give us the doctor's name."

"Can I please leave now?" Greg asked from the doorway.

"No!" both detectives blurted out.

"Shit! My girl's going to be pissed off at my being so late." He turned to leave.

"Tell her you're not coming tonight," Stan said. "We need you here."

Greg turned back. "Why do you need me? I'm just the guy's neighbor. I don't want to get involved with any of this."

"Listen, you little shit, a girl's life is in danger," Stan snapped. "Call your girlfriend, and then boot up this computer."

"I can turn it on for you, but if Frank's password hasn't been saved, I won't be able to get you on line."

Stan looked from the boy to his partner. "See if there's a file with passwords in it, or we're wasting our fuckin' time here."

"Why don't you call the hospital, and see if they know who Frank's doctor is?" Greg suggested.

Stan turned back to Greg.

"After I call my girl, if you want, I can call the hospital and say I'm looking for my uncle. Maybe he's been admitted for tests or something, before he sees the doctor."

"Kid, that was brilliant," Stan said, giving him a nod. "Maybe you should try out for the Police Academy and become a detective. It looks like you have a brain in your head, as well as those big muscles."

Greg smiled at the compliment. "I'll try the computer first. If I don't get on line, I'll find the hospital's phone number and make that call." He walked over to the desk, and sat down in front of it.

While Greg was working on the computer, Hawk continued to search the files. "There are some current bank statements in here. Mmm. Not bad. Dembeck looks like he has some dough. His last balance was over seventy-two thousand dollars."

"You're shitting me. Right?"

"Nope! He's made some large deposits this month. A little over ten grand on the fifteenth, and thirteen grand at the end of the month."

"Where the hell is he getting all that money from?" Stan said.

"I can't get onto his Facebook or Twitter sites," Greg said. "He didn't store his password in either of them."

"Shut it down," Hawk said. "We're wasting our time here." He rose and retuned the folders to the drawer. "Stan, we'll bring the computer and this drawer of files with us to the station. I want to go through them again, and make copies of these bank statements."

"Great. Can I leave now?"

"Not yet," Stan said. "We're going to search the rest of the house. We'll need your signature on the notes we write up, of what we'll be taking away with us."

Greg groaned, and turned away to call his girlfriend.

"Let's start with the master bedroom," Hawk said, walking past Greg and making a right in the hall. He stopped at the first room he came to and flipped on the light switch. "This has got to be it," he said, glancing down at the mattress that was lying on the floor.

"What's with Shortie?" Stan said, halting in the doorway and surveying the large room. "He's got one chair in the living room, and a mattress on the bedroom floor. I can't believe it. All that loot, and the midget won't spend a dime of it to buy some comfortable furniture."

Hawk walked over to the closet and pulled open the door. "His clothes are in here, and there's an open packed suitcase on the floor."

"A packed suitcase?"

"Come on," Hawk said, heading out of the room. "Let's check the garage to see if his car is still in there."

When Stan opened the door to the two-car garage, the car was still in it, and Frank was lying on the floor with his head twisted at a very odd angle.

"Looks like his neck's been broken," Stan said, standing over the little man. "Why the hell was he murdered?"

CHAPTER SIXTY

Stacy Jamison had just finished her third long swig of Scotch, when she heard a key jiggling in the front door. She bent down, and quickly hid the almost empty bottle behind the small trash container that was under the sink cabinet.

"I'm home!" Lizzy called out.

Stacy met her daughter in the front hall. "Where's Amber?"

"She's probably in her bedroom, Mom," Lizzy answered, tossing the large, black dance bag under the hall table.

"It's almost 9:30. Your sister is not at home and you're late, young lady," Stacy said, trying to keep her words from slurring.

"Mrs. Morrison kept us late. She was teaching us a new tap number for the National competition, and it took a little longer for the girls to get it right."

"And your sister didn't stay to learn the new routine? Why not? Why am I spending all that money, if she's cutting out of those classes?"

Lizzy was always covering up for her twin. Either Amber was taking off with her boyfriend instead of doing her share of the chores, or sneaking into a place that she wasn't old enough to be admitted.

Stacy Jamison put her hands on her hips, and blocked Lizzy's attempt to walk around her. "I'm waiting. Where is your sister? And don't give me any more of your lies. I know how you've been covering up for her. I'm not stupid, and the lying is going to stop. Now, where is she?"

"She said she was seeing Randy for a little while," Lizzy said, not adding that her sister was supposed to meet her after the class ended so they could walk home together.

"Well, she had better come through this front door within the hour, or she's going to regret it this time." Stacy stepped aside, and Lizzy rushed past her and down the hall to her bedroom.

After slamming the door shut, Lizzy walked over to her unmade bed and climbed on top of the rumpled blanket. She dialed her sister's cellphone number and let it ring until the recording came on, then whispered in case her mother was listening at the door: "Amber, Mom's been at the bottle again. You better get your ass home quick, because she's really pissed. And I had to tell her you were with Randy, so forget about lying this time. It won't work."

Stacy took another long swig out of the hidden bottle, then stashed it away again and headed into the living room. The television was already on, but the volume had been turned low. She grabbed the remote off the cocktail table and switched the channels until she came to her favorite reality show. Moments after she'd stretched out on the sofa, she was fast asleep, with spittle dribbling onto her blue silk blouse.

CHAPTER SIXTY-ONE

After two and a half hours of sitting and looking through magazines, a short, gray-haired nurse stepped into the waiting room.

"Are you the folks who are here about Ms. Plummer?"

"I'm Detective Delaney," Catherine said, getting up from the chair. "Is Amanda all right?"

"She's doing well. She's out of recovery, and being transferred to a room. You can see her in a little while." She turned to leave.

"Wait a minute!"

The nurse turned back.

"We were told a doctor would talk to us after her operation," Catherine said, clearly annoyed.

Cody and Jake stood up, and joined Catherine.

"I'm afraid he can't do that right now. Another emergency just came in, and Doctor Simpson had to rush back into surgery to take care of the new patient. It might take a while, but I'm sure he'll talk to you when he's finished."

"Can you tell me about Ms. Plummer's operation, and what was done to her?"

"I'm sorry. I haven't seen her chart. I'm just passing on the message that she's being transferred to a room. As soon as I find out what room she's been put in, I'll let you know where she is."

Cody turned to the old man after she left. "Jake, you look exhausted. Why don't I have one of my men come, and take you home?"

"I'm not going anywhere until I see my girl," he said, sitting down again.

Catherine collected the magazines that they'd dropped on their chairs and a side table, and stuck them back in the wall holders. "I wonder how long this is going to take, before she—"

"Ms. Plummer is in room 203A, on the second floor. You can see her now," the same nurse said at the doorway.

They walked slowly to Amanda's room to accommodate Jake, because he'd forgotten to bring his cane with him.

Amanda's eyes were closed when the three of them entered the small room. The only light in the dim space came from a long, narrow wall fixture above her bed. Its rays emphasized the whiteness of the thick plaster cast that covered Amanda's left arm and shoulder, as well as how deathly white her face was. An intravenous line of clear fluid dripped steadily into her hand, and two machines beeped to the right of her bed.

"She's so pale," Jake whispered, slipping his hand under the raised bed rail and grasping her fingers. "Amanda, Honey. It's Jake. I'm here."

Amanda's eyes fluttered open. Her lips moved a bit, but nothing came out.

Catherine walked over to the other side of the bed. "Amanda, please try... I need your help," she said, as softly as she could.

Amanda's head slowly turned to her. "Catherine," she whispered.

"Did you see who shot you?"

Amanda licked her dry lips. "No, it was too dark. I was letting Harry in..." Her eyes flickered. "Harry, is he ...? Is he?"

"He's fine," Jake said, patting her hand. "He saved your life. Don't worry about the dog; I'll take care of him until you're back home."

Amanda smiled and closed her eyes.

"Cathy, let's go. She's too drugged to tell us anymore. We'll come back first thing in the morning."

Catherine leaned over the rail and gently rubbed Amanda's cheek. "Amanda, please try again. Did you see anything? Anything at all?"

Amanda's eyes fluttered half open. "A flash of light before I fell. And... and a strange smell." Her eyes slid closed again, and her head tilted to the side.

"She's going to be out of it for hours," Cody said, his hand motioning that they should leave.

Jake and Catherine followed him out of the room, but Catherine grabbed hold of his arm and pulled him to a stop when they'd reached the nurse's station. "What about our waiting to speak to the surgeon? Amanda may have said something to him, before she was anesthetized."

Cody nodded, then turned and walked over to the long desk. "Excuse me," he called out to a nurse who was writing on a clipboard.

She came over to him, still holding the board. "Can I help you?"

Cody showed her his badge. "I'd like to ask you a few questions about Ms. Plummer. I also need the name and phone number of the surgeon who just operated on her."

"I was just updating Ms. Plummer's chart, Officer. Can you give me a minute? The surgical nurse gave me something to give to the police when one of you showed up this evening."

When Cody nodded, she walked away and into a side room.

"This is the bullet that was taken out of Ms. Plummer's arm," she said, when she returned. She handed Cody a small, clear plastic container. A white label with the word Plummer was pasted on the lid, and a bloody metal object was inside. "The nurse told me to tell you that the only thing that touched that bullet was a sterile instrument."

"Thank you," Cody said, nodding.

"That young lady is very lucky to be alive. If this bullet had hit her arm an inch higher, it wouldn't have broken her bone; it would have passed through the flesh above the bone and gone straight through her heart."

CHAPTER SIXTY-TWO

While driving to Jake's house from the hospital, Catherine and Cody listened to a dispatcher announce a homicide and the address where the victim was discovered.

"We're not going there, Delaney. We're going home right after we drop Jake off," Cody said, stopping the car at a red light. Cody's cell phone rang. "It's in my shirt pocket. Grab it, Babe."

Catherine pulled the phone out of his pocket and clicked it on. "Detective Delaney.... Stan, whose house?... What!... Slow down.... Are you sure of that?... Cody and I will be there as soon as we can. Leave everything the way it is, until we get there.... Yes.... Yes, I know. I'm as stumped as you are.... We'll be there as soon as we can." She clicked off and held the phone in her lap.

"What?" Cody said after a quick glance.

"Dembeck's been murdered."

"The little man?"

"Stan said it looks like his neck was broken. He and Hawk found him on the garage floor."

"Did Amanda tell you about that man's death?" Jake asked from the back seat.

"No," Catherine said, staring through the side window. When their car turned the corner and drove onto the block where Amanda and Jake lived, she saw a crowd of people standing in the street in front of Amanda's house. Four black-and-white patrol cars were parked at the curb, and two uniformed officers were attaching yellow crime-scene tape to two palm trees to keep the bystanders away.

Cody pulled the car to a stop behind the last patrol car. "Cathy, help Jake to his house," he said, unbuckling his seatbelt. "I'm going to check out what they've found."

"I have to get Harry," Jake said, as Catherine was helping him out of the car. "I promised Amanda I'd take care of him."

"Don't worry about the dog. I'll bring him to you right after I speak to the detectives." She tucked her arm through Jake's, then slowly prodded him toward his house.

He unlocked the door, then turned back to her. "Don't forget to bring me his food and bowls. The poor thing must be starving by now."

"I'll be back with Harry in a few minutes. Take it easy while I'm gone."

She found Cody standing in Amanda's back yard, talking to one of the CSIs. Flood lights had been set up to illuminate the entire area. Two men were searching the grass; another one was fingerprinting the rear door, and a fourth one was snapping photographs.

"Cody, what's happening?"

"They found a nine millimeter shell casing around twenty feet back from this kitchen door."

She looked puzzled. "Only one shot was fired?"

"He must have thought he'd killed her when she fell out of her wheelchair," the officer standing next to Cody replied.

"Cody, if her ex finds out that Amanda's still alive; he'll come after her again."

"Good. I just sent a couple of our plain-clothes guys to the hospital to keep an eye on her. I also arranged to have her moved to a new room on a different floor, but the old room number will still be listed at the receptionist's desk and on the information center's phone list. I hope the bastard does go for it, because we'll be ready for him when he shows up."

"As soon as I bring the dog over to Jake, I want—"

"The dog's not here."

"What? Where is he?"

Cody shrugged.

CHAPTER SIXTY-THREE

When Stacy Jamison rubbed her eyes open, she was disoriented. Other than the light coming from the television, the room was dark. She swiveled her body around, and sat up on the sofa. The same reality show was still on, and she was positive that she'd seen that exact scene and heard the exact words the characters were saying before she fell asleep.

The house was quiet. *The girls must be asleep,* she thought, rising. She shut off the TV and walked to the kitchen. Moon light streamed through the window, casting shadows across the spotless white room. She left the light off and made her way over to the cabinet below the sink.

"Just one little sip so I can go to sleep," she mumbled, reaching for the bottle. Before taking a drink, she glanced at the door to make sure one of the girls wasn't standing there. The liquor went down smoothly. It calmed her trembling fingers, and gave her a sense of peace.

After stashing the empty bottle beneath the other glassware in the recycle bin, she headed toward her bedroom. As she made her way down the hall, she noticed a streak of light under Lizzy's closed door, and knew her daughter had forgotten to turn off her light again. The room had its usual pile of discarded clothes and magazines on the floor, when she opened the door and tip-toed inside. Her daughter was on her stomach and fast asleep, with her cell phone still clutched in her hand.

Stacy walked over to the bed and gently pried the phone out of Lizzy's hand. After setting it down on the nightstand beside her Minnie Mouse clock, she glanced at the illuminated dial. When she saw it was 1:00 AM, it dawned on her how long she had slept. Before leaving, she looked around her daughter's room and smiled.

The twins may have been identical in looks, but that was as far as it went. Lizzy was the quiet, but messy one. Amber was adventurous, reckless, a first-class chatter box, but she was remarkably neat. Even the décor in the girls' rooms was different. Lizzy's pink room was a testament to her love of everything Disney. Shelves were filled with character dolls, ceramics, even plastic collectibles. In contrast, the walls in Amber's room were painted a vivid red, and they were covered with posters of the latest pop stars and handsome movie idols.

In the fall, Amber would be going off to Skidmore College in upstate New York. Lizzy was enrolled in a local beauty school, something that Stacy had to admit pleased her, because she didn't want to be left alone in an empty house.

She pulled the sheet up on Lizzy, then walked out of her room and closed the door again. Amber's door was closed, and no light peeked out from beneath it. *Good, she must have come in while I was sleeping,* Stacy thought, continuing on to her own room. *Now I won't have to deal with her excuses tonight.*

Stacy's bedroom was luxurious, thanks to an expensive interior decorator. Yellow silk drapes trimmed with fancy tassels hung from the two large windows, and a matching spread covered the queen-size bed. After she'd thrown Mark out for the last time, she got rid of the dark walnut furniture he insisted they buy when they were first married. Back then, Stacy idolized the strikingly handsome young man. Whatever Mark wanted, Mark got. She had supported him until he got his degree in dentistry, and continued to do so until his dental practice became profitable. Now she had to work, because he'd fought her in court and she wasn't receiving any alimony.

Just a little bit to let me sleep, she thought. She sat on the overly soft bed, then pulled out the night table drawer and reached inside for the bottle of vodka. "Just one little sip," she said with a sigh as she kicked off her high heels.

"Amber, please come home. I don't think I can stay awake much longer to let you in," Lizzy whispered into her cell phone.

CHAPTER SIXTY-FOUR

The wet crime scene tape was drooping down to the soggy grass, and the fierce wind was threatening to tear the last of the long palm fronds off the trees when Cody and Catherine arrived at Frank Dembeck's house. They rushed past the medical examiner and CSI vans that were parked on the driveway, over to the lone, dripping-wet officer who was standing guard at the front door.

"James, there's no reason for you to be standing in this downpour. No one's dumb enough to be out in this weather, other than us," Cody said, patting his shoulder. "Come inside and dry off."

As soon as the three of them entered the house, Stan Wilkins rushed over to them. "I'm glad you could make it."

"Looks like it's going to be another sleepless night," Catherine said, shrugging out of her raincoat.

"Let me show you around, before you go into the garage. I want you to get the full picture of Dembeck, before I fill you in on a few things."

Cody and Catherine dropped their folded rainwear near the door, and followed him into the living room.

"Look at this. Just one fuckin' chair, and all these filled snake tanks. Pretty weird shit, huh?"

Catherine and Cody walked over to the far wall.

"Are any of these poisonous?" Catherine asked, peering into one of the large tanks, that like all of the others, was covered by a wire mesh lid.

"No. The kid who's taking care of Dembeck's pets said Dembeck was bitten once and wouldn't go anywhere near a poisonous one."

Catherine walked slowly down the row of stacked glass tanks, stopping in front of a few of them "These tanks must hold hundreds of snakes," she said, watching as many of the multi-colored ones twisted and wound their scaly bodies around each other.

"Some people have weed grow-houses," Stan said, "but this weirdo has a fuckin' snake grow-house. And if this isn't weird enough, the dwarf's breeding thousands of mice and rats in a back bedroom."

Catherine and Cody walked back to Stan, who hadn't taken a single step into the room.

"Here's the really interesting thing. The kid told us that Dembeck sells a lot of his rodents to a collector who can't raise enough of his own to feed his large collection. And get this; the collector also collects poisonous snakes."

Catherine shivered, and glanced back at the tanks.

"A large collector?" Cody said. "Did you get that person's name?"

"No. We got Dembeck's files. Hawk's going through them right now. There's another thing that's weird. Dembeck has a fortune in his checking account. Over seventy thousand bucks, and more than twenty-five of that was deposited this month."

Catherine looked up at Cody. "No one keeps that kind of money in a checking account."

"Maybe he's getting a monthly inheritance," Cody said, "Or a pension. He can't possibly make that kind of money selling rodents."

"That's exactly what I thought. Someone needs to get his bank records and copies of the checks that were deposited. Then we'll know where that shit-load of money came from."

"Stan, what about his computer?" Cody asked.

"We got it, but we can't get onto his Facebook or Twitter pages, because he didn't store his password. Hawk and I think the collector who's buying Dembeck's rodents maybe ordering them through Facebook. We hafta get on there, and we hafta get his phone records fast!"

"I have a Fed friend who can help us," Catherine said, "I'm meeting with him tomorrow morning right after our briefing. Get the computer set up and ready for him. I'm sure he'll know what to do with it."

"They're about to take the body away," Hawk called out from the hallway. "If you want a look, you'd better come into the garage. Stan, I'm going to put this computer in the trunk. The files are already in there, and then I'm leaving with or without you, Pal."

"We're coming. Don't leave without me."

As the three of them stepped into the garage, two officers who were carrying paper evidence bags walked out through the open garage door. Burt was standing beside the body. He looked drawn and tired. His normally neat clothes were wrinkled and soiled, and his shoulders were sagging.

"Burt, you're a mess," Catherine said, walking over to him with a smile.

"I should have become a teacher like my mother wanted me to be," he said, pulling off the latex gloves and then shoving them into a paper bag.

Cody knelt down beside the corpse. "Doc, are you sure his neck is broken?"

"I'm positive," Burt answered, turning to him.

"Is it possible that with Dembeck's physical disability, it broke when he fell and hit the concrete?"

"No. There's heavy bruising around his neck, indicating his neck was forcefully twisted. When I rotated his head, I could tell multiple bones had been broken. Cody, breaking someone's neck isn't easy, but when you have that kind of break, there's a combination of muscle and other soft tissue damage caused by strangulation. See the hemorrhaging around his neck? He bled out until he died. When I do the autopsy, I'm sure I'll find significant petechial and lymph node hemorrhages and shattered bone fragments."

One of Burt's assistants who was standing on the driveway opened the van's door. The second one rolled a metal gurney with a black body bag on top of it into the garage.

"Are we ready to take him?" the man asked, unfolding the body bag.

"In a minute," Burt told him.

Cody rose, still staring down at Dembeck. "Doc, can you give me an idea of how tall or strong his killer might be, based on the little man's stature?"

"Unfortunately, no. But he must have known his assailant, because your men found no evidence of a forced entry."

"Stan, are you ready to leave?" Hawk shouted from the car that was parked at the curb.

"Yeah! Hold your horses, I'm comin'." He turned to Catherine and Cody before leaving. "Listen guys, my gut tells me that it's the money that got Shortie murdered. If you follow the money trail, you'll nab the bastard."

"We might get some good fingerprints," Catherine said.

"There are no prints," Stan said. "Our guys said everything has been wiped clean."

CHAPTER SIXTY-FIVE

As sunlight streamed through the venetian blinds in Stacy's bedroom, it cast zig-zag lines across her face and the wrinkled clothes she still wore from the previous day. Lizzy looked down at the empty liquor bottle that was clutched in her mother's hand. She desperately wanted to walk out of that bedroom and never talk to or see her mother ever again, but that would have to wait until she graduated from beauty school and got a job. "Mom, wake up," she said, shaking Stacy's shoulder.

Stacy mumbled and turned onto her side, facing away from her.

Lizzy pulled the bottle out from her mother's hand and flung it across the room. It crashed nosily against the wall, causing the shards of glass to scatter across the white tile floor. "Damn you, wake up!"

Stacy rolled over, mumbled incoherently, then slowly opened her eyes. "What... what broke?"

"Your booze bottle. That's what broke," Lizzy snapped, her face a mask of fury, her eyes red-rimmed and puffy from crying all night.

Stacy saw the anger on her daughter's face and the cellphone clutched tightly in her hand. She pulled herself up into a sitting position against her pillows. "Lizzy, honey, I can explain. I—"

"I don't want to hear your excuses. Amber's not here. She didn't come home last night."

Stacy gasped, and clutched the blouse over her heart. "That can't be. She has to be in her room."

"She's not in her room. She's not home. I've been calling her all night. She didn't answer her phone, and she never called me back."

"She must be with her boyfriend," Stacy said, climbing out of bed.

"I just spoke to Randy," Lizzy said with tears rolling down her face. "He said Amber never met him yesterday like she was supposed to, and she didn't call to let him know why."

"Your father... Amber's got to be with him," Stacy said, breathless and grabbing hold of Lizzy's shoulders. "She was angry that I wasn't nicer to him during dinner, so she's getting even with me by not coming home.

That's it. She's with him." She grabbed Lizzy's phone and punched in her ex-husband's cellphone number.

"Hello," his raspy voice replied.

"Mark, I want you to bring Amber home immediately! Do you hear me?"

"Amber?" he said, sounding half asleep. "Amber's not here."

Stacy dropped the phone. "Oh, my God… Oh, my good God. Lizzy, get dressed. We have to drive around and find her. Hurry!"

"Mom, we need to call the police."

"No! Not yet. She may be at a friend's house. I don't want to start something. Get dressed!"

CHAPTER SIXTY-SIX

"Holy shit! Cody, come in here now," Catherine shouted.

"What's up, Babe?" he asked as soon as he reached the kitchen door. A wet bath towel was cinched around his waist, and only half of his face had shaving cream on it. "Why are you smacking that newspaper on the table?"

"I'm furious. One of our team is a traitor. That reporter... Mary Kaye... Her story is on the *Sun Sentinel*'s front page." She unrolled and straightened the paper and then read:

Boca Raton Police are working with a psychic. My source said Amanda Plummer was shot last night, but she's alive. According to the doctors at the Bethesda West Hospital, Ms. Plummer is in stable condition, and may be discharged sometime later this afternoon.

"It had to be someone on our team," Cody said, shaking the razor he was holding so hard, the cream on the edge of it flew off.

"They were all warned to keep their mouths shut, but one of them blabbed. Now her husband knows for sure that she's still alive."

"Catherine, call the hospital. Update the men who are on surveillance. As soon as I finish shaving, I'll arrange to have her transferred to another hospital or private nursing facility." He turned around to leave, but quickly turned back. "When you finish with that call, make another one to the Florida State prison. Get the warden to give you the names of any relatives or friends her husband contacted in this area."

When Cody returned to the kitchen fully dressed, Catherine was sitting at the kitchen table with a puzzled expression on her face. "What's wrong?"

She stared straight ahead at the refrigerator, instead of looking at him. "Amanda's ex was captured three hours after he escaped." She turned to Cody. "He wasn't the one who fired that shot."

"Christ! Then who the hell did?"

"The person who found out she was working with us," Catherine said, an edge to her voice. "He wanted to make sure that Amanda couldn't identify him as the person who murdered those two girls. That's who tried to kill her."

CHAPTER SIXTY-SEVEN

Amber was still groggy, but coming around. Her eyes were burning and tearing, but when she tried to bring one of her hands down to her face so she could rub them, she discovered her hands were tied overhead to a headboard.

"It's about time you woke up, my pretty little Elizabeth."

Amber turned to him. The man was nude and holding his shriveled penis. She tried to yank her hands out of the restraints, but the rope was too tight. Her heart pounded, and his mistakenly calling her by her sister's name echoed in her aching head. "Let me go," she said, not correcting him.

He smiled down at her, and rubbed her bare breast.

"Stop that, you monster!" The tears rolled down the sides of her face.

"Not yet," he said, pulling on his penis as his other hand dipped into her curly mound.

Amber tried to buck up from the bed but couldn't, because her legs had been spread apart and her ankles were tied to a metal footboard. "Stop it! Stop it!" she shouted, as his fingers dipped into her pubic warmth.

"Your pussy's so nice and tight. I'm going to love fucking you," he said, sliding his fingers in and out, in and out, and smiling as his penis grew longer and harder.

Amber screamed as loud as she could.

"No one can hear you, Lizzy." He took his fingers out of her vagina, brought them in front of her face, and then slowly licked them to taunt her.

The contents of Amber's stomach suddenly erupted.

He jumped back, and slapped her face hard. "You ruined it for me, you little bitch. Look at what you did," he said, staring down at his deflating erection and the vomit on his chest.

Amber turned her head sideways to keep from choking on the vile-tasting vomit, and he stomped out of the room, cursing.

While he was gone, Amber franticly twisted and turned her wrists until they were slick with blood, but the rope wouldn't loosen.

When he walked back into the room, he was fully dressed and holding a syringe.

Amber stared at the needle. She could barely draw a breath into her lungs she was so frightened. "Let me call my father," she cried as he drew nearer. "Please."

He jabbed the needle into her upper arm.

"What is that stuff?" she cried out, as the burning liquid plunged into her.

He pulled the needle out, and didn't bother to wipe off the couple of drops that had leaked onto her arm.

"Please, please let me go," Amber begged, as her eyes began to flutter.

"I decided I no longer want you," he said, standing over her. "You make me sick. Grandpa would be ashamed of me if I touched you now."

His words were becoming fuzzy to Amber, but she refused to give in to unconsciousness. *What does he mean he doesn't want me anymore? Is he going to kill me?* She shut her eyes and let her head tilt to the side. If what he injected into her was supposed to kill her, Amber decided she'd let him think that it had.

CHAPTER SIXTY-EIGHT

Jason Pollack was waiting in the police station's reception area. He smiled and waved to Catherine when she and Cody entered the large area, then held out his arms in welcome.

"Jason," Catherine squealed, rushing into his embrace and hugging him tight. "I can't thank you enough for sticking your neck out for me."

"Your hug is worth it," he said, setting her back, and giving her a long once over.

Cody cringed when he saw her enveloped in the tall, muscular man's arms, and wanted to punch his white teeth right down to his throat, He knew that Catherine had dated the Fed in the past, and it gnawed on him that she still had his personal phone number.

"Jason, this is my partner, Cody O'Dell," she said, turning to Cody.

Cody shook the man's hand when it was offered. The shake was firm, and he hated him more.

"Come inside," Catherine said, ignoring the daggers the men were giving each other. "We have that computer that I need you to look at."

"Cody, the chief was looking for you a little while ago," a detective said as they were passing by his cubicle. Cody stopped mid-step.

"Where is he now?"

"He's in the conference room, getting the group ready for the briefing."

"Thanks." Cody started off again, and Catherine and Jason went with him. "Cathy, take care of that computer business," he said when he reached the conference room. "I'll catch up with you after the briefing."

He left them, and walked inside. Chief Delaney was standing in front of the room, and the large group of detectives and technicians were already seated and quiet.

"Did I miss much?" Cody asked the chief when he reached his side.

"I was just going to start. Don't go anywhere after the meeting. I'm waiting for a call about that copter."

"You got it?"

"The pilot's transferring a young patient from a Miami hospital to Delray Community's trauma center. He should be there within the hour. When I get his call, he said you're to meet him at the Delray Hospital's helipad. Let's get started. I don't want you to leave before this meeting is finished."

"Yes, Sir." Cody turned to his audience. "Okay, boys and girls, before we start on official business, I want to tell you that I'm royally pissed off that one of you spilled the beans to the *Sun Sentinel* reporter. I don't know who did it, but you've set our killer after Ms. Plummer again."

Murmurs filtered around the room, and curious eyes glanced around, looking for answers.

"I thought there was a BOLO out on her ex-husband," a sharp voice called out from the back of the room.

"He was captured three hours after his escape," Cody said. "Our shooter has to be the person who murdered the two girls. That bullet was meant to silence Ms. Plummer, so she wouldn't be able to identify him."

Again the room became noisy.

"Quiet down," Cody shouted. "We need to move on."

The room immediately became silent.

"We have another wrinkle in this case. As all of you know, we've been looking for someone who collects snakes, because Ms. Plummer saw the girls in a snake-filled room. We had a connection to find that collector. Unfortunately, Frank Dembeck—our source—was murdered last night."

"What?" the chief muttered beside him.

"Mr. Dembeck's neck was broken. Our CSIs found no evidence of a forced entry into his house, and the killer's fingerprints were wiped off."

Catherine walked into the room, and sat down in the front row.

"Cody," Dexter called out.

Cody turned to him. "Yes, Dex."

"I was going to wait until later to tell you, but years ago, when I was working the gangs unit in the South Bronx, I remember the news reporting a serial killer in Florida that was targeting young, black women."

Catherine gasped, and rose quickly. "How long ago?"

"I don't remember," Dexter said, flipping a few dreadlocks off his shoulder. "I only remember that black girls' bodies were found every couple of months, and some who were registered as missing hadn't been found. I don't know if it's related to our victims, because they're white, but I never heard a word about the police catching that killer."

Cody turned to Catherine. Her mouth had dropped open, and her face was pallid. "Catherine, what is it? What's wrong?"

"Amanda said she saw a lot of hands—black hands—trying to claw their way up from beneath the earth."

CHAPTER SIXTY-NINE

She'd been driving around for a little more than an hour, but it felt like six long ones to Stacy. Her hands trembled on the steering wheel, and rivulets of sweat ran down between her breasts. She needed a drink, and needed it soon, or her body would begin to shake.

She glanced at Lizzy, who was sitting beside her, intently staring out of the side window, searching for her sister. "Honey, I'm going to make a quick stop in the supermarket for some water and crackers. I'm feeling sick. I need something in my stomach."

Lizzy glanced at her mother, then back at the window. "Whatever. I'll call Randy again. Don't take too long."

Stacy practically ran into the Publix's after parking the car as far away from the store as she could, without making Lizzy suspicious. She needed time to buy a bottle of wine and a couple of other things, then pay for it and take the package into the lady's room for her quick fix.

The lines at each of the six cash registers were long, and looked like they were moving at a snail's pace. Stacy chose a line that looked the shortest, and prayed it would move fast.

"The oatmeal is a buy one, get one free," an elderly woman said, as she was being checked out. The cashier called for a price check, and everyone waited until the sale price was confirmed.

Stacy shifted from one foot to another, growing more impatient by the minute. By the time she reached the head of the line with her wine and two boxes of cookies, her blouse was sticking to her back and her heart was racing.

"I'm sorry. My register is out of paper. It will only take me a minute to fix," the frizzy-haired cashier said. She dashed over to the service desk. On her way back with the roll of white paper, Stacy spotted Lizzy walking through the automatic door. Her heart nearly exploded as she watched her daughter head directly over to her.

"Mom, what's taking so long?" she said, and then looked down at what her mother was buying. When Lizzy lifted her head, her face was red, and her nostrils flared.

"Lizzy, I…"

Lizzy turned around and quickly walked away.

Stacy was much calmer when she returned to the car. After stowing the bag with the wine bottle in the trunk, she climbed into the car and tossed the two boxes of cookies onto the back seat. She waited for Lizzy to open the door and get in, but her daughter stood outside, glaring at her through the window.

Stacy rolled down the window. "Lizzy, get in. I can explain."

"I don't want to hear any more of your Goddamn excuses," Lizzy shouted, taking two steps back. "You're a sick alcoholic!"

"Lizzy, I—"

"You're not the one who's important now! I don't give a shit about you anymore! All I care about is my sister!"

"We'll find her," Stacy said, leaning across the passenger seat and pushing the door open.

Lizzy stepped forward, and slammed the door shut.

"Lizzy!"

"I just called Dad. He's coming for me. We're going to the police," she said, and then ran toward the store.

CHAPTER SEVENTY

"Cody, do you think Dexter will find the some information on those missing and murdered black girls?" she asked as they were walking toward her office.

"I don't know. Dex said he thinks it happened about twenty years ago, and twenty years is a long time. He's calling a few newspapers to find out where it took place, and then the station that handled the investigation to see their files." Cody sighed. "Those files were probably locked away in storage years ago. It could take forever to find them, and we don't have forever."

"Stan and Hawk may find something when they get a look at Dembeck's banking records. Maybe they'll get a name from one of those large deposits that were made."

"Let's hope so. When I—"

"Cathy, Cody," the chief called to them from the doorway of his office. "I need to talk to you. Come in here. After they entered the room, Cody was told to lock the door so they wouldn't be disturbed.

Instead of sitting down in front of his desk like she usually did when she was summoned, Catherine walked over to the bookcase and leaned back against it. "What's up?" she asked, when he was seated behind his desk.

"I wanted to ask your opinions."

Cody turned one of the wooden chairs around, and straddled it. "Ask away."

"What do you think about my running for mayor?"

Catherine started to choke.

"I guess that's a no," he said, pressing back against his chair.

"It's not a no," Catherine quickly said. "You just caught me by surprise."

"Sir, you told me a few months ago that you were thinking about retiring."

"Yeah, I know," he said, tilting his chair forward again. "That's when I was feeling sick. But now... Now that I'm perfectly well again, I keep asking myself how I can let Clarkston run for reelection. If that asshole gets to serve another term, the entire police force will be whittled down to nothing." He got up from his chair and turned to look out the window. "Thanks to him, folks around here have lost their respect for cops, and that puts our men in danger. In good conscience, I can't let that happen. A mayor's got to have his men's backs. I have a good reputation, medals for valor, and with a little help from a few influential people I know, I think I would have a good chance of beating him. So, what do you think?" he asked, turning back to them.

Catherine glanced over at Cody, then at her uncle.

"I think you'll both say yes, after you hear what I'm gonna' tell you. I've got a confession to make."

"Uncle Steve, I don't know what this is about, but—"

"I think it was Clarkston who called that reporter. In fact, I'm almost certain he did it."

"What do you mean?" Catherine asked.

"Remember me telling you two that I had just gotten off the phone with him?"

"Yes. So? He's always calling you and bitching about one thing, or another."

"Well, this time he insisted I tell him where we were getting our information about the killer, and I stupidly said from a physic and then gave him Ms. Plummer's name."

CHAPTER SEVENTY-ONE

Catherine was sipping coffee from her mug when Jason Pollack walked into her office with a grim look on his face.

"How can you drink that sludge?" he asked, pushing some folders aside on her desk and then perching on the corner of it.

"This isn't too bad. You should taste the coffee at the end of the day," she said, smiling up at him.

"Catherine, I couldn't crack into that computer," he said, shaking his head. "I tried, but I don't have the right equipment with me."

"You have to get on that computer, Jason, it's urgent. We think the killer may be on Dembeck's Facebook site."

"I took the hard drive out of it." He got off her desk.

"And?"

"I'm taking it up to Tallahassee. I have what I need in that office to read what's on it. I'm sorry; I wish I could do it here. It would be a lot faster, but I can't."

"How long do you think it will take you?" Catherine asked, getting up.

"I don't know. It's going to take me a couple of hours just to drive upstate, and then…" He shrugged. "I'll work as fast as I can. I promise."

"Tell me that I'll have that information by tonight. Please, Jason. Another kid is about to be kidnapped."

"I'll try my hardest."

"Catherine. Oh!" Cody stopped at the door when he spied Jason standing next to Catherine.

"Jason can't get into Dembeck's Facebook account," Catherine said, turning to Cody. "He removed the hard drive, and he has to take it up to his Tallahassee office."

"Oh, crap! That's going to take forever. Jason, we must have that information. And we need it… we need it in a blink of an eye or sooner."

Catherine heard the desperation in his voice. "Cody, what's happened?"

"I just got a call from the admitting officer. A father and his daughter are in the reception area. They're waiting to talk to us."

A chill ran down Catherine's arms and spine. She stared at Cody for a few moments, afraid to ask if he knew this father was waiting to report a missing daughter. She finally nodded. "I'll go out and get them."

"Good. You handle that." He turned to Jason. "Forget about driving up there. I have the use of a helicopter this morning. I'll get the pilot to drop you off at your office."

"Cody, what about searching the open land?" Catherine asked. "Won't flying him up there take too long?"

"Waiting an extra hour might actually be better. The ground needs to absorb last night's rainfall, or I might not be able to see those ruts."

"What do you want me to do while you're gone?"

"Stay put. I'll keep in touch as soon as I start the search. If I spot something, anything, I'll give you the location. Then get a team together and meet me." He turned to leave, then turned back. "I almost forgot. Here's the medical examiner's report on the body parts. I didn't get a chance to read it," he said, pulling a folded sheet of paper out from his back pants pocket.

Catherine took the fax, unfolded it, and scanned down to the bottom where the ME had typed: RESULTS. "He says the DNA of the head matches the body parts that we fished out of the Intercostal. They're also a positive match with the burned man who was found in Lillian's house." She looked at Cody. "How could her brother be such a monster? How could he cut her up, and then throw her away? I'm sick thinking about Lillian. She deserved better than that."

"Catherine…"

"I'm all right." she said, brushing past Jason. "There's a worried father and kid waiting for me."

Cody grabbed her arm as she reached the door. "Are you sure, Delaney?"

"Quit wasting time, O'Dell. Get Jason to his office. And then get the hell over those open fields, and find that fucking snake house!" Her cell phone rang. "Delaney, here… Yes… Yes… Thank you for calling, and please tell Amanda I'll take care of it."

"What was that about?" Cody asked.

"Amanda told a nurse to call me, because she doesn't have a phone in the room. She said he has her, but he's left the house and the girl is still alive. Cody, we have time. We have to find her before it's too late."

CHAPTER SEVENTY-TWO

The tall, strikingly handsome man who was waiting in the police reception area was pacing back and forth like a caged animal. His jaw was clenched, and his dark eyes looked haunted. Catherine assumed the slim teenager who was sitting on the bench, nervously biting her fingernails, was his daughter, because she looked like him.

"I'm Detective Delaney," she said when she reached him.

"My sister is missing," the girl said, jumping up, dashing over to Catherine, and grabbing hold of her arm. The girl's eyes were red and swollen from crying, and her face was ashen. "You have to find her." She broke into sobs and was quickly pulled away from Catherine, and enveloped in the man's arms.

"It's all right, Honey. The police will find her." He looked at Catherine, waiting for her to confirm what he said.

"Yes, of course." Catherine nodded, but her heart felt like it had dropped down to her stomach. "Why don't you follow me into my office," she said, softly. She led them through the interior door, past the detectives' cubicles with their staring eyes, to her office rather than into one of the intimidating interrogation rooms. "Please have a seat. Would you like something to drink?" she asked while they were sitting down.

"No, thank you," he said, shaking his head and reaching for his daughter's hand. "My name's Mark Jamison. My daughter Amber is missing."

Catherine sat across from them. "How long has Amber been missing?"

Jamison looked at his daughter. "Lizzy, how long? Talk to the detective."

The girl's lips were trembling, and tears were streaming down her face. She swallowed. "Yesterday, she was supposed to meet me after dance class so we could walk home together, but she didn't show up. I thought she was with her boyfriend Randy, so I went home by myself."

"Around what time was that?"

"Around 9 o'clock."

"Then what happened?" Catherine asked, as her palms and forehead began to moisten.

"I tried to call her all night," Lizzy said, swiping the tears off her cheeks, only to have more stream down her face. "She never answered her phone, and in the morning I called Randy. He said she never met him, and he didn't know where she was."

"My daughter and I have been driving around the neighborhood for hours, thinking Amber may have fallen or been hit by a car. And Lizzy called all of Amber's friends. No one has heard from her or seen her. We're desperate, detective. You've got to help us find her."

"Is it possible that Amber ran away from home?"

"She'd never do that," Lizzy said adamantly, starting to sob again.

Mr. Jamison wrapped his arm around his daughter's shoulders, and pressed her head against his chest. "Detective, Amber and Elizabeth are very close. We're positive that Amber is in trouble. She'd never, ever leave her sister like this. Never!"

"Can you give me a description of Amber?" Catherine said, reaching for the pad and pen on her desk.

"She looks like me," Lizzy said with her head raised. "We're identical twins."

CHAPTER SEVENTY-THREE

The drive over to the Bethesda West Hospital seemed like it was taking forever. Catherine didn't turn on the siren, or stick the flashing bubble-light on top of the unmarked car, fearing it might tip off the killer if he was driving close by. The hospital's parking lot was filled. She circled around half a dozen times before she could park. When she reached the lobby, she rushed past the reception desk and the elevators to an exit door, and then bolted up the steps to the second floor. She had to see Amanda, before Cody called.

The long hallway reeked of ammonia and cleaning fluids. It was crowded with visitors and a few slow-walking patients who were being assisted by nurses or relatives. An upright, large metal food cart that held shelves stacked with the patients' breakfast trays, stood outside the room that Amanda had originally been put into. Catherine stepped inside. The room was dark and empty.

"Hold up!"

Catherine grabbed the holster on her right hip and spun around. "Roger! Jesus Christ. Why'd you sneak up on me like that? I could have shot your lazy ass, Buddy."

"Sorry. I wanted to catch you before you walked in here."

"I like your green scrubs," she said, giving the crew-cut detective a once over and removing her hand from her gun. "Where's your piece?" Roger turned slightly, so she could see the bulge at his waistband. "I couldn't ask at the desk, so I was looking for one of you. What room was Plummer transferred to?"

"We got her out of that new room about an hour ago. She's at the Delray Abbey Rehabilitation Center."

"Good. Who's there with her?"

"Simons and Murphy. Don't worry about Plummer. She's covered. No one is going to mess with her. She's even got her pooch with her."

"Huh? What'd you say?"

He smiled. "Somehow that mutt snuck into this hospital and found her room. She wouldn't leave without him, so we let him go with her."

"And they're going to let him stay there?"

He shrugged. "Don't know. Why are you looking for her?"

Catherine headed out of the room and down the hall, and he went with her. "Another girl is missing. I wanted to show Amanda her picture."

"Aw, shit! When the hell is this going to stop?"

Catherine stopped in front of the same exit door. "When we catch the bastard," she said, looking at the detective. "Keep your eyes open. If he shows up, make sure he doesn't get away, even if you have to beat the shit out of him."

Amanda was sitting in a wheelchair by the window, looking up at a TV screen. She was dressed in a blue and white hospital gown, and had a white blanket over her legs. Her hair had been plaited into one thick braid. It hung over her shoulder and reached down to her waist. Harry, who was curled in her lap, lifted his head and barked shrilly the second Catherine, stepped into the sunlit room.

"Harry, quiet," Amanda said, patting his head.

The plainclothes detective, who was sitting in the corner, tilted his chair forward and rose. "Delaney."

"Everything quiet, Murphy?"

"Yeah, but the food is lousy."

"Catherine, I need to ask you a big favor."

Catherine sat down on the freshly made-up bed. "Sure, Amanda. What do you need?"

"Can you bring Harry to Jake? They just told me that he can't stay here."

"No problem."

"Tell Jake that he has to make sure that Harry doesn't run away again. This time he might get run over by a car."

"I'll be sure to tell him. Amanda..." Catherine licked her dry lips. "Amanda, another girl was just reported missing."

Amanda's pressed her casted arm against her chest. She squeezed her eyes shut for a moment or two, then opened them and stared at Catherine without saying a word.

"I have a picture. I want to show it to you," Catherine said, noting how Amanda's chest was suddenly rising and falling rapidly. She reached into her pants pocket and pulled out her cell phone, then clicked on her stored pictures until she found the one she'd snapped of Lizzy in her office. "Here it is," she said holding the phone out to Amanda.

Amanda wouldn't touch the phone, but stared at the picture. "That's her," she whispered, peering up at Catherine. "That's the girl I saw on the red bed."

"No, Amanda. This girl is Lizzy. The one you saw on that red bed was Amber. It wasn't a double image you were seeing that night when you were letting Harry into the kitchen. What you were seeing was identical twins."

Amanda's hand reached out for Catherine's. She grasped them tightly. Her lips quivered, and she shut her eyes. Harry jumped off her lap, and cowered by her legs.

Catherine waited. Her heart was pounding. She could barely draw a breath into her constricted lungs, because the room suddenly felt like the air had been sucked out of it.

Murphy stared from one woman to the other. His eyes had widened, his mouth had dropped open.

"She's in the snake room," Amanda finally said, after opening her eyes. "She's still alive, Catherine. Find her. Dear God, please find her before it's too late."

CHAPTER SEVENTY-FOUR

He read the short note Grace left on the hallway table saying she had gone to church, and would be home in time for dinner. He crumpled the slip into a tight ball, and carried it into the bedroom. As he stripped off his clothing, he thought about his religious and boring wife. Grace was still attractive and had kept her figure, but for some reason he couldn't stand to be around her, no less fuck her. Either the woman was on her knees praying for world peace, or she was involved in some ridiculous cause like releasing whales and pandas from captivity. Organizing bake sales and neighborhood garden tours with the other church ladies were her specialty. Their phone rang endlessly when he was at home. It drove him nuts, but he tolerated her and those calls because she never questioned why he was leaving the house at odd hours.

This morning was a big disappointment, he thought, stepping into the hot shower. He grabbed the bar of soap, and scrubbed his chest and arms vigorously. *Damn girl. She got vomit all over me. All that planning was for nothing. Now I'll have to find another one.*

It was past the lunch hour when he arrived at Duffy's Restaurant, but the place was still busy and very noisy when he got there.

"How many will you be?" the young hostess asked.

"Just me. I want a table where I'll be able to see the TV."

"Follow me, please," she said, taking a rolled up napkin that had silverware in it and a menu with her.

He followed her to the furthest row of booths and sat in the last one, so he could watch the large television that was hung high on the far wall.

She placed the menu and silverware down on the table. "Your waitress will be with you shortly."

He nodded, and she walked away. He was watching a tennis match on the TV, when a waitress stopped at his table. She was young, very attractive, and his eyes were drawn to the jutting nipple nubs that were pressing against her tight, knitted top.

*   *   *

"Are you ready to order, or would you like a couple of minutes?"

He felt himself growing hard under the table, and smiled up at her. "I'll have the baby back ribs well done, fries, a side of coleslaw, and a cold Coors."

She jotted his order down on a pad. "I'll be right back." She smiled, then walked away, unaware that he was watching her tight ass swing from side to side.

When she was out of sight, he looked up at the television, and slipped his right hand beneath the table to his crotch. He rubbed his hardening penis, while staring up at the tennis.

"Here's your beer," the waitress said, returning and placing the tall glass on the table. "Your food will be out shortly." She left again.

He reached for the glass of foam-topped beer with his other hand, then took a long drink and expelled a satisfied sigh.

The program he was watching was suddenly interrupted and the words: NEWS ALERT flashed across the screen.

"We need your help to find this young lady," the male announcer said, holding up a photograph. The cameraman panned in, enlarging the young girl's face.

He smiled, picked up the glass, and took another sip of his beer.

"Amber Jamison is five-feet, four-inches tall."

His glass tipped over. Some of the beer spilled onto the table.

"Amber has been missing since yesterday, and we…"

"Amber? No… That can't be."

He didn't hear the rest of the announcement.

"I got the wrong one," he mumbled with his eyes bulging wide. "The venom may not have worked." He quickly slid out of the booth, dropped a twenty-dollar bill on the table, then dashed out of the restaurant, almost knocking the hostess off her feet.

CHAPTER SEVENTY-FIVE

Something tickled her nose. Amber tried to swat it away, but whatever was doing it, did it again. Her eyes flickered a few times, then opened wide, and she let out a blood-curdling scream. A green and yellow snake's head was poised inches away from her face. She grabbed the snake when it darted toward her and flung it away, then saw the long brown one that was winding its way up her leg. She screamed again and tore it off, but when she turned to toss it away, she lost her balance on the pile of cartons, and tumbled down to the snake-filled floor. Her blood-curdling screams echoed around the room, as she tried to raise herself up on her shaking-weak legs. Upright and trembling from head to toe, Amber shook her head to clear the fuzziness from her brain, while frantically kicking at the hissing snakes that were slithering toward her.

Amber's heart pounded, and her chest got so tight she could barely draw a breath into her lungs. Tears streamed down her face, and her eyes burned, but she kept kicking the snakes away, trying to not fall down again into the squirming mass. *Is he in the house? Did he hear me scream?* She looked at the door on the opposite side of the room, expecting him to come through it at any moment. When he didn't, she bolted to it, her bare feet stomping on snakes in her panic. The door was locked when she turned the knob. She spun around and looked at the window. It was barred on the outside.

I'm locked in. I'm a prisoner. He's going to kill me when he finds out I'm still alive, she thought, panting and kicking, terrified to her core. The snakes kept slithering close to her, and Amber kept kicking them away. She forced herself not to scream again, pressed her ear against the door. The only thing she heard was the hissing of the snakes, and their bodies rubbing against the wooden floor. And then an even more frightening thought filled her mind. *He thinks I'm Lizzy. If he finds out I'm not my sister, he'll go after her. Oh, God, please help me. I have to get to her, warn her, save her from this crazy man.*

Tears were running down Amber's face, and her eyes were burning. Although the room was stifling-hot, goose bumps covered her slim, nude body. Her mind no longer groggy from whatever he had injected into her arm, Amber scanned the room and spotted the open doggie door near the floor on the right wall. Snakes were wriggling in and out of it. Were the colorful ones poisonous?

"There's only one way out of here," she told herself. "You have to get to Lizzy before he does."

With a new-found strength, Amber dashed over to the doggie door, lowered herself onto the snake-filled floor, and then—pushing some snakes away—she squeezed her body through the narrow opening. She rose when she was inside the new room and pressed her back against the wall to catch her breath. There were even more snakes in this room, some large, some small, many colorful, all of them wiggling and slithering, hissing and winding their scaly bodies around and over each other. She kicked the snakes away as she ran to the door. This one was unlocked. After opening it, she peeked both ways in the hall. Other than some creaks that were coming from the attic, the house was silent. Amber left the door open, and silently crept over to the staircase. When she still heard no sign of the man, she inched her way down the worn steps one at a time, trying to be as silent as she could.

As soon as Amber spotted the front door, she made a mad dash to it, only to find it was locked. Her heart skipped a beat, sweat poured down her body. She spun around. Some of the snakes from the upstairs bedroom room were slithering down the steps.

She darted to a door on her right, pressed her ear against it, and listened. She didn't hear him, just muffled, soft sounds. Her fingers were shaking when she grasped the doorknob and pulled the door open. She gasped and staggered back a step. The entire room was lined with floor-to-ceiling metal shelves, and on those shelves there were enormous glass tanks filled with large, coiling snakes. She shivered, saw the window across the room, then ran into the room and over to the lone window.

The hissing grew louder as Amber's fists banged on the window to open it, but the frame and sill had been painted so many times, it was glued shut. She glanced back at some of the tanks, because the hissing was growing louder. Many of the snakes had uncoiled their bodies, and were now smacking their heads against the glass. Amber spotted a metal folding chair leaning against the far wall. She snuck past a line of tanks, grabbed the chair, and then dashed over to the window. Her arm hurt when she lifted up the chair, but she swung it as hard as she could against the glass, and it shattered. She kept hitting the shards, until the remaining glass was out of the frame. Ready to climb out of the window, Amber flung the chair back. It crashed into one of the tanks. As the rattler slithered out of the broken tank and onto the floor, Amber climbed out of the window, and ran into the open field.

CHAPTER SEVENTY-SIX

After leaving Amanda at the rehabilitation facility, Catherine drove to Jake's house to drop off Harry. Unfortunately, the old man wasn't home, so the mutt was back in Catherine's office, whining and scratching the door to get out.

"Harry, sit your ass down, or I'll tie you down, you miserable hound."

Her phone rang. She lifted it off the cradle. "Detective Delaney."

"Catherine, I still don't see any ruts."

"Cody, it's only been an hour… Shut up!"

"What?"

"Not you, Cody. That stupid mutt is back in my office, and he's driving me crazy. But forget about him. Can you fly closer to the ground?"

"Babe, if we get any closer, we'll be mowing the grass with the rotor blades."

"I got a call from Wilkins a few minutes ago."

"What did he have to say?"

"He and Whitehall went to Dembeck's bank when it opened this morning. They checked his accounts. Seems the little man has been depositing more than ten grand in his checking account for the last six months."

"We already knew that."

"Yeah, but what we didn't know was, it was always in cash."

"That means we can't trace where it came from."

"The guys are heading over to the phone company to get his phone records. You know what I think, O'Dell? I think that little man may have been blackmailing someone, and that someone got tired of shelling out that money."

"That's an interesting theory, Delaney. Guess we'll know more when we get those phone records."

"We got the new kid's picture on every television station. Her father has offered a fifty-thousand-dollar reward to the person who finds her. Unfortunately, no calls have come in. Hold on. My cell phone is ringing.

Delaney... Yeah, I hear you... Really?... How soon can you get it?... Call me the moment you have something. Bye." She clicked off. "Cody, that was Jason. He got into the hard drive. Someone going by the name of 'Grandpa's Boy' was the last one on Dembeck's Facebook page."

"That's fantastic. Who is he?"

"Jason doesn't know. Thanks to Edward Snowden and the new law that Congress just passed, Facebook insists we get a subpoena before they release the person's name or any information on his profile."

"Oh, crap!"

"You got that right. The last thing 'Grandpa's Boy' wrote to Dembeck was: "See you in an hour. Leave garage door open. Have surprise for you."

"And what time was that sent to him?" Cody asked.

"Exactly one hour after Whitehall and Wilkins shut down their computer, and left the station."

CHAPTER SEVENTY-SEVEN

If he wasn't ruffled enough by learning he'd snatched the wrong girl, he was even more upset after he got a speeding ticket.

"Fuckin' cops!" he muttered, turning off the motor in front of the old house, and climbing out of his car. "What the hell is that?" He stopped in his tracks and stared at the sun-lit shards of broken glass on the side lawn. "She got out! The venom didn't kill her. Fuck."

He rushed over to the side of the house and inspected the broken window, then looked down at the grass. Droplets of red blood tipped some of the grass blades. He walked farther, looking at the trail of blood as it headed into the fallow field. "You bitch. You won't get away from me." He rushed back to the car and started it up.

Amber was exhausted and so dehydrated, she felt dizzy. She stopped a few times for only a couple of moments, to pull slivers of glass out of her bleeding feet, and then took off again as fast as she could.

Her body was slick with sweat, and flies bit her mercilessly. They swarmed in front of her face and eyes, and if she opened her mouth to suck in air, they flew into her mouth and she swallowed them.

She peered to her right and left as she ran, looking for a building or a road where she could flag down a car or truck in spite of her nakedness. All she saw was flattened fields of coarse, dried-out vegetation— vegetation that pierced her feet and made them bloodier. She stumbled once or twice, but forced herself to get up and go on, not for herself, but for her sister, who she believed was in mortal danger.

Amber heard the car's rumble in the distance behind her. She knew it could only be him. He had to be after her. She ran faster. The car got louder. She saw a canal directly in front of her. She had to cross it, so the car couldn't follow her. She ran faster. Her lungs burned—her eyes teared—the bugs and mosquitoes gnawed at her. When she reached the canal, she stopped and turned back. A little more and he'd have her. She jumped. The current was strong. She tried to swim to the other bank, but she was too weak. She heard the car stop—heard its door open. She didn't turn around. She swam. Her life depended on it.

CHAPTER SEVENTY-EIGHT

After being dropped off at the Delray Community Hospital, Cody had to trudge across a messy construction site to get to the helipad.

"They're building a new four-story building," the pilot said as Cody was attaching his five-point harness. "The new helipad's gonna be on top of it. It'll be much better for the patients. They won't have to be transferred by ambulance to the emergency room; they'll just go down an elevator."

"I never realized there were so many dials and gauges in a helicopter," Cody said, mesmerized by the instrument panel, and the collective and cyclic controls that maneuvered the aircraft.

"This model was specifically outfitted to transport critically ill patients. Cody, put on your helmet, and I'll connect your boom mike so we can talk when we're airborne." He waited until Cody had it on, then secured his own helmet and chin strap. "Palm Beach tower," he said, talking into his mouthpiece. "This is Tango 3118. I need permission to take off from Delray Community Hospital."

"Roger, Tango 3118, you're clear for takeoff."

Cody had never been in a helicopter before, so he paid close attention to how the pilot manipulated the sticks and foot pedals. As the copter rose a few feet off the ground, the rapid rotation of its four blades created a windstorm down below.

"Where are we heading?"

"Head west," Cody said. "We found two bodies in a canal west of Route 441."

The copter swerved to the right, and rose to five hundred feet.

"We need to search open, undeveloped land. Delray is our center point, and our search is within a forty-mile radius."

"What are we looking for?"

"Deep tire ruts."

The pilot glanced at him. "Your psychic told you to look for ruts?"

Cody groaned. "You heard about her, huh?"

"Hey! Don't sweat it. I believe in them, UFO's, and alien visitations."

They were nearly two hours into their meticulous grid search, and Cody's long legs and feet were getting numb from their tight confinement. "Lenny, let's take another fly-by two hundred feet closer to the canal. After that, you're going to have to set this thing down, so I can stretch my legs."

"Will do. This time look through the small window between your feet. It will give you a better view of the ground," Lenny said, tilting the copter's nose down and swerving toward the left, to run parallel to the canal.

Ten minutes later, Cody was ready to ask for that break when he spotted something bobbing in the canal below him. "Lenny," he shouted, pointing down. "Go back! Something or someone is in that canal."

Lenny nosed the copter down, and circled back, flying even lower this time.

"It's a girl!" Cody shouted. "Set it down fast!"

"No, I have to go down stream a few hundred feet, or you'll miss her," Lenny said, his voice also tinged with excitement.

Before the copter's skids had even touched the ground, Cody's helmet and shoes were off, his restraint was unfastened, and he was waiting by the side door to slide it open. The blades were still rotating when he jumped out of the copter. He ducked under them, and ran as fast as he could to the canal. He saw her coming toward him, her arms flailing as she tried to reach shore. He shouted that he was coming, and jumped into the raging water just in time to grab her arm.

"I've got you," he said, his heart pounding. "You're safe, sweetheart. You're safe."

CHAPTER SEVENTY-NINE

Catherine arrived at the Delray Hospital in record time after receiving Cody's call, saying he had Amber and was flying her there. She parked the black-and-white patrol car in a reserved doctor's slot, and rushed into the building. The emergency waiting area was full and noisy. She bypassed the reception desk, and followed a visitor through the door to the examination area.

"Has Amber Jamison arrived on the helicopter?" she asked a nurse, before she could walk away.

The nurse looked at her.

Catherine flipped open her badge. "The girl who's coming in on a copter. Is she in here?"

"It's landing now, and an ambulance is waiting for her. She'll be here in a couple of minutes."

Catherine thanked her and rushed back outside to wait by the door. She was thrilled that Amber was alive, but extremely anxious about her condition, because Cody hadn't told her anything. *Was the girl raped or brutalized,* she wondered. Whatever happened to Amber Jamison while she was held in captivity, Catherine knew the youngster would be traumatized for years like she still was, twenty years after her own rape.

Shifting from one foot to the other while she waited, Catherine kept scanning the roads that led into the emergency area. Amber's father would arrive soon, because she asked Betancourt to pick him up and rush him over to the hospital. When she looked to her right a couple of minutes later, she saw an ambulance arrive, and then back into another entrance. Catherine rushed over. As soon as the driver parked, the ambulance's rear door opened and a wet and haggard-looking Cody climbed out.

He looked at her. "She's alive, but in shock." He stepped out of the way, so the driver and second paramedic could take the gurney out of the ambulance.

Amber was wrapped in a gray woolen blanket, and had an IV line inserted into her bare upper arm. Although two straps were holding her down, her body convulsed so hard, the jerking movements had the gurney shaking.

"He thought I was Lizzy," she said, wide-eyed, staring up at the sky and turning her head from side to side. "He's going to kill Lizzy. I have to get to her. I have to save her. I have to," she babbled, as she was wheeled inside.

Cody and Catherine watched Amber's gurney be pushed into a cubicle and close to a bed. Then the bag of IV fluid was taken off her blanket and hung on a pole. After removing the two restraints, Amber was transferred from the gurney to the bed, and the side rails were pulled up. A nurse walked in as soon as the paramedics pulled the gurney out, and she drew the privacy curtain so Cody and Catherine could no longer see what was happening.

"Let me out of here. I have to get to Lizzy," Amber screamed, banging on the side rails, trying to get out of the bed.

Two doctors rushed in to the hysterical girl, and tried to calm her.

"Don't touch me. Lizzy! Lizzy, watch out! He's coming for you!"

Catherine pulled Cody aside, but didn't take her eyes off the curtain. "Talk to me. What happened?" she said, tugging on his arm. "Did she identify him?"

"I couldn't get anything out of her other than what you've been hearing. She's been hysterical and ranting, since I grabbed her in the canal."

"What did she mean when she said, 'he thought I was Lizzy'?"

Cody pulled his arm free, and watched another nurse rush into Amber's cubicle, holding a hypodermic needle.

"No!" Amber screamed. "No more needles! Take that away from me! Let me go!" She screamed for a few minutes, and then became silent.

One of the nurses and both doctors walked out from behind the curtain. Catherine rushed over to the doctors.

"I'm Detective Delaney. How is she? What did you find?"

"She's in shock," the bearded doctor replied. "We gave her a sedative to calm her down. We can't do more, until a parent gives us permission to treat her."

"A police officer is rushing her father to the hospital. He'll be here in a few minutes. Doctors, will the girl be all right?"

The second doctor—his nametag read Butler—answered. "She has glass and other matter embedded in her hands and feet. As soon as we get that approval, we'll remove them surgically and stitch up her cuts."

"We'll need samples of that glass and the other stuff you remove for evidence," Cody said. "Please have someone call the Boca Raton station when it's ready to be picked up."

"We'll do that," the same doctor replied.

"I saw the nurse taking vials of blood out of that room," Catherine said. "Was it taken for standard tests, or are you looking for something else?"

"Some of it was for standard tests like blood type, and clotting stats. But we took an additional one, because her arm was extremely swollen and discolored. It looks like something has been injected into it. We need to find out what that substance was, before we can anesthetize her. I'm sorry, but I can't tell you any more at this time," he said, and then he and the other doctor walked away and into another curtained-off cubicle.

Seconds later, Amanda's father and sister rushed inside and over to them.

"Where's my daughter?"

"Amber will be all right," Cody said. "She was just given a sedative to calm her down."

Jamison swallowed. Tears flowed down his unshaven face.

"She's behind that curtain," Cody said, pointing to where Amber was lying. "But I need a minute," he said, taking hold of Jamison's arm. "Your daughter said something about the man thinking she was Lizzy."

Lizzy's eyes widened, and she grabbed hold of her father's hand.

Jamison's mouth dropped open.

"We think he abducted the wrong girl, and he might come after Lizzy."

Jamison pulled his daughter to him, and clung to her, shock registering on his face, and not a word coming out of his mouth.

"You and your daughter need to stay here. Don't leave the hospital. We're going to protect you and your two daughters."

"You're going to watch us? Thank you."

"No. Other officers will be assigned to protect the three of you around the clock," Cody said. "Detective Delaney and I will be looking for the man who abducted your daughter."

CHAPTER EIGHTY

He had watched the girl thrashing wildly in the fast-flowing water, until she rounded a bend and he could no longer see any sign of her in the canal.

"It's just as well," he muttered, shielding his eyes from the sun. "Your drowning will save me from wasting any more of my precious venom on you."

He got into his car, and drove back to the house. When he got there, he left the motor running, climbed out of it, and left the door wide open.

"I made a mistake, Grandpa," he said, rushing to the house. "It won't happen again. I'll be more careful with the next one, I promise."

When he opened the front door, he gasped and clutched his chest. The floor was swarming with snakes, and more were slithering down the stairs from the upper landing.

Tears filled his eyes. "My poor babies," he said in a soothing tone, as he reached down and scooped up two handfuls "What has she done to you?"

Pushing more away with the tip of his shoe, he carefully made his way up the steps and to the bedroom door that Amber had left open. He entered the room with the wriggling snakes still clutched in his hands, and saw strands of long, dark hair snagged on the doggie door's wooden frame.

"So that's how she got out." He walked over to the opening and shoved the snakes through it and into the other room, then turned around. More of his beloved pets were still making their way out of the room. "I have to stop them," he said, frantic. He rushed into the third bedroom, where he raised his mice and rats. Without bothering to put on his rubber apron, he grabbed a few mice by their tails, brought them over to the metal table, and then hacked them into small bits. After scooping up the scraps of flesh and dropping them in the metal pail, he raced out to the hall.

"Come to daddy," he coed, carefully placing one bloody part on the wooden floor, and then another and another, creating a trail into the other bedroom. Like starving children following cookie crumbs, the snakes turned and followed the morsels and bloody droplets into the bedroom.

He was thrilled by his clever ploy. He laughed aloud and patted his thighs as he watched them climb over and under one another to reach the food. "See, Grandpa. Your boy's not so stupid after all." When all of the upstairs snakes had been safely locked away, he rushed back into the other bedroom and chopped up more rodents so he could lure the ones below into buckets that he could carry upstairs.

When he was satisfied they'd all been rescued, he headed downstairs to his special play bedroom. The door was slightly ajar. He opened it wide, and walked inside, and over to the bed. The sight of the rumpled red sheet made his heart race. He shut his eyes, unzipped his fly, and stuck his hand in his pants and around his flaccid penis.

"Grandpa, I'm twelve years old today. It's my birthday, remember?" he said in a little boy's whiney voice. He felt himself growing hard, and opened his eyes. "Yes... Yes, that always does it." As he continued to stare at the bed, he slowly stripped off his sweaty, bloody clothes. When they were puddled on the floor, he climbed onto the bed, shut his eyes, and took hold of his penis with both hands.

"Do it now, Grandpa," he said, pulling his stiffening rod back and forth, back and forth, faster and faster. "Stick it in her. Ram her hard. Yes! Yes! Keep doing it, Grandpa. Faster! Harder! Don't stoppp..." he shouted louder and louder, drowning out the sound of the helicopter that was circling above.

CHAPTER EIGHTY-ONE

"It's got to be that old farm house," Catherine called out from the helicopter's rear bench. "It's not far from the canal, and the ground looks like it's covered with old sugar cane stalks."

"Lenny, do a 360, and get closer to the house this time. Catherine might be right," Cody said.

The pilot nosed the copter down and circled around the wooden house, its skids barely missing the roof.

"I see broken glass on the ground. Over to the right," Catherine said, pointing. "This has got to be it. Set this thing down," she said, jabbing the pilot's shoulder.

"Got ya. Hold on. I need to get clear of the house." The helicopter lifted higher and swung to the left. Five hundred feet away from the house, he set it down.

Cody removed his helmet and harness and quickly turned to her. "His car is there, and he must have heard the copter. We're not going make like we're Superman and Wonder Woman, charging in there and acting like super heroes. We're going to do this by the book, so the bastard doesn't get off on a technicality. Are you with me on this? If you're not, you're staying in the copter."

She nodded. "I'm with you, O'Dell. Call the chief. Give him our location, and tell him to send the troops." She released her safety strap, slid the door open, and jumped onto the ground.

"He's on his way," Cody said when he was beside her. "Ready?"

"Ready," she said, pulling her gun out of her holster. "Let's get that bastard."

With their guns held out before them, Catherine and Cody slowly made their way toward the house. Their eyes scanned the grounds, then the windows in the house, to make sure a gun wasn't pointed at them. The car's motor was still running when they got to it. They glanced at each other, acknowledging he was close, then took off again.

Catherine silently pointed to the right side of the house, where she'd seen the broken glass. When they reached the corner, they bent low and took short, quiet steps along the side of the building, until they were beneath the broken window. Catherine pointed down to the droplets of blood on the grass and on the shards of glass, evidence they'd have to collect before leaving there. Cody nodded he understood. She nodded back. They were both certain this was the right place.

"No!" a man screamed from the inner room.

Catherine and Cody bolted upright, and pointed their guns through the window. Their mouths dropped open. A rattlesnake dropped down from a curtain, landed on the nude man, and then sank its curved fangs into his neck.

"Help me," the man cried out, trying to dislodge the snake.

"Hold it up!" Cody shouted. "Hold it away from you!"

Catherine rose, and sprinted toward the front of the house.

When the fangs were finally pried out of his neck, the man held the snake's head up as high as he could. Cody aimed the Glock, and pulled the trigger. The bullet splattered the rattler's head; its body was dropped on the side of the bed.

Catherine ran into the room, and over to the bed.

He saw her. "The antivenom… I need it," he gasped, pointing across the room.

Cody saw her walk over to a small, white refrigerator. Then he turned and scanned the room to make sure there weren't other snakes crawling on the floor, or hanging from the red drapery above the bed.

Catherine opened the refrigerator door. A filled syringe was lying on a small, plastic tray. She picked it up, and carried it over to the bed.

"The… the needle," the man said, grabbing his chest, desperately trying to draw air into his lungs.

Sirens blared in the distance.

"Is this what you want?" she asked in a velvety-soft voice.

"Please," he whispered, staring at the syringe. Blood trickled out of both sides of his mouth, and out of his ears. "Please… my arm… stick it in."

"Did you rape and kill those two girls?"

"Please… I beg you…"

"Did you rape and kill those two girls?" Catherine repeated, staring down at his sweat-slicked body, and holding up the antivenom that would save him.

"I'm sorry," he whimpered, grabbing on to his discolored, swelling neck and gasping for air.

"What about the black girls? Did you rape and kill them, too?"

"Grandpa did," he said, his voice fading to a whisper.

"Are they buried here?"

The man's eyes suddenly stared up at the red drape. The hand holding his neck dropped down on the bed. This time he didn't answer Catherine's question.

Catherine opened her hand, and the hypodermic needle fell to the wooden floor, shattering.

"Catherine!"

She turned to Cody, then walked to the window and let him pull her through it.

The sirens were growing louder. Their team was almost there. They reached the front of the house as eight police cars and vans pulled to a stop. Their doors flew open. Alvarez, Betancourt, Wilkins, Whitehall, and a fully out fitted SWAT team spilled out of them.

The chief was the first one to get to them. "Are you two all right?"

"No one can go in the house," Catherine said, loud enough for all of them to hear. "I saw tanks of snakes, and some of them are poisonous. One was loose and Cody shot it, but more of them may be crawling around. Animal control's got to clear them out first, before any of you step in there."

"What about him?" the chief asked.

The others waited, their expressions fierce, their guns gripped tight and ready to be fired.

"He's dead. One of his snakes got him."

"Do we know who he is?" her uncle asked.

She nodded. "Sheldon Clarkston."

"Sheldon Clarkston," her uncle gasped. "The mayor's son?"

CHAPTER EIGHTY-TWO

For once, the mayor was not the one to announce a killer had been caught; it was Chief Delaney. About an hour after he'd returned to the station, he called for an emergency press conference. It was dark outside by the time everything had been set up. Swarms of reporters and their cameramen were waiting for him outside the station.

"I'm going to make this brief," he said when he reached the bank of standing microphones. "The man who abducted and murdered those two young ladies has been killed today, and the third young lady, Amber Jamison has been found and is recovering."

"Who is he? What's his name?" a redheaded reporter from WXEL shouted out.

"We have to verify the man's identification, before I can release that information."

"I don't understand, Chief Delaney. Haven't you taken his fingerprints?" A female reporter in the front of the crowd asked

The chief cleared his throat. He hated lying, but they needed a little time to tie up a few loose ends in their investigation. "My detectives told me who the man is. However, we haven't been able to retrieve his body because his house is filled with poisonous snakes. Animal control is presently removing them. When we get their nod that it's safe to enter, we'll conduct our investigation. After the man's family has been notified, we'll be able to tell you more."

"How did he die? Did one of your men shoot him?"

The chief smiled wanly. "Actually, it was one of his own poisonous snakes that killed him. That's it boys and girls. Be back here at two tomorrow afternoon, and I'll give you the name of the killer." He waved, and walked away, not answering any more questions.

The Boca Raton police station was a hive of activity the following morning. At noon, the conference room was filled to overflowing for their briefing. Detectives, technicians, and even traffic cops filled the room.

There were high-fives, and laughter. Jokes about the mayor's son turning out to be the killer had them patting each other on their backs because none of the police liked him.

"Quiet down, boys and girls," the chief said, walking into the room with a wide smile on his face. "There's a press conference this afternoon, so let's get our facts together."

Jason Pollack walked into the room, and stood to the side. Cody and Catherine followed him in and stood beside him.

The room quieted, and everyone stared at the chief, waiting for him to start. "Catherine, you're first," he said, giving her a nod.

She walked to the front of the room, and faced the group. "Sheldon Clarkston was a pharmacist. He wasn't on a time clock. His hours weren't monitored. He worked for CVS, and when other CVS stores were short a pharmacist, he'd fill in for them. Therefore, he had access to a lot of records, and the records he was most interested in were the ones that listed attractive young ladies who had allergies. I spoke to some doctors who specialize in allergies. They told me that a person who has asthma would definitely die if they were injected with a large amount of poisonous venom, because it would constrict their lungs and virtually strangle them. Hillary Blackstone and Madeline Kefler had asthma. Their bodies will be exhumed as soon as we get court approval, and tests will be taken to check for hemotoxic and neurotoxic properties. Now here's the kicker. Elizabeth Jamison, one of the identical Jamison twins, has asthma, but Clarkston mistakenly grabbed the wrong girl. Amber survived, because she didn't have the allergy and that's why she was able to eventually escape." She looked over at Cody. "You're next."

When Cody walked to the front of the room, Catherine joined Jason again. "Animal control has cleared the farm house, and our team is in there collecting evidence." he said. "Sheldon Clarkston's body has been transferred to the morgue, and is probably being autopsied as we gather here. Detectives Whitehall and Wilkins are at the farm. Yesterday, they checked out Frank Dembeck's banking records, because there were large monthly cash deposits made in his checking account. We've just confirmed that same amount of cash was withdrawn from Sheldon Clarkston's brokerage account on those same days. We believe Dembeck was blackmailing Clarkston, but we have no confirmation of that fact at this time. We also suspect that it was Clarkston who shot Amanda

Plummer, because we found her name and address in his car. His car was towed to our facility, and a gun was found in his glove compartment. Ballistics are now comparing the bullets fired from his gun, with the one that was removed from Ms. Plummer." He turned to Jason.

"And now I'd like Federal Agent Jason Pollack to fill you in on his findings."

Jason walked over and shook Cody's hand, and then Cody walked over and stood beside Catherine.

"Ladies and gentlemen," Jason began. "I'd first like to commend all of you on a job well done in finding this man, and putting an end to his killing spree." He smiled briefly, and then continued. "My agency has checked Sheldon Clarkston's records. We believe he first started his killing spree when he was attending Albany College of Pharmacy and Health Sciences, in Albany, New York."

Murmurs and whispers circulated around the room.

Jason held up his hand to quiet them. "Our records indicate six young women's bodies were discovered in that upstate New York area while he attended that school. We have the names of those individuals, and we will be exhuming their bodies for testing for traces of venom." He looked over at Cody and Catherine. "I'm sorry, but I didn't have time to tell you the rest of it, because I just got the information." He turned back to the group. "Frank Dembeck was the attorney who drew up and witnessed the signing of Stewart Clarkston's will, giving the farm property to his grandson, Sheldon Clarkston. After comparing Stewart Clarkston's signature on his quick claim deed and other recorded instruments with the signature on the will, we've come to the conclusion that the signature on the will was a forgery. That's probably the reason behind the blackmail, but we'll have to check into it further."

"What about the hard drive?" Catherine called out. "Tell us what you found on it."

Jason expelled a deep breath. "Catherine, the hard drive confirmed the cash payments. Dembeck used his Facebook page to demand the cash, and Grandpa's Boy—Sheldon Clarkston—would give him the date he'd drop it off. The last correspondence between them was to set up another date, and that meeting got Dembeck murdered to stop the payments. And last, but not least: K-9 cadaver dogs and their handlers are combing the Clarkston farm property for the missing black girls that we believe his grandfather murdered. That's it for me. Chief, it's all yours."

The chief stepped forward. "Thank you Jason," he said, shaking his hand and then turning forward. "Well, boys and girls, we did it. I, too, want to thank you for all the hard work and long hours you've put in to solve this case. I'm proud of each and every one of you. If there are any further questions, please see me later. The reporters are waiting outside, and they get testy if they're kept waiting in the sun too long."

As he was walking out of the room, he stopped in front of Catherine and Cody. "Don't forget the Cancer Care Gala tonight. I'm looking forward to seeing you both all prettied up."

CHAPTER EIGHTY-THREE

"Catherine, what's taking you so long?" Cody called out, dropping the folded newspaper on top of the cocktail table. "We only have fifteen minutes to pick up your uncle."

"I'm ready," she said, her voice soft and seductive.

He turned around. She was standing in the living room doorway. His lips curled into a smile, and his eyes twinkled. The slinky, red evening gown that he'd purchased clung to her full breasts and accentuated every curve of her lush body. "I like your hair up," he said, walking toward her. "Delaney, I knew there was a woman hiding under your boring detective-clothes. You look gorgeous, Babe." He gently lifted her chin and peered into her eyes. "You look absolutely delicious. Good enough to eat."

She returned his smile, and straightened his bowtie. "And you look very handsome in your tuxedo, O'Dell."

"Boy, do I wish we could forget this event and stay at home."

"Me, too," she said with a sigh. "But my uncle needs us beside him, when he announces he's running for mayor."

Cody's cellphone rang in his pants pocket.

"Aren't you going to answer it?"

"No. We're off duty tonight. We're gonna dance and have some fun for a change."

"It could be my uncle saying he's gotten a lift, or he's going to be late."

Cody reluctantly dug the phone out of his pants pocket, and glanced at the caller ID number. "Yes, Chief.... Huh?... I don't understand... Are you sure that's right?... Did you know about that?... Yes, I understand.... Yes, I'll take care of it... Yes, you can count on me. We'll see you as soon as we can. Bye."

"What was that about?" Catherine asked. "Is he all right?"

Cody clutched the phone tight. "He's fine, but—"

"But what, O'Dell? Spit it out. What's wrong?"

"Your sister has been shot, and is in Memorial Regional Hospital."

"What? Is this supposed to be some sort of sick joke?" she said, backing away from him. "If it is, I don't think it's funny."

"Your father just got off the phone with him."

"My father? He called him? That can't be. My uncle and I haven't spoken to that man in over fifteen years."

"Catherine, your sister—"

"I don't have a sister!" she shouted. "I'm the bastard's only child. The child he treated like shit and ignored right after I was raped like it was my fault!"

Cody placed his hands on her shaking shoulders. "Catherine, Honey, listen to me." She tried to break away, but he held on tighter. "You do have a sister. Your uncle didn't know about her, until he received the call minutes ago. He said your father told him that he has a second family."

"A second family," she repeated, bitterly. Tears streamed down her face. She turned away from Cody. "This really is a joke. That man made me feel guilty that I was raped. Like I'd brought it on myself, and now you're telling me that he's a fucking adulterer with another family."

Cody wrapped his arms around her, and brought her body up against his. "She's been shot, Hon. Your sister never knew about his second family or you. She just found out. She's asking for you."

Catherine broke into sobs.

"Don't take your anger out on her. Like you, she had no idea that she had a sister."

Catherine turned around within his arms, and pressed her face against his chest.

"Her name is Susan," he said, softly. He lifted her face so she'd have to look up at him. "Catherine, your sister is your good friend Susan."

THE END.

THE INDEX KILLER
by
A.R. Alan

PROLOGUE

Friday evening, Sanford—nicknamed Sandy by all his friends and family—picked up his eight-year-old son Bryce for his usual weekend visitation. After devouring cheeseburgers and super-sized portions of fries at Burger King, the two went to Sandy's apartment, where they slathered peanut butter and grape jelly sandwiches together for their usual Saturday treasure hunt at a remote section of beach in Boca Raton.

Sheila, his ex-wife, didn't approve of their searching the sand with a metal detector. "Looking for gold and silver only teaches your son that you can make a quick buck without working hard," she complained each time he collected the freckle-faced boy. "Take him to the library, a book store, a museum. Someplace that will prepare him for a college education and high-paying job."

"Lighten up, Sheila. He's only a kid," he'd tell her, always ruffling his son's mop of red hair. "The beach is fun. All you have him doing is reading and homework. The kid needs some fun in his life. He needs to be outdoors getting some fresh air in his lungs, instead of watching TV and doing school work."

"Yeah, Mom. I need some fun in my life," Bryce would echo. To the boy, his father was a living, breathing action hero instead of a sanitation worker.

When Sandy and Bryce laid their towels and the blue cooler bag down on the sand at 7:30AM the following day, only a few hardy walkers strolled on the beach.

"You ready to find us some gold and diamonds?"

"I can't wait. Will you let me hold the detector this time?"

"It's too heavy for you. Besides, you're the one who digs down and finds the treasure. Isn't that better than carrying this heavy thing around?"

Frowning, Bryce kicked the toe of his sandal into the sand. "Guess so, but next year I'll be bigger, so it won't be too heavy, and you'll have to let me carry it."

Sandy patted his son's head, then switched on the detector and headed toward the sandy dunes.

"Why we going over there, Dad?"

"Thought we'd try the base of the dunes first. Sometimes the tide washes things way up on the beach. Let's see if we find anything. If we don't, we'll go closer to the water like we usually do."

Fifteen minutes later, the needle indicated a buried metal object. "See! Told you we'd find something here. Maybe it will be a real treasure, and we can take that trip to Disneyland. What do you say?"

Bryce smiled up at his father, then got down on his knees and dug the small, yellow plastic shovel into the warm sand. The deeper he dug through the sand and bits of shells and coral, the louder the detector pinged.

"Keep going. You're getting closer," Sandy said, laying the detector down on the sand, and kneeling beside his boy. A moment later he froze, and his son screamed and scrambled away.

They'd found gold all right, but the small bow-shaped ring was on the bone of a long-nailed, dead woman's finger.

CHAPTER ONE

The three red Macy's paper shopping bags sitting on the kitchen floor were full, but it wasn't with new clothes, trinkets, or household gadgets. They were filled with day-old bread, wilted salads, and bruised fruits that

Lillian had scavenged from a local Publix Supermarket dumpster, rather than go to the food bank or sink low enough to apply for food stamps.

The small, two-bedroom house that she and her younger brother had inherited from their parents was mostly furnished with shabby furniture she'd purchased from the local Goodwill Thrift store. And because Lillian was out of work for the third time in six months, every room smelled of mildew, because she couldn't afford to keep the air conditioning on.

"Damn brats. It's after ten," she mumbled, walking over to the kitchen window. She peered into her moonlit back yard, where shrieks of laughter echoed up from beyond the hedge that separated the two properties. When the new neighbors and their four teenagers had moved in six months earlier, the first thing they did was to have a large above-ground metal pool installed at the very end of their yard. Every night, even nights when it drizzled outside, their kids and hordes of friends frolicked in the pool. Lillian had called the police a couple of times when the racket continued past midnight, but the cops' warnings hadn't helped one bit. Finally realizing there was nothing more she could do about the commotion, Lillian began to unpack her groceries.

"These apples and pears aren't bad." She paused, then turned toward the kitchen door. "Oh, it's you, Stanley. I see you haven't shaved for a change. Don't look at me like that. I don't want to hear anything from you, you lazy bum. Go in your room and don't bother me." She opened the refrigerator door, then turned back to the bag and resumed her unpacking. "Mmm. This mango looks good. I'll just cut off the brown spots when I'm ready to eat it." She dropped the over-ripe mango and the other partially rotting fruits into the lower drawer of the fridge. Next, she pulled out an oval plastic container. "Well look at this. I got me a real Greek salad with lots of feta cheese." She lifted the lid and sniffed. "Stupid fools. There's nothing wrong with this seven-dollar salad." Her mouth watered as she set the container down on top of the counter. "I'll eat this later, when Stanley's not around."

After everything had been emptied into the refrigerator and bread box, and the folded bags placed in one of the lower cabinets for another day, Lillian headed into her bedroom.

In front of the bedroom window was an old wooden chair and a makeshift desk. Four stacks of college textbooks supported a white-and-red marbleized Formica tabletop that she had grabbed off the curb, before the garbage men could toss it into their truck.

After hiking her black skirt above her bony knees, she sat down at the desk and stared at her laptop, which was open to the *Sun Sentinel's* employment section. To the right of the computer was a yellow legal pad with a list of firms and contact names that she planned to mail out or e-mail her resumes to.

"Why am I bothering?" she said to herself. "What did that lousy college degree in accounting do for me, other than leave me with student loans? I need something, anything to tide me over. The car payment and electric bill are past due." She slammed her hand against the desk top. "The check-book's almost drained. What am I going to do? Why do those bastards keep firing me?" She rose from the chair, stormed over to her bed, and started punching the throw pil-lows to plump them up and relieve some of her frustration.

Hearing the sound of slippered feet in the hall as they drew close to her room, she turned toward her bedroom door. Stanley was standing there, his hands tucked into the pockets of the creased tan slacks that he always wore, his bloated stomach protruding over his cheap black belt. "You again? You're nothing but a worthless piece of shit, brother. You don't work, you don't clean the house, all you do is putter around in the tool shed. How many times do I have to tell you to leave me alone? Get out of here and let me think." She threw the red-fringed pillow she was holding at him. Stanley ducked, leaned back against the door frame, and smiled his twisted, coy smile.

"That's it!" Lillian's eyes widened. "Why didn't I think of it before? People who have jobs and are single need someone to clean their place, shop, cook them some meals, and do their laundry and odd jobs. See, Stanley," she said, tucking a strand of mousy-brown hair behind her ear. "It took me to think of the solution, not you, dummy. How would you survive without me? Huh?"

After rushing over to her computer and clearing off the screen, Lillian switched onto Craigslist. Half an hour later, her ad with the heading: "Part-Time Wife For Hire" was posted on the site.

The story continues in
THE INDEX KILLER
by A.R. Alan
ISBN: 978-1-61720-736-5

A.R. Alan is a born storyteller. Even in first grade, she became notorious for scribbling stories on scraps of paper. When she wasn't doing that, she'd have her nose buried in a book, soaking up other peoples' stories. Reading and writing stories became lifelong passions, and she's currently finishing her eleventh novel.

Worldwide travel and a career that brought her in touch with a never-ending stream of interesting personalities and celebrities fanned her already fertile imagination over the years, and validate the vivid, multi-dimensional characters that people her novels.

She is also an avid environmentalist, and played a major role in saving a New Jersey/New York mountain range from developers. It will remain open space forever.

Previously writing under the name of B.B. Carter, she has had many short stories, poems, and five novels published. She has also penned comedic material for Joan Rivers.

CPSIA information can be obtained
at www.ICGtesting.com
Printed in the USA
FSOW01n0049030117
29127FS